Done.

Juliet Rose

ABOVE THE RAIN COLLECTIVE

Above the Rain Collective

2025

Above the Rain Collective

abovetheraincollective@gmail.com

North Georgia, USA

Contributing Editor: J.A. Sexton

Publisher's note:

ISBN: 979-8-9899186-4-5

First Printing March 2025

abovetheraincollective.com

authorjulietrose.com

Cover graphics and interior formatting by J.A. Sexton

Original cover photo by Ingrid Sindt

Above the Rain Collective logo artwork by Bee Freitag

Chapter art by Jack Freitag

Contents

For those brave enough to face their demons

Domestic Dispute Call - 328 Beachside Drive, Crestview

Officer Jepsen was dispatched to the residence after a neighbor called in a domestic dispute. The neighbor reported hearing a baby crying and adults yelling.

Officer Jespsen arrived at the home at 9:09 pm. He knocked, and the male resident of the home answered the door. He was in an agitated state and told the officer he and his wife were arguing, but that was all.

Officer Jepsen asked to speak to the wife. The female resident of the home came to the door with signs of physical assault. Officer Jepsen asked to speak to her alone. She was holding a child of about eighteen months of age.

She said the male suspect hit her, then hit the child. The child, a boy, had bruises and was crying. Upon further investigation, Officer Jepsen found the male suspect was stationed at Camp Lejeune and deferred to their procedure, contacting the suspect's commanding officer.

The suspect was escorted from the home and was transported to the base for further investigation there. The female resident and child were transferred to the hospital for treatment and observation.

CHAPTER ONE

If the sun and surf could grow wings, Casey would be soaring. He caught the next wave, laughing back at his friend Smith as they darted through the tunnels caused by the impending hurricane. Smith wiped out and disappeared into the angry water, only to surface a few feet away. He waved his hand at Casey with a grin to let him know he was alright as he climbed back on the board and began paddling out to catch the following swell.

Casey grinned and turned his face to the sun as the wave he was on leveled out and became part of the surrounding water. He sat on his board, then headed into the storm crest. Outside of the waves at least doubling in size, it was hard to believe a hurricane was brewing out in the ocean. The sunshine was bright and warm, hiding the approaching inclement weather off the coast. It was days like these, anything seemed possible.

It was perfect.

Casey rose to his feet and balanced on his board, eyeing the incoming wave. He set his footing and relaxed his knees as he felt the wave rise beneath him. This would be the one, he could sense it. The one that would make him feel like he could conquer anything. The one that made him able to find a sense of peace outside of substances.

Outside of ketamine.

The wave lifted him with his board as Casey braced himself to ride it all the way into shore. He felt it as he became one with the motion. The high. He wanted it to last forever, but it only lasted for a moment before the swell petered out and caused him to lose his balance, dumping him headfirst into the brine.

Smith came up beside him on his board, laughing. "Almost had it that time, man."

Casey pushed himself up and straddled his board, peering out over the ocean. "So close. I thought it was the one. You want to keep going for a bit?"

Smith grinned and began the long strokes to push himself out over the waves. "Yeah. We need to head out in a few, though. I've got to grab a shower, then pick some stuff up before the party."

"Special K?" Casey asked, even though he already knew the answer.

Smith wiggled his light brown eyebrows. "You know it. Wouldn't be a party without K."

Casey followed him out toward the approaching waves, knowing one way or another, he was going to capture that feeling tonight. The one he was always chasing inside himself. Well, since he and Smith became friends again a few years back. They'd known each other as kids but had drifted apart when Smith hit high school and Casey was still a child in Smith's eyes. Before then, they'd hung out riding bikes and getting into shit as kids.

Smith was three, almost four, years older than him and had taken Casey under his wing when Casey showed up on the party scene when Casey turned sixteen. Casey was already smoking weed and drinking by then, but he rapidly began experimenting with whatever drugs he could get his hands on, finally settling on ketamine and the dream-like state it put him in. Since then, that had been his go-to drug of choice.

Now, at eighteen, Casey saw him as an older brother as well as a friend. Smith was a mess, but he never turned his back on Casey. He always made sure he was taken care of. Casey didn't feel so alone when he was hanging out with Smith. That's why they'd hit it off. Smith was a social loner, and Casey was an anti-social partier.

It fit.

By the time they were exhausted and heading for the beach, Casey knew the only way he was going to fly today was with a little help. He had brief moments of pure happiness when he was surfing. Where nothing else mattered and he could hold the world in his hand. Moments free of the darkness that held him down. It didn't last long, though. It always faded after a few breaths.

Nothing like what ketamine gave him. That's where he found himself, in the layers of the drug's hold on his brain. Or as he lost himself in the sensation of falling between planes of reality.

It was one and the same.

The rest of the night was a blur, Casey getting fucked up as fast as his body would let him. He remembered snippets, like fast-forwarding through a movie. Talking to a girl about music and art, standing by the bonfire as people stumbled around him. Smith cracking jokes and flirting with the girl Casey had been talking to before. Jumping off the pier, fully clothed, and swimming to shore. Drinking way too much, taking more ketamine. Laying in the sand, staring up at the stars, as he considered other worlds with other beings watching him from the distance. Making out with some girl, not the same one from before.

Kylie? Claire? He couldn't remember. She was there, then she was gone. Moments came and went in a flash, and Casey wasn't sure when, or even if, things happened. That was part of the appeal. Nothing really mattering, time taking on its own dimension.

His favorite part was when ketamine made him feel like he was floating outside of himself, yet still seeing from the inside. Part here, part there. The disconnection felt like taking deep breaths of pure oxygen.

He didn't remember how he got home or where his shoes were, but that was par for the course. He woke up in his bed, covered in sand, his head pounding like a jackhammer. He groaned and rolled over, trying to shut out the sun.

His parents didn't push the issue of him being out all night, assuming he was simply hanging out with friends. He usually made it home and was in bed by the time they got up in the morning. They let him sleep in most times, as long as he got his chores done and didn't sleep the day away. They were on him about going to college or finding a decent job but had given him some leeway over the summer to figure things out. What they didn't know was that Casey figuring things out, treading water so he didn't slip under, was him running away from reality and flying under the wire.

His little brother, Aidan, on the other hand, didn't have patience for Casey's antics. He wanted his big brother to pay attention to him, to be there for him. To keep the promises Casey made in the moments between waking up, parties, and passing out. At those times, the promises came easy, and Casey meant them. It was the other times, they fell to the wayside, leaving Aidan disappointed and upset.

Casey hoped Aidan would sometimes forget those promises so he could sleep off the bad decisions from the night before. The mornings were rough, Casey not knowing when to stop himself from taking it too far in the foggy distraction of pills and alcohol the night before. He always told himself he'd chill out, but somewhere along the way, he let himself and Aidan down.

It wasn't that he didn't want to be there for his little brother. Nothing was more important to Casey than spending time with Aidan. It was that he was still trying to figure out how to balance the dark, doubtful parts in himself with the part of him that loved his family and wanted to feel like they were enough.

For him to be enough for them.

His family loved him and never made him question that, but his inner voice told him he didn't fit. That he didn't make sense in their perfect bubble. Despite their unending support, Casey couldn't help but feel like he was often on the outside looking in. That behind their smiles and affection, lay something waiting to push him out. To recognize he wasn't like them.

He was the one thing not like the others.

He was so afraid Aidan would discover the real Casey and not want him in his life anymore. Not want him to be his big brother. To recognize the failure Casey had become and hid behind a wall of pretend. Casey couldn't live up to the pedestal Aidan put him on. So, Casey made promises he didn't always want to fulfill.

However, Aidan never forgot.

CHAPTER TWO

"**Y**ou promised!" Aidan whined over Casey's bed, his eleven-year-old body tense with frustration. "I let you sleep in, but you said you'd take me surfing today."

Casey groaned and uncovered his head buried in the pillow. He *had* promised his little brother he'd take him surfing. That was before he tied one on at a beach party the night before. He tried to think of a good excuse, but Aidan's desperate eyes let him know he wouldn't get out of it that easily. He sat up and rubbed his head, making his dark curls frizz wildly around his face. "Yeah, let me get a shower first."

Aidan frowned. "A shower? You're just going to get wet and sandy, anyway. Why do you need to take a shower?

Come on, Casey!"

"Aidan, I'll take you surfing, but you have to get out of my face. Give me a chance to get moving. Okay?"

Aidan looked hurt but nodded and stepped back. "We are going surfing, right?"

Casey grinned through his pounding headache. "Yeah, buddy. Sorry, just give me a minute. I promise. Why don't you go make us a couple of sandwiches while I shower? Grab some drinks, too."

Aidan eyed him, his almost black eyes reading Casey's face for honesty. Seeing that Casey was being truthful, he darted out of the room for the kitchen. Casey lay back on his pillow and willed the room to stop spinning. What the fuck did he take last night? He had a few drinks, then the pills started getting passed out. Ketamine for sure, maybe a little coke, then were those bluish pills. He didn't even know what those were, but that didn't stop him from popping them, anyway. Once the flow of substances started, it was hard to stop. He lost all sense of reason, and the only thing stopping him was passing out.

Smith had been in rare form. He'd climbed on top of the lifeguard station roof and jumped off. How he didn't break his legs, Casey had no idea. Then again, it was like they were invincible when they were high. Casey groaned as he remembered he'd also taken a running leap off the end of the pier. That would explain all the scratches and bruises on his arms and legs. He pushed back the blanket and stared at his body. He'd dropped weight.

Stumbling out of bed, Casey headed for the shower, bracing himself on the wall as he went. The idea of surfing made him nauseous. As he rounded the corner to the bathroom, he moved faster, feeling the contents of his guts making their way out. He leaned over the toilet and vomited, his stomach cleaning itself of what it could. The acrid stench of undigested alcohol hit his nasal passages, causing him to dry heave after there was nothing left to expel. He again considered how he could get out of taking Aidan surfing.

He couldn't. He'd let that kid down way too many times. He crawled into the shower and let the hot water rinse away the stink of last night. He loved Aidan, that was the truth. He never expected to be a big brother, but when his mother remarried, he hoped she and Isaac would have children. He was tired of being alone. They had Aidan when he was seven, and it was the highlight of his life. He thought back to when they brought Aidan home.

"I want him to sleep in my bed," Casey begged, holding the squirming bundle of blankets and Aidan.

They chuckled and shook their heads. "Not your bed, but we can put his crib in your room. As long as you promise not to keep him up all night," Isaac offered.

"I promise!" Casey insisted.

Like he'd promised Aidan he'd take him surfing today. Damn. He needed to keep his word.

He scrubbed his skin and drew in a deep breath. Hungover or not, he would keep that promise. Maybe a little nip off the bottle would help. He finished showering and turned off the water. As he stumbled back to his room, he could hear Aidan excitedly chattering with their mother in the kitchen. *Their* mother.

It had been only Casey and her until he was almost five years old. That's when she met Isaac. After a whirlwind romance, they married and had Aidan two years later. Casey liked Isaac but never felt like he was his father. Casey wanted him to be, but something kept him from letting Isaac in.

Not that Isaac didn't try.

Reaching under his bed, Casey drew out a half bottle of vodka and took a couple of swigs. The liquid burned going down as he closed his eyes and let the alcohol absorb into his system. By the time they'd get to the beach, he should be feeling better. Nothing like the hair of the dog he bit to get him moving.

He stashed the bottle back under the bed and yanked on his board shorts and a t-shirt. The shorts were too loose, so he pulled the drawstring as tight as he could to keep them up. No sense in flashing the beachgoers.

His mother frowned when he walked into the kitchen, eyeing him with concern. "You are too thin, Casey. You need to eat more."

Casey grinned and kissed her on the forehead. "I will, Mom. Speaking of, Aidan, did you pack us food?"

Aidan was practically bouncing in place and bobbed his head. "Peanut butter and jelly sandwiches, cookies, and chocolate milk."

The words chocolate milk made Casey feel like he would hurl again, and he pushed it down. "Water?"

Aidan tipped his head, his smooth, dark hair falling over his eyes. "Who wants to drink water when you can drink chocolate milk?"

That did it.

Casey ran to the sink and puked up bile. Afraid to meet his mother in the eyes, he wiped his mouth on a dishrag and glanced at Aidan. "Me."

Their mother came over and placed her hand on Casey's forehead. "Are you coming down with something?

Do you feel alright?"

That was his mother, a chronic worrier. Casey took a swig of water and swished his mouth out, spitting it in the sink. "Must be something I ate. I feel fine."

She watched him, her eyes saying she didn't believe what he was saying. Casey could see she was smelling the booze on him and shook his head. Their eyes met, and he prayed to not see disappointment in hers. He never wanted to let her down. He only saw concern.

"Casey-" she began, but he cut her off.

"I'm fine, Mom, don't worry. Come on, Aidan, we gotta go. Grab the food, and let's head out."

Aidan didn't have to be asked twice and bolted for the door, the bag of sandwiches and snacks clasped tightly in his hand. Casey hugged his mother, avoiding eye contact when she placed her hand on his arm.

"I worry about you, Casey," she whispered.

She should, he thought. He was a speeding train, heading for a brick wall. He smiled and shook his head. "Nothing to be concerned about. Let me get going before Aidan loses his mind."

She dropped her hand, knowing the conversation was over. "You can take my car. Be safe and keep an eye on him."

"I always do, Mom."

The beach was fairly empty when they arrived, and Casey was glad for it. He couldn't stand when tourists camped out and acted like they owned the beach. They pulled the surfboards off the rack on top of the car and headed down to the water line. The coast of North Carolina didn't get big waves, but they were good for the younger kids and light surfing. When storms rolled in, the more experienced surfers hit the rougher, larger waves.

Today would be good for Aidan, the water was consistent but not turbulent.

The vodka had taken the edge off Casey's hangover, and he felt like he could manage a good session despite the night before. He set the board down. "Hey, hand me one of those sandwiches. Can't paddle without energy."

Aidan stared at him impatiently but handed him a sandwich, anyhow. "Come on, Casey."

Casey grinned, taking two large bites of the sandwich. Man, he loved that kid. Aidan took no shit. "You want me to pass out and drown?"

Aidan shook his head, though his face didn't seem convinced. "No. Just hurry."

Casey watched his brother, and a feeling of sadness passed through him. He couldn't explain it, but it was something he'd learned to live with. "Alright, let's do this."

Aidan was already running for the water. Casey caught up to him, and they got their boards onto the surface. Casey watched with admiration as Aidan's thin arms pumped through the waves like someone much bigger and stronger than him. The waves flipped Aidan over, dumping him into the ocean. Casey's heart skipped a beat, but Aidan surfaced and climbed back on the board as if nothing happened.

Casey liked to stay behind Aidan to make sure he was alright, however, as the boy grew, he was becoming a force to be contended with. Casey had always struggled with feeling insecure and unsure about his abilities. Aidan suffered none of that. He took on the world fearlessly. Casey sometimes felt like the younger brother when he was around Aidan.

Aidan was an old soul.

Aidan stood on the board and braced himself expertly.

Casey followed suit, and they spent the next couple of hours becoming one with the ocean. Casey wondered why he questioned coming that day. He needed it. As he weaved through the waves, he forgot about drinking and pills. This was all he desired.

This and hanging out with Aidan.

By the time they were exhausted and ready to go in, the beach had filled up, and Casey was more than happy to leave. They gathered their things and headed for the car when a slim, brunette girl passed them, smiling coyly at Casey.

"Hey, Casey. Surprised to see you out here today after last night. Figured you were sleeping it off."

Casey didn't remember the girl's name, and his cheeks flamed at her words. He didn't want Aidan to know about his other life. The one where he was willing to throw away everyone and everything for a fix. He waved Aidan on and paused. "Yeah, good times."

"You were the life of the party," she said, alluding to something Casey couldn't remember.

"How's that?"

"You don't remember?"

Casey rarely did. "What? Jumping off the pier?"

The girl tipped her head, her eyes confused. "Well, there was that. I meant, fighting that guy."

Casey wracked his brain. Fought what guy? She must be confused with someone else. Casey wasn't a fighter. "You sure it was me?"

"Uh... yeah. There's only one Casey Duncan. You beat

the hell out of him."

Casey stared at his knuckles and noticed they were cut and bruised, but he honestly didn't remember fighting anyone. Why would he have done that? "Who was he?"

She shrugged and waved to her friend, who'd walked away. "Gotta go. Not sure. He wasn't from here. I think he was saying some shit about the locals. He started in on Smith, and you jumped in. It was less of a fight and more of you whooping his ass."

Casey frowned. He'd never fight someone sober. Smith accused him of being a free spirit, a hippie. He nodded at the girl. Heather. That's right, she was one of Smith's friends. Casey hung out with a group when he was with Smith but never hung out with them separately. Smith always had a crew around him. Probably because he was their source. Aidan was leaning on the car watching them, his expression analytical and a little bored.

Casey raised his hand to him. "It was good seeing you. I need to take my brother home."

She glanced at Aidan, then back at Casey, a strange smile on her face. "You coming tonight?"

Casey remembered Smith telling him they were doing some night surfing. "Yeah, maybe."

"Bring your little brother."

"He's eleven."

The girl tipped her head. "Oh, thought he was a little older. Bring him, anyway. I'm sure he'd have fun."

A wave of rage passed through Casey, and he glared at her. "What the fuck is wrong with you? He's a kid."

She shrugged and began walking away. "So were you when you started coming around."

Casey watched her retreating form and thought

about that. He was young, but not eleven. Thirteen when he started sneaking booze. A couple of years later, it was pills and anything else he could get his hands on. He'd do everything he could to keep Aidan away from all of that. To prevent him from getting sucked into the abyss.

He ran to the car and fastened their boards on the roof rack. Aidan was staring at where the girl had gone. "Who was that girl?"

"Some chick Smith knows. I don't really know her. Don't worry about it."

Aidan shrugged with disinterest. "I wasn't. What do you want to do now?"

Casey looked at his little brother, the one person he'd do anything for. "Whatever you want, little dude."

CHAPTER THREE

C asey tripped and landed face-first in the sand. The sun was beginning to turn the sky a myriad of colors, and he knew he needed to find Smith before the early beach walkers made their way out. They'd started the night out together, but after a cocktail of pills, booze, and who knew what else, Casey lost track of Smith. Smith was known to wander away to sleep it off.

That wasn't the problem.

Their small-minded, conservative town was. If anyone found Smith passed out on the beach with substances in his body, he'd lose his job and likely get locked up. Especially since he was the one providing the rest of them with their party supplies. Smith's parents had been some of the most well-off people in the town before they left, and their son turning out to be a dealer and an addict would cause a major uproar.

That, and Casey liked Smith. They'd connected from the first time they met as kids, and there wasn't a time in recent years Casey couldn't call on Smith and have him there for him as fast as Smith could come. Casey loved Aidan more than anything in the world, but Smith filled in him the connection of an older brother. Something he always felt like he was lacking growing up.

Casey picked himself up, brushing the sand from his face, and stumbled down the beach. Smith could be in the lifeguard stand, but for some reason, his tall, lanky friend liked to crash in the sand. Casey scanned ahead of him, attempting to make the wavering reality around him form into a functional path. His feet and brain seemed to not be on the same course.

"Smith!" he yelled into the night, listening for any sign of his friend. He was greeted with silence.

Fuck.

Hopefully, Smith was alright. He never seemed to know his limits, though, neither did Casey. They egged each other on and often went over their ability to slow down.

A bumpy shape up ahead caught Casey's attention, and he willed his body to move faster. The tide was coming in, and if the shape was Smith, he was dangerously close to being dragged out to sea. Casey's legs and brain finally became one, and he began to run. As he came up on the hump, he could tell it was Smith and he was unresponsive.

"Fuck, man. Smith?" Casey said as he knelt and rolled his friend over.

In the dark, it was hard to make out Smith's face,

but from the dead weight of his body, Casey feared he might be too late. He began to come up with explanations if he needed to call for help, but fear froze him in place. If anyone came and found them like this, they'd both be in a world of hurt. Casey gently slapped Smith's face, like he'd seen in movies, but like in real life, it did nothing.

"Please, wake up. Dude, stop fucking around for real. I need you to wake the hell up," Casey whispered, pushing the anxiety away.

It seemed to go on forever with no change when Smith suddenly twitched as water came out of his mouth and nose. He rolled over and began vomiting and coughing. The tide was now covering parts of their bodies, and Casey knew they needed to move. Smith tried to sit up but fell over in the water. Casey yanked him back up.

"Smith, thank fuck you're alive. We need to get up the beach."

"Fuckin' leave me alone," Smith answered, his voice strained and tired. "Just go."

"Not going to happen, man. You're stuck with me." Casey put his hands under Smith's arms and started dragging him, inch by inch, out of the surf. It would have been comical if it wasn't damn near impossible.

"I got it," Smith finally said and turned over onto his hands and knees, crawling up the beach like a baby. He made it far enough out of the tide to be safe, then collapsed onto the sand in exhaustion.

Casey followed and sat next to his friend. He leaned over to make sure Smith was breathing. Smith was a lump, but he was breathing. Casey pulled his knees to his chest and wrapped his arms around them. He'd stay with Smith until he was able to get up and go somewhere else.

That's what friends did.

Casey watched the sunrise and marveled at the beauty of it. He wished he could bottle it and drink it down. In a way, he mused, that's exactly what drugs did for him. Created a beautiful place he couldn't find anywhere else.

Every few minutes, Casey made sure Smith was alive. As the beach walkers came out, Casey pretended they were just hanging out to watch the sunrise. A few people eyed them, but most paid them no mind. Some even smiled and waved as they strolled by.

An incredible thirst came over Casey after a couple of hours, and he knew he needed to get some fresh water. Smith seemed more like he was sleeping versus passed out, and Casey nudged him. "Smith, wake up."

A groan erupted from his friend. Smith rolled over and peered at Casey from under his elbow, his mouth in a smirk. "You should've let me die."

"Yeah, well, I didn't, so deal with it. I've gotta get some water. You want to walk over to Natalie's place with me?"

Smith sighed, shaking his head slowly. "Not really, but okay."

They made their way down the beach like a pair of old married people. Except with drugs still coursing through their veins. Neither spoke as the crash was beginning. Usually, Casey tried to sleep off the come down, but he never made it home and had to face it out in public. That wasn't going to be fun.

Since he didn't make it home and now it was morning, his parents were going to be so pissed. They'd let go of the reins once he turned eighteen, but he still had to call to let them know if he wasn't coming home. He didn't the night before. He'd see if Natalie would let him use the restaurant phone.

Natalie's place was a beachside restaurant called By the Sea. During the day, it was mostly tourists, but the locals took it over at night. Natalie had been a fixture in the town as long as Casey could remember. She was always brusk but kind. She didn't take any shit, however, would be the first to be there for them when times got tough. She was like everyone's badass aunt in town.

Speaking of Natalie, she was behind the counter when they fumbled through the door, her eyes saying she knew what they were up to. She pushed her sweaty, golden hair out of her face and sighed. "Morning, boys, up to surf?"

They could tell she knew that wasn't what was going on, but she was trying to give them some leeway. Smith practically fell into a chair, and Casey went to the counter. Natalie eyed him and stopped wiping the counter for a moment. Her thick forearms wrung the rag out, and she dropped it in a bucket behind the register as she moved over to where he was standing.

"What can I get for you today, Casey?"

"Uh... two number fours with coffee." Casey stuck his hand in his grimy pocket, hoping he still had a little money. Relieved when his hand landed on the crumpled bill, he drew out the twenty and handed it to Natalie.

Natalie yelled the order back to the cook, Jimmy, then leaned in close to Casey. "You're going to end up dead if you keep going like this. You and Smith."

Casey chuckled like she was joking, knowing she wasn't. He cleared his throat and glanced back at Smith, who looked like he could pass out at any moment. "It's fine. We'll slow down."

Natalie made what sounded like a grunt and poured them each a coffee, sliding the mugs over to Casey. "Don't shit in my hand and call it a cookie."

Casey almost burst out laughing, however, he could see from her expression she wasn't having it. He could pull the wool over his parents' eyes but not Natalie's. It was like she could see right into his soul. He couldn't explain why, but he liked that about Natalie.

He hung his head and clutched a mug in each hand, making his way back to the table where Smith appeared as if he was using the table to brace himself. Casey sat down, watching Smith to make sure he wasn't going to pitch out of his seat.

Smith took the mug as Casey shoved it toward him, then grimaced and pushed it away. "Shit's terrible."

"That it is, but don't go and hurt Natalie's feelings," Casey agreed.

Smith snickered and glanced at Natalie, who had her back to them. "Can't hurt that woman's feelings. In a past life, I think she was some kind of headhunting warrior."

They both chuckled but didn't make eye contact when she brought their plates over. They admired her as a person, but they feared her even more. They their muttered thanks and ate. Well, Casey ate. Smith pushed the food around his plate, his skin looking a little green.

Casey leaned in. "You alright, man?"

Smith met his eyes, a flicker of anger appearing for a moment, then disappearing. "Yeah, thanks to you. I mean it. I had accepted my fate last night. Welcomed it even. I sure the fuck didn't expect to come to with you sitting right next to me like a mother."

Casey couldn't tell if Smith was trying to lighten the mood or was chastising him. It didn't matter either way. What was done was done. He'd do it again.

"I couldn't just leave you there. You're my friend, my brother. You would've done the same for me."

Smith watched him, his empty fork in midair. "That's true, I guess. I knew what I was doing, though."

"Yeah, I know. Smith, you can talk to me. You know that, right?"

"About what? About the fact that my parents want nothing to do with me? That all I have is a shit job in this shit town? You at least have a family who worries about you, wants you around."

Fuck. His parents.

Casey didn't want to leave Smith mid-thought, but if he didn't call home, his parents were going to freak out. He set his fork down and took a swig of coffee. "Hold that thought, I need to call home before Isaac comes out looking for me."

Smith nodded and waved his hand as if to say, "Go on."

Casey went to the counter and reached over to pull the phone toward him. Natalie glanced at him but made no effort to say anything. Casey dialed his home phone, anxiety making his hands tremble. When his mother answered, the lies came out easy and fast.

"Hey, Mom, sorry I didn't call last night. I was staying at Smith's place, and we fell asleep before I had a chance to call to let you know I was staying over."

At first, the line was silent, then his mother's soft voice came through. "I'm glad you're alright. I was very worried. Isaac left to go look for you."

She was always so calm, he never knew the level of anger his actions caused in her. However, if Isaac was out looking for him, she was very upset. He cradled the phone to his ear and rubbed his forehead. "If I see him, I'll let him know I'm alright. We stopped off to get a bite to eat at By the Sea. I'll be home soon."

"Okay. Casey, I love you. I didn't sleep much last night, waiting for you to come home. All you need to do is call."

It was such a simple thing. Why couldn't he do it? Like Smith, he seemed hellbent on destroying all the good things in his life. "I'll do better. Love you, Mom."

They hung up, and Casey pushed the guilt down into the part of him that held all his misgivings. It was always full, yet he did nothing to change it. He turned back to go to the table, thinking about what Smith said about having no one. It wasn't true. He had Casey. The table where they were sitting was empty, and Casey glanced around for his friend.

Smith was gone.

CHAPTER FOUR

C asey wandered the streets toward home, thinking about if he hadn't found Smith. Would he have drowned? OD'd? He didn't seem to be breathing when Casey found him, but was able to come around. How long had he been out there? Casey shook his head, trying to remind himself he did get there in time. Smith was alive. Even if he didn't want to be.

Casey could relate. At times, he thought about how easy it would be to simply take too much and stop breathing. Allow himself to float away from everything. He considered what that would do to his mother. To Aidan. Sure, at first they'd be upset, but eventually, their little, happy family would move on without him.

Like his biological father did. That dude walked out

when Casey was only a toddler and never came back. In the beginning, he'd send cards on Casey's birthday and holidays and saw him for court-ordered visitations every now and then. However, by the time Casey was five years old, that all ended. He never heard from his father again.

Casey used to cry and ask his mother why his father never saw him. She tried to explain some people were selfish, that it wasn't Casey's fault. Yet, night after night, he'd lie in bed, and his brain told him otherwise. If he'd been well behaved, if he was smarter, his father would still be around. Now, he knew better, but it didn't hurt any less. He leaned into humor to deflect the painful feelings clawing their way out, and when that didn't work, he turned to drugs.

Casey found himself a few blocks from home and slowed his pace, not ready to face the inquisition. His mother loved him, but she was a worrier and would grill him on every detail of his night. He worked out his story as he dragged his feet toward home.

Right before he got there, a car slowed near him, and the window rolled down. It was a blond girl who hung out with Smith a lot and was at most parties they went to. Casey didn't know her well but was used to seeing her around. She was loud and outspoken, drawing attention wherever she was.

She waved him over, her glitter-painted nails catching the sun. "Casey, right? Tucker is looking for you."

"Who the hell is Tucker?" Casey asked, not familiar with the name or why he was looking for him.

"That guy you wailed on the other night at the party? The one you beat up," the girl explained, flipping her hair off her shoulder.

Jesus, did everyone but Casey remember him beating the guy's ass? "Oh. What the fuck ever. I don't have time for that shit. Who even is this guy?"

The girl shrugged and glanced away. "I don't know. He started showing up at parties in the last few months. He's pissed you whooped his ass. Not his words. He claims you jumped him."

Casey laughed. He was not known to go around beating people up for no reason. He certainly would never jump someone unexpectedly. He wanted people to be aware what they did wrong. "Thanks for letting me know. How do you know him?"

"Just from the scene. Like I said, he started showing up. Sometimes he has some good shit on him."

Casey frowned. "Is he dealing?"

"Now and then. He wants to take over and push Smith out, I know that. That's why he started shit with him the other night. He's trying to take him down."

Casey rubbed his eyes. "It's not like Smith is some huge drug kingpin. He only brings enough to keep the party going. Does this guy seriously think he's going to get rich off this podunk town?"

The girl watched him for a moment, not responding. Casey understood. No one wanted to believe their little town could dry up and be flicked away like a crusty booger. But it could. It was no different than a hundred other small southern towns with not much to offer. They had the beach, but that didn't keep the locals out of poverty. A shiny fantasy for those who came only long enough to fulfill their yearly vacation dreams.

This guy Tucker was one of a series of people who

came in thinking there was more to it than there was. There wasn't. Even Smith, who was their sole source, was pretty much homeless. He crashed on people's couches and slept in the lifeguard stand when it was warm enough.

Casey shook his head. "I'll keep my eyes out. Thanks for letting me know, uh-"

"Miranda. We went to school together. Remember?"

"We did. Sorry, I don't remember much from those days. Were we in the same class?"

She chuckled and tossed a cigarette butt out the car window. "Nah, I was a few years ahead of you in Smith's class. You were a freshman when I was a senior. I recall seeing you, though."

"So, how do you remember me from back then?" Casey asked, having zero recollection of the girl in front of him, outside of seeing her with Smith at parties. Even then, they didn't interact more than general greetings.

She stared him dead in the eye, then batted her eyelashes and grinned. "You were young, but you were fine as hell. Still are."

Casey blushed. "Yeah, uh, that's weird. Well, thanks for letting me know about Tucker. I'm not too worried about it. I'm sure our paths will cross at some point; the town isn't that big."

Miranda shook her blond head and smiled suggestively. "That it is. So, Casey, if you ever want to, you know, fool around... I'm game."

Was she offering to have sex with him?

It wouldn't be the first time a girl came on to him, but not usually so bluntly. Unfortunately, Casey didn't feel the same about Miranda. Sure, she was pretty, but she didn't do it for him in that way.

31

He didn't want to hurt her feelings, though, so he smiled and nodded. "Yeah, maybe. I gotta get home now. My mom is upset I didn't come home last night."

Miranda tipped her head, knitting her brows. "You're an adult, right?"

Casey resented the implication and her nosing her way into his business. "I respect my mom."

Miranda cackled and shook her head. "No, you don't, or you wouldn't do the shit you do."

With that, she rolled up the window and drove away. She wasn't wrong. She had no business getting so personal with him, but her words stung. He treated his family like shit, sometimes. Casey set his resolve and walked up to the house. He needed to pull it together. To be the son and brother his family deserved. It was a cycle he repeated over and over. Fuck up, feel bad, commit to changing, then fuck up again.

He was surprised when he went inside and no one was home. Relieved, actually. Isaac was already at work. There was a note on the table saying his mother had taken Aidan shopping for school clothes and supplies. School. Casey had graduated two months earlier but didn't know what was next for him. Aidan would be going back to school in a month, and Casey had no set life plans.

Isaac was supportive but had become increasingly concerned about Casey's future. Casey would tell them different things to get them off his back, but he truly had no idea what he was supposed to do in life. College didn't appeal to him. While he worked jobs here and there, nothing called to him as a career.

Nothing mattered except getting fucked up.

He went to his bedroom and lay down, falling asleep

almost as soon as his head hit the pillow. When he woke up hours later, he could hear Aidan talking to Isaac. How long had he slept? He sat up and sniffed himself. He reeked of sweat and chemicals. Not ready to face the family yet, he slipped in to take a shower and practice his excuses. Where he'd been, who he was with. Keep it simple and as close to the truth as possible, so he didn't trip himself up.

Satisfied he was settled, Casey joined the family for dinner and did his best to be the stellar son. Isaac eyed him from the other side of the table, his face unreadable. Finally, his stepdad set down his fork and cleared his throat.

"Are you staying in tonight?"

As far as Casey knew, he was. He bobbed his head. "Yeah, I need to get some rest."

Aidan laughed. "You slept all day."

"Nah, I was listening to music a lot of the time."

Aidan clearly didn't believe him. "What were you listening to? ZZ Top?"

"Haha, I get it. Zs. Anyway, I'm home tonight. Why, did you need something?" Casey asked, putting on his best obedient child expression.

Isaac shrugged. "No, I only think you need to spend some time with your family. We can all watch a movie together after dinner."

"Sounds good," Casey replied, waiting for the other shoe to drop.

Did they know something? Was Issac trying to trick him into admitting what he was up to? Casey scanned their faces to see if they were on to him.

Isaac smiled. "Glad to hear it. We haven't had a family night in a while."

Casey's mother rose and gathered their plates to take them to the kitchen. Isaac jumped in to help clear the table, and the boys went to pick a movie. Casey started going through the cabinet where the movies were stored, sliding ones they didn't want out of the way as they tried to make a decision. They'd watched most of them numerous times. He finally settled on Jumanji, which was Aidan's favorite.

Seeing they were alone, Aidan turned to Casey. "You did sleep all day."

"No, I was doing other things, too."

"Casey, I saw you. I kept checking because I wanted to see if you wanted to go skateboarding. You were asleep, and you smelled bad," Aidan insisted.

Casey met his eyes. Aidan had a way of looking at people like he could read into their souls. He'd been that way since he was little, lacking the usual baby innocence. Sometimes, it was unsettling. This time, though, it was comforting. It made Casey feel less alone.

It made him feel seen.

"You're right. Look, don't say anything to Mom or Isaac. I don't want them thinking anything is wrong," Casey whispered.

"Is there? I mean, is something wrong?" Aidan asked, concerned. His small face was so serious and worried, it broke Casey's heart.

"No, little dude, everything's fine. I'm just tired today. We can do something fun tomorrow, okay? We can go skateboarding around town."

That was enough to distract Aidan's attention as Isaac and their mother came in to watch the movie. Isaac made popcorn, and their mother carried bowls for each of them. She smiled at her boys and sat down.

"This is so nice, all of us spending the evening together. I'm glad you are here tonight, Casey," she said, her voice carrying no hidden intentions.

"Me too, Mom."

They settled in, and Casey felt a sense of peace wash over him. As if everything in life was perfect at that very moment. He didn't need drugs to enjoy life. He needed his family and this. The quiet ease of being together with no expectations. He could let it all go and embrace what he had in that room. It was enough. The feeling of completeness filled his soul and allowed him to breathe.

Except he knew it wouldn't last.

CHAPTER FIVE

C asey didn't see it coming. There was no way he could have. His attention was focused on getting home on time to show his mother how much he appreciated all she'd done for him. Truthfully, he was also thinking about his biological father and wondering where he was now, what he was doing with his life. It didn't matter, though; Casey hadn't seen him in thirteen years.

Casey was thinking about how hard it must've been for his mother raising him alone after his father walked out on them, when the sound of squealing tires snapped him out of his thoughts. Headlights blinded him, and his sneaker slipped off the curb as he tried to regain his senses.

He squinted to see who was behind the wheel but

wasn't able to make out more than a shape of a guy. Casey put his hands over his eyes to diffuse the bright lights preventing him from seeing. He took a step back when he saw a shadow coming toward him, but he had nowhere to go.

He was cornered.

Angry laughter erupted as something hard smacked Casey in the head. He fell to his knees, still blinded by the headlights. He rose his hand to shield his face when cold metal struck him across the cheekbone. Hitting the ground, he felt a boot kick him in the chest. He was repeatedly struck until he began to black out. Not before he made out the face of his attacker. Or, at least, one of them.

Tucker.

That fucking asshole from the party. Now Casey remembered him. The one who started in on Smith and Casey took down. Tucker waited until Casey was alone and unsuspecting, then he and his friends took their opportunity to get revenge. Casey slipped in and out of consciousness, hearing the car tires peel out and the clank of metal as they threw the weapon out of the window. Casey felt the fuzzy darkness draw him down, letting his mother down once again.

"Hey, man. Wake up. Fuck. Casey!" A voice was yelling over him, causing Casey to wince in pain. The numbness of unconsciousness was being replaced with very real pain and confusion. His head felt split in two pieces, and his eyes were swollen shut.

Casey groaned and vomited. Hands turned him on his side so he didn't choke. Right now, Casey would kill for ketamine to take away the pain. He tried to speak.

"Fuck off, dude. Let me be."

"I have no clue what you just said, but we gotta get you out of here. It's getting late. Can you stand?"

Could he stand? He couldn't even open his eyes. What happened? Oh yeah. Tucker. He was going to kill that guy. Casey pried his eyes open with his fingers, the world spinning madly around him. However, he could make out the distinct outline of Smith. Smith was leaning over him, peering into his face.

Casey put his hand up. "Back up, Smith. I'm going to hurl."

Hot bile and what tasted like blood spewed out of his mouth. He was sure he had broken ribs. How the hell was he going to explain this to his mother? She was going to flip out. Casey eased to a sitting position, his head throbbing.

"I'm seriously fucked up."

"What happened, Casey? Miranda called me and said you were dead on the street. I hauled ass down here."

"Tucker."

Smith frowned, the memory dawning on him. "That dick from the party?"

"That's the one. He wasn't alone. I could hear other people with him. They jumped me," Casey explained. "I didn't even see it coming."

"Fuck, man, I'm sorry. He wouldn't even know who you were if it weren't for me. Do you need to go to the hospital?" Smith asked, his long fingers rubbing his chin in concern as he checked Casey over.

Casey shook his head. "I can't let my family know what happened. My mother will freak out, and Isaac will insist on tracking them down. I want to leave my parents out of this."

"You want to come to the lifeguard stand? I'm sleeping there tonight. We can build a fire on the beach."

"I don't know what I'll tell my mom. I promised I'd be home on time tonight," Casey replied.

Smith stood up straight, his thin back cracking with the movement. "Just tell them we are hanging out. I mean, it's true or can be."

Casey chuckled, the motion causing his head to pulse. "Okay, that might work for tonight, but what am I going to tell them tomorrow about how I look?"

"We'll figure it out. Let's call them and let them know you are spending the night with me. We'll camp out in the stand and come up with a plan. That work?"

Casey grimaced. It would have to until he had a better explanation. "You have any K on you?"

Smith nodded, then grinned. "Always. Come on, I'll help you up."

By the time they got Casey up on his feet, he was sweating profusely, and the world around him refused to stay still. He took a deep breath and attempted a step, burning pain shooting through him. "You have your car?"

"Yeah, it's right over here. I'm glad Miranda called me when she saw you."

Miranda. Something about that stuck for Casey. She saw him lying in the street but called Smith instead of helping him? No, there was more to it than that, Casey thought. "I think she was in on it."

"Miranda? Why?"

"I don't know. She's popped up since the party. She seems to show up where I am, even though we never really talked before. I think she was with Tucker."

"I don't know, Casey. I've known Miranda for years. Tucker just started coming around," Smith countered. His lanky legs were moving too fast for Casey.

Casey shrugged, sending shooting pains into his shoulders. "Whatever, then. Call it a hunch."

They made it to Smith's car, and he helped Casey get in. Every movement was like a knife cutting off pieces of him. Bones were broken for sure, and he was covered in head-to-toe bruises. He rested his head against the back of the seat. "Hey, Smith? Do you have that K on you? I'm fucking hurting bad."

"Shit, yeah. Hold on. It's in the back." Smith climbed out and went to the back of the car, pulling out a dirty duffle bag and rifled through it. He came back clutching a baggie of pills. "Let me crush this. It will work faster if you snort it."

Casey closed his eyes as he heard Smith turning the tablets into power. Smith touched his arm, and Casey peered at him. Smith held up his hand, which had a small pile of white powder in the palm. Casey knew what to do. He leaned forward and placed his thumb over one of his nostrils, then took a deep snort of the powder with the other. It burned like hell, but at least psychologically made him feel better, knowing he'd have physical relief soon.

He dropped his head back against the seat and nodded. "Thanks, man."

Smith snorted the rest of the powder and started the car. "We'll run by the gas station to call your parents, then head to the lifeguard stand. I have a stash of beer and pills in there."

Casey nodded weakly, his head feeling like it could roll off his shoulders at any point. "Sounds good."

By the time they got to the gas station, Casey was fully feeling the effects of the ketamine and didn't remember exactly what he said to his mother. Something about him and Smith wanting an early surfing session, so he was going to stay over with him so they could get up before the sun.

She didn't seem upset or concerned, so at least for tonight, Casey didn't need to explain what happened to him. Tomorrow was a problem for tomorrow.

The lifeguard stand was taller than Casey remembered. Or his body was so beat up, each step up the ladder was like a mile. Smith had a beer waiting for him when he got to the top, and he chugged it as fast as he could. Anything to take away the pain. Smith cracked another beer for him, and they leaned on the railing, looking out over the ocean. Even though he'd grown up there, Casey never got over the immense beauty of the coast.

"Did you see what kind of car they were driving, or who else was with Tucker?" Smith asked, taking a long swig of his beer.

"No. I was in my own world, and then all of a sudden, I was blinded by the headlights. I only caught a glimpse of Tucker when I was knocked to the ground. He spit on me when he left."

"Jesus Christ," Smith muttered. "Don't worry, we'll find his little bitch ass. Make him pay."

Casey knew they would. It was a small town, paths would cross. The thing was, he wasn't dying for revenge. They could find Tucker and beat the shit out of him, but it wouldn't change anything. It was a stupid cycle that would continue long after they were all gone. They were like trapped animals in a claustrophobic cage, biting each other, instead of the ones that put them there.

He wanted to hurt Tucker, but at what cost?

Casey shook his head. "I need to leave this fucking town. Go out and see the world."

Smith took another swig of beer, then lit a cigarette. "Where you going?"

"I don't know. Somewhere. This can't be all there is. Maybe New Zealand."

"New Zealand? I thought you meant like Raleigh."

They both laughed. Their tiny North Carolina town wasn't even on most maps. Sure, Raleigh was a big city, but Casey wanted to see things. Other cultures, natural wonders. He desired to travel the world.

He glanced at Smith. "Don't you want to leave?"

Smith took a long drag, the tip of the cigarette glowing like a firefly. "For what? It's all ideas, anyway. Every place is just like the other. Streets, towns, homes, bills. Why bother? I have no plans. I just need to get through today, you know?"

Casey braced himself against the railing, realizing he needed to sit before he fell. He crept into the lifeguard stand and was relieved to see Smith had set up a cot with blankets and pillows. He sat on the cot, using it like a couch, and rested his back against the wooden wall. Smith stood in the doorway, his tall frame filling the opening. He rested his hands against the top of the door frame and yawned.

"To keep close to the truth, we should go surfing in the morning. Then tell your mother you wiped out and hit one of the pilings."

Leave it to Smith to know how to spin the best lie.

That excuse held up, but Casey doubted he could get on a surfboard. "That works, except for the surfing part. Not even sure I'll be able to walk in the morning," he answered.

Smith chuckled and sat down on the cot next to Casey. "Fair enough. Didn't think about that. Either way, it's totally believable. I've seen some surfing injuries that'd make your bumps and bruises look like child's play."

So had Casey. "Broken bones. Pretty sure he cracked a few of my ribs."

Smith sighed, turning to Casey. "I'm sorry, man. Seriously. Tucker's issues are with me, not you. I feel like total shit about this."

Casey shrugged. "Maybe they used to be, but he and I have issues now."

"Yeah. We'll set this right. He won't get away with it," Smith insisted.

"Then, what? He and his friends come after us again? Or worse, come after my little brother? Come on, Smith. We need to let it go before it gets out of hand and drags other people into it. It doesn't change anything."

Anger flashed across Smith's face. He lit another cigarette and stared out the door. "So, what? We let him get away with this? He could have killed you. I'll leave you out of it, but I'm not done with him yet."

"Look, I understand where you're coming from. It pisses me off, too, but I can't let this spiral out of control. Aidan is everything to me, and I need to protect him first and foremost. It's a small town. What's to say Tucker wouldn't see Aidan walking home from school and decide to go after him? I can't risk it. I'm not like you, I have-" Casey stopped himself before he said anything else, regretting even thinking it. He slammed his mouth shut, but it was too late to take back what he said. "Family? Yeah, yeah, I get it, dude. I have no one," Smith added miserably.

Casey felt like shit. He didn't mean to hurt Smith like that. "You have me. We're brothers."

Smith grinned, his face looking more vulnerable than he realized. "Thanks, Casey. Brothers, it is. So, you want some more K, bro?"

Casey laughed. "You know it."

CHAPTER SIX

T he next morning, Smith and Casey did a light surf session, despite Casey barely being able to walk. Casey could hardly stay on the board and gave up after about thirty minutes. Deep breaths were excruciating and his balance was shit. Smith helped him tape his ribs, which only made movement even more restrictive.

Either way, he wasn't lying to his mother about surfing that morning. He did it. Now, the lie would come easier. They rested on a blanket in the sand when they were done and watched tourists flooding onto the beach.

Smith turned to Casey, his eyes distant. "I'm going to find Tucker and beat his ass. His beef was with me, to begin with, so I'm going to refocus his anger that way. I'm sick of people trying to come in and take over my area."

"Does it happen a lot? People trying to push you out?" Casey asked, lying flat on the blanket to give his ribs a break. It didn't help much.

Smith shrugged, digging a hole in the sand with his foot. "Not really. There isn't much money in dealing drugs here, so it's the small-time assholes who think they are going to make big bucks. Clearly, I'm not rolling in dough."

Casey laughed. His ribs screamed in response. That was true. Smith didn't even have a stable place to live. He floated around, crashing on couches, sleeping in the lifeguard stand, even passing out on the beach. His parents acted as if they didn't have a son. Casey felt for Smith in that regard. His own family was at times overbearing, but always cared about where he was and what was best for him.

He glanced at Smith. His friend was staring out over the waves, his brow furrowed in thought. Most people saw Smith as the party guy, but Casey knew better. He knew him well enough to know Smith was struggling. He showed Casey his sensitive side, sometimes. Not intentionally, but no one could keep up the facade forever.

"Hey, thanks for coming for me," Casey whispered.

Smith's eyes focused back in, and he smirked at Casey. "Guess we're taking turns, right?"

"Yeah. If I leave this town, will you come with me?"

"Maybe. I don't know. I mean, there's nothing really keeping me here, you know? But what's out there for me? Most times, it's easier to think about getting through today and not plan for the future."

Casey understood that. When he dreamed about

leaving, he didn't have a set plan. It was simply a way to not feel trapped there. To think that maybe there was a place where he wouldn't feel so alone in the world. He rolled over, using his arm to push himself into a sitting position.

Everything hurt.

"I need to head home soon."

Smith stood up, shaking sand out of his hair. "You got your story straight?"

"I think so. I was surfing, got distracted, and hit the piling," Casey answered. Keep it simple, so he didn't trip himself up.

"That about does it. I can be your alibi if you need one. Make it more dramatic, though. You were surfing when a wave caught your board and smashed you into the piling. Your injuries are pretty severe, so the story needs to be." Smith put his hand out to Casey to help him up.

Casey took Smith's hand and let him guide him to his feet. Smith made sure he was stable, then gathered the blanket. They walked off the beach, Casey moving like a ninety-year-old. No matter how hard he tried, he couldn't stand up completely straight. His mother was going to freak out when she saw him. Surfing, piling. He hoped she bought it.

He cleared his throat. "Smith, about Tucker, though. Can't you let it go?"

Smith stopped walking and turned to Casey, his eyes flashing. "Then, what? Do you think he'll stop? I just need to send him a message. Let him know he doesn't belong here. That I won't take his shit."

"Where did he come from? Like, how did he end up here?" Casey asked, pausing to catch his breath and try to take the pressure off his ribs.

"I don't know. Heard rumor he was someone's relative, but who cares? He doesn't get to show up here and act like he owns the place. He's not local. He's not one of us."

Casey knew there was no talking Smith out of tracking Tucker down, but he didn't like that he was the reason for it. If he hadn't interceded at the party, Smith likely would have set him straight right then and there. But he did, and here they were. Guys like Tucker showed up every couple of years, acting like they were God's gift to the locals. They usually moved on once they realized there was nothing going on there. The locals always knew that. It was an insignificant tourist town with no prospects and no growth.

They made it to Smith's car, and Smith helped Casey get into the passenger's seat. The drive was silent, each in their own thoughts, when Casey turned to Smith.

"Can you at least wait til I'm healed, so I can have your back? I caused some of this and don't want you dealing with Tucker alone."

"What about Aidan?" Smith questioned.

Aidan. There was that. Casey didn't want to involve his little brother, however, he wasn't sure he could completely prevent that. It seemed like Tucker was bound and determined to make his presence known. If he touched Aidan, though, Casey would kill him.

That much he knew for sure.

Smith pulled up in front of Casey's house. Isaac was out doing yard work, and Casey felt panic growing in him. He hated lying to his mother but knew the truth would only open a can of worms. He'd need to stick with the lie. Casey pushed the door open, steadying himself for the onslaught of questions he was about to endure. Isaac glanced over, then looked away, not noticing Casey's injuries. A millisecond later, his head whipped around, and he stared at Casey. Casey had yet to see himself more than in the reflection of the car window and could only imagine how bad he looked.

Isaac dropped the shears he was holding and ran over. "What happened?"

Smith spoke up before Casey could. "We were surfing, and this crazy, random wave caught his board and threw him into the pilings under the pier. It was bad. By the time I got to him, Casey was barely conscious. I had to drag him and his board onto shore."

Isaac wasn't a surfer and took Smith's word for it. "We need to get you to the hospital."

Casey shook his head. "No, I'm okay. Smith helped me tape my ribs, and it's not as bad as it appears."

"No, you need to go. You could have internal injuries. How long ago was this?"

"A couple of hours, I guess," Smith answered. He was always better at lying than Casey. "I took him to the lifeguard stand for treatment and checked him over. It looks worse than it is, I think."

Isaac frowned, glancing between them, not convinced. "Still, you can't risk internal bleeding. We should go have you looked at. Your mother will insist on it."

Internal bleeding. Casey hadn't considered it last night. If that would've killed him, he'd already be dead. However, he knew Isaac was right, his mother would make him go to the doctor. "Fine. Can I at least go inside for a bit? I need to go to the bathroom."

Isaac seemed unsure, knowing Casey's mother would be the final say, but motioned to the door. "Do you need my help getting inside?"

Casey waved him away, wishing he wasn't under the microscope. If he thought he was now, he was in for it once his mother saw him. As if she sensed his presence, she appeared at the door. Her face scanned all three men standing outside and landed on Casey. Her eyes grew wide as she threw open the storm door.

"Casey! What is going on? Who did this to you?" Her voice was frantic as she bolted across the lawn.

Casey glanced at Smith, letting him know it was alright to leave. This was going to be a whole production. Smith took a step back, his eyes darting between them, then gave a short nod. Casey's parents didn't even seem to notice him there, so he backed toward his car.

As soon as Smith was near it, he jumped in and drove away with a wave of his hand. Smith was always polite to Casey's family, but it was clear he wasn't sure what to do around them.

Casey let his mother fuss over his injuries for a minute, then put his hand up. "Mom, I need to go to the bathroom. Can you give me a minute?"

She knitted her brow and glanced at Isaac. "He needs to go to the hospital. Isaac, did you tell him he needs to go to the hospital?"

"I did. Let him use the bathroom first, then I can take him over there."

"You? I am going, too," she insisted.

"What about Aidan?" Casey mumbled, wanting them to chill out.

"He'll just have to go with us," she stated.

So, it was going to be a family outing. Great.

After Casey went to the bathroom, they loaded up in Isaac's car like they were going to the movies. Casey's mother kept staring at him, and he wished she'd stop.

"Mom, it won't go away just because you watch me like a hawk," Casey said.

Aidan laughed, then clammed up when Isaac gave him the dad-eye. Casey appreciated his brother bringing a little levity to the situation. Aidan had a way of doing that. Casey closed his eyes and practiced his story in his mind again. Surfing, wave, piling.

Got it.

Being a small town, the closest hospital was a town over and still no bigger than an elementary school. They were able to get right in to be seen, and Casey's mother hovered around him as the doctor asked questions about what happened and his injuries. When the doctor asked him to take off his clothes and put on the paper gown, that was the line in the sand.

"Mom, I'm not taking off my clothes in front of you. Can you please step out?" he asked.

She appeared panicked for a moment, then the doctor smiled and motioned for the door. "It's okay, he's in good hands. From what it looks like, these injuries will heal on their own, and there's no risk of internal injuries. The X-rays look good. A couple of broken ribs but no organ damage and no need for surgery at this point. I just need to check a few other things before he can leave."

Casey was grateful for the interference and breathed a sigh of relief when his mother left the room. He could see the finish line and couldn't wait to get out of there and go home.

The doctor came back over and sat down in front of Casey, checking over his injuries as he made notes on a chart. He set the chart down and met Casey's eyes, his own concerned. He looked younger than Casey first thought when he came into the room. Casey sensed there was more to the doctor asking his mother to leave and tensed up. The doctor cleared his throat and frowned.

"Do you want to tell me what really happened?"

CHAPTER SEVEN

C asey's heart leapt to his throat, and he stared at the doctor. What gave it away? What part of the lie should he stick with, and what part should he admit? He shook his head. "I'm sorry, I don't know what you mean."

The doctor rubbed his chin, his eyes focused on Casey's face. He gazed at the chart for a second, then back at Casey. "Look, I don't know what happened, but I know your story doesn't add up. These injuries didn't happen a couple of hours ago. I'd say at least eighteen hours ago, with how they are presenting. That, and you have multiple narcotics in your bloodstream."

Fuck.

They drew blood when he got there. Casey didn't think about the ketamine and other drugs in his system.

His mind raced, trying to come up with a believable lie. He swallowed hard and stared at his hands. "Maybe someone slipped me something."

"Come on, Casey," the doctor replied, his voice developing a sympathetic familiarity. "I'm not your enemy, and you're an adult, so I'm bound to not say anything to your parents. However, it looks like you took a serious beating, and the amount of drugs in your system tells me this isn't the first time you took them. I'm only trying to help."

Casey glanced up, not sure how honest the doctor was being. He half expected him to call the police. He dropped his eyes to the doctor's name tag. Dr. Bender. Ironic. He wiped his sweaty palms on his pants and decided a partial lie and a little truth might be enough to get him out of this. "This guy beat me up yesterday for getting between him and my friend. I took ketamine for the pain."

Dr. Bender tipped his head, reading Casey's face. "Alright, fine, we'll go with that. Do you want to tell me where you got ketamine from, then?"

Casey flushed, not wanting to get Smith in any trouble. His throat tightened, and he stared at the wall, not answering the question. It was one thing to be called out for his drug use, Casey wasn't taking anyone else down with him. Dr. Bender waited a few seconds, then sighed, knowing he was not getting an answer out of Casey. He picked up the chart and scribbled some notes on it. Casey wished he could see what the doctor was writing in there.

Dr. Bender looked back up, meeting Casey's eyes that were now on him. "I'm going to give you a steroid for the swelling and some antibiotics. I want to give you some pain meds, however, since you have been taking ketamine,

I worry the levels of drugs in your system will be too much. I know you don't want to give anyone away, but you need to comprehend that ketamine is a very powerful drug. You or someone you know could die from using it. Do you understand?"

Casey nodded, dropping his gaze. Shame was coursing through him, and for some reason, it mattered to him what the doctor thought of him. Why did he even care? Dr. Bender handed him the prescriptions and stood up.

"Come back if you have any issues. I included a sheet of warning signs for your healing. Casey, please reach out to me when you are ready to get some help. Believe me when I say you can trust me. You're young and don't want this hanging over the rest of your life."

At this, Casey met his eyes and wanted to cry. Part of him reasoned he was just having a good time and would leave it all behind when he got a little older. But another part of him was telling him he did have a problem. That he was running from something deep inside by using. Something he wasn't ready to face. He stood, slipping on his shorts, and pulled his hoodie over his head, liking the sensation of shutting out the world. He put on his public face and smiled.

"Thanks, Dr. Bender. You have nothing to worry about. I won't use it again."

They stared at each other, both knowing that was a lie. Casey clutched the paperwork and headed for the door. He was glad he was at least eighteen, so the doctor wouldn't, or couldn't, say anything to his parents.

Dr. Bender called out to him as he reached the door. "I don't know what you are dealing with, Casey, but if you ever need to talk or a referral for a therapist, I am here."

Casey didn't turn around and practically bolted out the door. His parents and Aidan were in the waiting room and rose when Casey came out. They glanced at him, then at Dr. Bender, who was following behind.

Casey's mother chewed her lip, her face twisted with concern. "What did they say?" she asked Casey.

"I'll be fine, Mom. A couple of broken ribs and some bruises. They gave me a prescription for steroids and antibiotics."

"What about for the pain?" Isaac asked.

Casey's face felt hot, and he glanced at Dr. Bender, praying he wouldn't say anything. Dr. Bender met his eyes, then focused on his parents. "Ibuprofen should be fine. If the pain gets too severe, we can assess something stronger at that point. For now, I think it's best if we start minimally for the pain. It can be a good indicator of healing progress."

Casey's mother seemed relieved by this and touched his arm, her dark eyes searching his face. "You must be more careful, Casey. You could've been hurt much worse."

Casey was afraid she would make an issue out of surfing and made a quick diversion. "I'm okay, Mom. I'll surf away from the pier from now on."

She smiled, her face tired and worried. "Please do."

Aidan was clearly bored out of his mind and came over to Casey, tugging on his arm. "Can we go now?"

Casey chuckled and ruffled his little brother's hair. "Thanks for the concern, dingus."

Aidan grinned and shrugged. "You aren't dead, Casey, so let's go."

"If I was dead, I wouldn't be going anywhere."

At this, Aidan laughed and pulled Casey by the arm toward the door. Casey looked back at Dr. Bender, who flicked his eyes between Aidan and Casey. As if to say, *you would hurt more than yourself.* Message received. Casey would try to stop or at least cut back. He bobbed his head and let Aidan drag him through the door.

On the ride home, Casey fought dozing off as Aidan talked nonstop. For some reason, Casey found his brother's energy soothing. By the time they got home, Casey was running on fumes and excused himself to take a nap. His mother made him take his meds first, and he had to admit, her hovering was comforting this time around. He crawled into bed and slept for almost twelve hours.

When Casey woke up, he wished the doctor had given him pain meds. Every inch of him ached and felt like they were on fire. He stumbled to the bathroom and took ibuprofen. He'd kill for some ketamine right about then and considered reaching out to Smith for some. He tried Smith on the phone at his latest crash spot but got no answer. Hopefully, the ibuprofen would take the edge off.

The house was quiet when he went downstairs. It was after two in the morning, and everyone else was sound asleep. He didn't like being up alone at this time. When he was, part of him wondered if he was actually dead and didn't know it. It had been that way since he was little. He'd wake up in the dark and think no one could hear or see him until his mother held him and reminded him he was there. However, since he'd grown up, he had to convince himself he was real.

He fished a pair of headphones out of the drawer in the kitchen and plugged them into the stereo in the living room. Music always helped him feel less disconnected from the world. He sorted through Isaac's records and landed on John Coltrane. Putting the record on, he sprawled out on the floor with his eyes closed.

As the music filled his senses, he felt his anxiety abate. Like ketamine, music helped Casey find a place within himself where he felt home... like he belonged. His muscles relaxed, and he found peace. At some point in the night, he fell asleep, and the record player turned itself off.

Aidan was standing over him when Casey woke up, still on the floor. The sun was bright and high in the sky as he gazed up at his younger brother. Casey pulled the headphones off. "What's up?"

Aidan grinned and nudged him with his foot. "Mom said to leave you alone, but that was hours ago. You wanna play video games with me?"

Casey sat up, his back screaming in pain. "Get me some ibuprofen, and you have a deal. Oh, and make me a sandwich, little dude. I'm starving."

Aidan ran out of the room, coming back in with the pill bottle and what looked like a mostly jelly sandwich with a wad of thick peanut butter dead in the center. Casey choked it down as Aidan set up the console. Within minutes, Casey was letting Aidan destroy him at Pro Skater. He could easily win the game, but he enjoyed seeing Aidan razz him more. It was totally worth losing to see Aidan jump up and down with excitement.

By dinnertime, Casey was craving K hard and thought about his promise to himself to not use. He couldn't go cold turkey and decided he could monitor it. Only take a little at a time, wean down. He knew Smith would be at the lifeguard stand after his shift.

He ate dinner with his family, then cleared his throat.

"Hey, I need to meet up with Smith for a little bit tonight. He might have a lead on a job for me."

Isaac raised his eyebrows. "Do you think that's wise, considering your condition?"

Casey tried to act nonchalant. "It'll only be for a bit. He wanted to introduce me to a guy who does the hiring for the town."

"A job at the lifeguard stand?" his mother asked.

That was where it got sticky. Casey was great at tiny lies, but the deeper they got, the less consistent he was. He shook his head. "I don't think so. Sounded like construction. I don't know. Just some dude Smith knows who is looking for someone to help out."

"Casey, I don't want you out late. You are still healing," his mother insisted.

"I promise I'll be back by nine. Okay?"

She didn't seem convinced but nodded. "Nine. Do you need a ride?"

"No, I'm good to take my skateboard, I think. I need to be moving some, anyway, to loosen up my body. I'll take it easy, I swear."

He helped clean up after dinner, then headed out to the lifeguard stand. He was on his skateboard and in incredible pain, so it took longer than he was expecting. By the time he got there, it was after eight. He'd have to see if Smith could give him a ride back home.

He climbed up the ladder, each step harder than the previous, as he tried to take steady breaths around his cracked ribs. "Smith, you in there?"

Smith came to the door and peered down. "Damn, Casey, I didn't expect to see you anytime soon. What did your parents say about everything?"

"They made me go to the hospital. Broken ribs and some other shit," Casey replied as he got to the top. "Drugs showed up in my system, so the doc wouldn't give me pain meds. I'm seriously hurting. You got any K on you?"

Smith waved him in. "You want some now? You want to hang out for a bit?"

Casey shook his head. "Can't. My mother is still freaking out and I promised I'd be home by nine. Let me buy some, though. Would you mind giving me a ride home? Skating over here was excruciating."

Smith dug through his bag and threw Casey a packet of pills. "On the house for covering my ass."

When he threw the packet, Casey noticed Smith's knuckles were freshly bleeding and bruised. They hadn't been that way when Smith dropped him off before at the house. He glanced at Smith. "Tucker?"

Smith nodded, his lips pressed together. "Tucker. I set him straight for what he did to you."

"Damn."

"Let him focus on me for a while. Anyway, let's get you home, dude. You look rough."

On the ride home, Smith told Casey how he found Tucker downtown and dragged him into an alley. He pummeled him and told him to back the fuck off. Tucker swore he would, but they both knew otherwise. It was a stay of execution was all.

Tucker wasn't smart enough to move on.

Smith pulled up to Casey's house and let the car idle. His eyes watched the brightly lit house, his face unreadable.

Casey shoved the door open and made sure the packet

of pills was tucked securely in his pocket. "Thanks for the ride home, man... and for the pills. It was going to be a long, rough night without them."

Smith's eyes flicked from the house to Casey, his mouth frozen in a partial grin. "No problem."

"You alright?" Casey could sense something brewing under the surface.

"Yeah. You have a good family, you know that, right?" Smith asked, his voice distant.

Casey did.

He didn't know why it wasn't enough. He still had more than Smith at the end of the day. He had people who cared about him, who wanted him around. On the outside, he had the perfect life. Hell, even to him, it appeared like the perfect life. He loved his family and knew they'd do anything for him.

When it was only him and his mother, he thought he never wanted it to change. However, when Isaac, then Aidan, came along, Casey felt like his family grew and never felt slighted by them. It was a good life and a good family. He knew he was lucky for that.

Yet, he still felt empty.

CHAPTER EIGHT

T he pain was unbearable. Casey sat on the edge of his bed, clutching the mattress with all his might. He really wished the doctor had given him pain meds. His back felt like it was twisted in knots, and those knots were getting tighter and tighter. He still had a few pills from Smith and debated whether or not he could push through the pain or needed to give in and take them.

His ribs were on fire and every breath was like trying to suck a marble through a straw. No matter what position he tried, the pain was consistent. It had only been a few days since seeing the doctor; however, at times, Casey thought it would never get better.

Finally, at the end of his rope, he crushed one of the pills and snorted it, praying for fast relief. As the ketamine gave him the sensation of falling through levels of reality, Casey felt his muscles loosen and lay back on his bed, letting breath into his lungs. That was better. Dr. Bender may have been trying to help Casey by denying him anything other than ibuprofen, but it was only driving Casey to use more ketamine. More than he wanted to.

He fell asleep, allowing the ketamine to take him away from himself and the pain. He only had one pill left and hoped it was enough to get through the night. By morning, that pill was gone, and Casey knew he'd need to get more if he was going to keep the pain at bay. He wasn't sure how much it was taking away the pain or simply causing his brain to not realize it. Either way, it was helping him cope.

He rifled through his wallet and stared at the last two twenties he had. That would cover him for a bit, but he needed to come up with more money. Unlike Smith, he'd never held a job for more than a few weeks. They never mattered to him, so usually, he just stopped showing up, then told his parents they didn't need him anymore. His mother always believed him, though Isaac's doubt was growing.

Casey didn't know what he wanted to do in life, however, he knew he wanted to leave the only town he'd known. It was suffocating him. He and Smith talked about it all the time, but at the end of the day, Smith didn't seem in a hurry to leave. On the other hand, it was all Casey could think about. The problem was, he didn't know what he'd do to get out or what to do once he did.

Casey rolled out of bed and slipped on a pair of board shorts and a tank top. His sneakers were only a couple of feet away, but reaching for them made his ribs scream, so he opted for the closer flip-flops instead. His dark, curly hair was wild around his face, and he ran his fingers through the mass, trying to tame it.

He slipped his hand into his bedside stand and felt around for any runaway pills. There weren't any, but his fingers brushed his journal, and he pulled it out. He used to write in it every day before the attack, however, hadn't felt like it the last few days. He opened the crinkled pages, flipping past drawings and half-assed poetry. Finally, he took out a pen and scribbled a few words and a drawing of a skeleton, skateboarding.

We can't fly if we don't break. We won't break if we don't take the leap.

Whatever that meant.

Most of his poems and thoughts were fragmented. He definitely felt broken and only sensed like he was flying when he was surfing or took ketamine. That was the problem. Like the words, Casey couldn't get to or express what he desired. It was always just outside of the goal, out of touch. He could see it, he couldn't find his way to it.

Frustrated, he slammed the journal shut and got up. It was stupid, anyway. Just another attempt at releasing something trapped inside him he couldn't quite reach.

Casey stretched slowly and peered out his window. Isaac's car was gone. It was later than Casey expected, so he went to the kitchen. His mother was on the phone and gave him a half smile. She finished the call and turned to him, her eyes scanning his face.

"Are you hungry? I let you sleep so you can heal. I need to go to work shortly. Isaac already left for work. Can you keep an eye on Aidan today?"

Casey nodded and grabbed a banana off the counter.

He peeled it as he measured his words, not wanting to give anything away. "I'm good. Not as sore, so I need to take care of a few things. Aidan can tag along."

She tipped her head, her face concerned. "Do you want to drop me off at work and take my car, so you don't have to walk? You should be taking it easy."

"Yeah, I can do that. Hey, do you have any cash? I need to get some more gauze and medicine."

She took her purse off a hook by the door and handed him thirty dollars. "Is this enough? Can you get Aidan lunch while you're out?"

Casey did the math quickly and nodded. He could get Aidan a burger at By the Sea and still have twenty left over. That would give him sixty for pills. He wouldn't eat. "Sure."

She smiled and placed her hand on his cheek. "I'm glad you are starting to feel better, you have some color returning to your cheeks. Don't overdo it. I'll have Isaac pick me up on his way home from work."

"Thanks, Mom. Where is Trouble?" he asked, referring to his little brother.

She gestured to the door. "He went outside to play."

"I'll round him up. When do you have to leave?"

"In about ten minutes. I need to pack a lunch still, so go get Aidan. I should be ready by then. I'll meet you at the car as soon as I'm ready."

Casey went out but didn't see Aidan anywhere. His bike was still lying in the grass, and it wasn't like Aidan to wander too far. His parents were nothing if not overprotective. Casey wandered up the street. In the distance, he could hear the retreating jingle of the ice cream truck music. Ah. Aidan must have seen the ice cream truck and gone after it.

Casey went in that direction, and sure enough, he saw Aidan standing with a dripping bomb pop in his hand, licking the sticky mess off his fingers. If their mother knew he'd gone that far without telling her, she'd be upset.

Casey moved toward Aidan when he observed something that stopped him in his tracks. Aidan wasn't alone. He was talking to some guy who had his back to Casey. Casey frowned and began walking faster in their direction. He knew that outline.

Tucker.

"Aidan!" Casey called out. "Come on."

Aidan glanced over, his cheeks flushed. He knew he wasn't supposed to leave without telling anyone. He ran toward Casey, his eyes worried. "Sorry. That guy was asking me if I knew where someone lived."

"Why the fuck did you come over here? Mom would be pissed if she knew."

Aidan's dark eyes looked like they might tear up. "I didn't mean to. I was trying to catch up to the ice cream truck and went too far."

Casey reached Aidan and placed his hand on his shoulder, his eyes on Tucker the whole time as they walked back toward the house. "What did he say to you?"

Aidan's dark eyebrows knitted, and he shook his head. "He, he was just asking if I knew some guy's name and where his house was."

"Who?" Casey's voice was crossed between panic and fury. He tried to remain calm for Aidan's sake.

"I don't remember. I didn't know the name. I'm sorry, Casey. Please don't tell Mom."

Casey was seeing red and didn't know what to do. Did Tucker know Aidan was his brother? He obviously wasn't looking for Casey because Aidan would have known that. He stared at Tucker, who had now turned and was watching him with a smirk. Casey wanted to bash his face in, but not in front of Aidan. He led Aidan by the shoulder back toward their house, his anger causing him to not think straight.

"Don't ever talk to that guy again," he barked at his little brother.

Aidan's eyes welled with tears, and he shook his head. "I didn't know. I'm sorry."

Casey immediately felt bad for letting his anger at Tucker spill over to Aidan. He turned Aidan to face him, his face softening. "I'm not mad at you, Aidan. That guy is bad news, do you understand? He's up to no good. I'm trying to protect you. Okay?"

Aidan nodded. The bomb pop was now a dripping mess, and he dropped it in the grass, wiping his hands on his shorts. "Do you know him?"

"I know *of* him. He likes to cause trouble. Just stay away from him, alright?"

"I will."

Casey's anger began to subside, and he glanced back. Tucker was gone. By the time they got to the house, their mother was waiting by the car. She took one look at Aidan and shook her head. "Ice cream truck?"

Aidan blushed. "Yeah."

"Go get cleaned up, your clothes are a mess. Casey is taking you with him to run errands and get lunch. If you didn't spoil it."

Aidan ran inside to change. Casey made sure he had

his wallet and climbed in the driver's seat. His mother slid in next to him, meeting his gaze. "Was he far?"

"Nah, just down the street," he lied.

She smiled, and her face relaxed. Aidan came out and crawled into the backseat, eyeing Casey and his mother, his angled face looking older than his eleven years. Seeing his mother wasn't angry at him, he sighed in relief and stared out the window.

After they dropped their mother off at work, Aidan moved up to the front seat next to Casey and whispered, "Thanks, Casey."

"For what?"

"For not telling on me."

Casey chuckled. "Trust me, if I had, we'd both probably be stuck at home. It's for the best."

Aidan grinned. They both knew their mother all too well. She was only caring for them, but her version of caring was very overwhelming at times. As they drove to the restaurant, Aidan chattered about a new trick he'd learned on his skateboard, and Casey watched him with a mixture of appreciation and admiration. Aidan moved through the world with confidence and freedom. Without the weight Casey always felt he had slowing him down.

They pulled in and parked by the restaurant. Casey was relieved to see Smith was on shift at the lifeguard stand, his tall outline leaning on the railing. He raised his hand to Smith, who nodded back. A silent message passed between him and Casey knew he'd be able to find some relief now.

First, though, he needed to feed Aidan.

They climbed out of the car and meandered down the boardwalk to the front of the restaurant. Casey moved intentionally to not cause himself pain. Or more pain. Despite his best efforts, every step was excruciating. He hid it away from Aidan, who would likely say something to their mother by accident. All Casey could think about was getting more ketamine to take it away.

Aidan turned to Casey, his eyes deep in thought. "I think I remember who that guy was asking about."

"Oh yeah? Who?"

"Some guy named, like, Ernest or something like that. Do you know who that is?"

Casey hadn't heard the name before but committed it to memory. He had a feeling he needed to remember that name.

A bad feeling.

CHAPTER NINE

"**C**asey, the phone's for you!" The sound of his mother's voice yelling up the stairs woke Casey from his slumber. He forced his eyes open, his head pounding.

What time was it?

A glance at the clock and he realized he'd slept until after one in the afternoon. Surprised Isaac didn't make an issue of him sleeping so late, Casey swung his legs over the edge of the bed. They'd been letting a lot slide with him since the attack, but that was a few weeks ago, and Casey was almost back to normal.

Even his ribs didn't hurt when he breathed in anymore. Granted, he'd been taking more ketamine than before, even as the pain subsided. He promised himself he'd cut back as soon as the pain was under control, but he hadn't yet.

Stumbling down the stairs, he grabbed the cordless phone off the counter and gave his mother a short wave to let her know he had it. She was sorting a bag of clothes on the couch and nodded at him, her face ever watchful. Seeing he was fine, she went back to putting clothes in piles.

Casey turned away and put the phone to his ear. "This is Casey."

"Hey, man. Recovering from last night?" Smith asked, referring to the bonfire party they'd attended.

"Yeah, I'm good. Enough, anyway. Surprised you're up and moving around, though. Last I saw, you were passed out under the lifeguard stand. You were breathing, so I left you alone to sleep it off."

Smith chuckled. "I appreciate that. Woke up with a gull pecking at my feet. Little fucker drew blood. What are you up to today?"

Casey frowned. What was he up to? His mother kept a calendar in the kitchen, so he wandered toward it to see if he was required for anything. It said *thrift store,* which explained why his mother was going through clothes. His clothes always went to Aidan, so he was free and clear. "Nothing. Why?"

"I need to drive down to Jacksonville to make a run and wouldn't mind some company. You want to go along for the ride?" Smith asked.

A run meant to pick up more ketamine and whatever other party drugs Smith could get. Usually, it was brought to them. Casey glanced at his mother and lowered his voice as if she knew what they were talking about.

"Jacksonville? Yeah, I have been wanting to check out a little shop there. You mind if we pop in while we're there?"

"Sure, I'm not in a rush. What shop?"

"I can't remember the name, but it's like a metaphysical store," Casey explained.

Smith began laughing. "Seriously? Going all new age on me, Casey?"

Casey flushed. Smith was his closest friend, but even he didn't know how much Casey struggled with finding his path. "Fuck off. I just want to check out a couple of things. Why are you having to go there? Don't they usually come to you?"

Smith was quiet, then answered, "I'm taking on some additional responsibilities."

Casey wondered what that meant. Smith always provided the locals with party drugs, but he never went bigger than that. Until now. If he was running the drugs, that meant he had a larger stake in it. "Alright. Let me get dressed and eat something. Come by in like an hour."

"Will do."

After they hung up, Casey went to the kitchen to scrounge for some food. His mother had made pancakes, so he choked down a few with orange juice. He wandered back out and saw his mother roped Aidan into helping with the clothes. He didn't look too thrilled about it, either. Aidan probably couldn't wait to go back to school.

"Hey, Mom. I'm going to ride with Smith to Jacksonville today to keep him company. You need me for anything?" Casey asked.

She paused midair, holding a t-shirt to Aidan's chest. "No. I'm going through your old clothes to see what fits Aidan and taking his old clothes down to the thrift store.

Will you be home for dinner?"

Casey did the math and shook his head. "I don't think so. With the drive and being there for a bit, it might be later this evening."

"Alright. You have an appointment with Dr. Bender tomorrow, so make sure you are home tonight."

They both knew Casey could disappear at times. Casey winked at Aidan. "Wouldn't miss it for the world."

She set the t-shirt down and frowned at him. "No need to be snide, Casey. They need to do x-rays to see how your ribs are healing."

"Sorry, Mom. I appreciate it." Casey felt like shit for being sarcastic with his mother. She was only trying to help.

By the time he was dressed, Smith was waiting outside. Casey grabbed his stuff and locked the door behind him. His mother and Aidan had left a few minutes before, and Casey was glad to not have to let anyone know he was leaving. He always felt like he was lying to them. Telling partial truths. Smith was drumming his fingers on the steering wheel, matching the rhythm of the music he was listening to.

Casey slid into the passenger's seat and threw his bag into the back seat. Smith grinned and glanced at him. "Thanks for coming along. I owe you one."

"Nah. If we stop by the shop, we're square. I needed to get out of the house, anyway."

"You need to get a job, man. Can't be home all the time. It's bad for your brain," Smith replied as he pulled away from the curb.

"Yeah. Nothing speaks to me."

Smith laughed, his head tipped back. "Speaks to you?

Fuck. I don't think work speaks to anyone. Labor for pay, that's all."

"You don't get something out of being a lifeguard?" Casey asked, embarrassed by what Smith said.

"Ninety percent of the time, no. When we save someone, yeah, I guess so. But it's not like my calling in life."

That surprised Casey. As long as he'd known Smith as an adult, he'd been a lifeguard. "What is your calling, then?"

At this, Smith blushed. Casey had hit a nerve. Smith slid a pair of sunglasses on and kept his face straight forward. "I don't know. Sometimes, I think I'd like to own my own restaurant, be a chef."

This time, Casey laughed. "A chef? Seriously? Can you even cook?"

Smith gripped the steering wheel harder, his knuckles turning white. "Fuck yeah, I can cook. Been doing it since I was a kid. You don't know everything about me, dude."

Casey stared in disbelief. He'd known Smith on and off for years, starting back when they were kids, however, he had no clue not only could he cook, but that he wanted to be a chef. "Oh, damn. I had no idea. So, why don't you?"

"Why don't I what?"

"Become a chef?"

Smith lowered his glasses and stared at Casey, a smirk on his face. "You know of any fine dining establishments around here?"

That was true. All of the restaurants served beach food. Fried, grill-type food the tourists loved when they were on vacation. Casey pushed. "Why only here? I'm waiting on the day I get the hell out of here. You could go, too."

Smith focused back on the road, his mouth in a straight line. "I think about it, sometimes. I don't have the money to go, though. Barely getting by as it is. At least here, I can sleep on people's couches and in the lifeguard stand. I'd need to straighten the fuck up to save any more to leave. I'm not there yet."

Neither was Casey. He dreamed of leaving but knew he didn't have the motivation to do so. "So, what's the deal with Jacksonville? Are you moving up the ladder?"

Smith chewed his lip. "I guess so. Taking on more responsibility. With Tucker sniffing around, I thought it would be wise."

Tucker. He'd slithered back into his hole since the day Casey saw him with Aidan. That reminded Casey of what Aidan told him. "Hey, do you know a guy named Ernest?"

Smith slowed his speed and eyed Casey, frowning. "Where'd you hear that name?"

"Oh, Tucker asked Aidan if he knew where an *Ernest* lived. At least, that's what Aidan thought he said."

"Fuck," Smith whispered.

"What?"

"Ernesto is my dealer. That's who I'm making this run for. He's where I get my stuff."

Ernesto, not Ernest. Aidan was close. Casey couldn't shake the feeling in his gut. "Do you trust him?"

Smith sighed. "As much as you can trust a dealer. So, no, but what choice do I have? He's been good to me and is a nice guy... but business is business."

"Does anyone else deal in town?" Casey asked.

Smith shook his head. "Not at this time. Tucker has

been trying to get his foot in the door, but Ernesto runs a pretty tight ship."

Casey fell silent. It was one thing to take ketamine to have a good time, it was another to be dealing it. He didn't know an Ernesto, and he thought he knew everyone in the town. "Does he live here?"

"Man, he lives like two blocks from you. Ernesto isn't his real name, though. Not sure I even know what it is, but you'd recognize him if you saw him," Smith explained.

That made Casey feel worse. This could be someone Aidan talked to, walked by his house. "Can you point him out sometime? I don't want Aidan around him."

"He almost never leaves his house except to make runs, and it seems like I'll be doing those now."

"Even so, if you see him, let me know. Seriously, Smith," Casey insisted.

They were to the outskirts of Jacksonville, and Smith lowered his speed. "Yeah, okay."

They wound through the streets until they pulled up in front of a worn-down, two-story house with a sagging front porch. It looked like no one was home, but Smith seemed to know better.

He left the car running and turned to Casey. "You coming in or chilling here?"

Casey shook his head. "No, this is all you, man. I'll stay in the getaway car."

Smith laughed and climbed out, leaning back down. "Just don't leave without me."

He loped up the cracked sidewalk, his long legs making it a mere few steps, then disappeared inside the home. Casey peered around the neighborhood. Kids around Aidan's age were playing stickball in the street, laughing without a care in the world. Casey was glad his mother was so protective of Aidan. These kids might not even know what was going on in their own neighborhood. Or maybe they did, and it was simply everyday life.

One of the kids caught Casey's eye and raised his hand in a wave. Casey gave a short wave back, then looked away. The boy reminded him of Aidan. Still young enough to believe all was right with the world while living next to a drug house.

Smith came out carrying a grocery bag and put it in the trunk before hopping into the driver's seat. "Alright, let's get you to the voodoo shop."

"Haha. Man, they sell like incense and gemstones, not shrunken heads. It's not as weird as you're making it out to be," Casey said, getting defensive.

"I'm just messing with you."

They found the store, and Casey got out, looking back at Smith. "You coming?"

Smith glanced at the trunk and sighed. "Yeah, but like only for a minute. I don't want to leave this shit unattended. Too risky, you know?"

A small bell chimed when they walked in, and Casey felt immediately at home. The shop looked like it was once an old house, each room having different items. Books in one, rocks and crystals in another, and so on. The smell of incense calmed him as he wandered around, picking up different rocks and minerals. Smith kept glancing toward the door, so Casey knew his time to browse was limited.

The girl behind the counter paid them no mind, which intrigued Casey. Usually, girls gravitated to him, but this one was busy pricing some books. Casey went to a display of wooden bead strands and ran his fingers through them, liking how smooth the orbs felt. He could almost sense a vibration coming off them. He turned the rack, admiring each one when he heard Smith clear his throat.

Casey looked over, and Smith gestured his head to the door. "You about ready to go?"

The girl glanced up at this and gazed between the two of them, seeming to pick up on Smith's agitation. She smiled. "Anything I can help you with?"

Casey shook his head, taking a string of mala prayer beads off the rack. They had carvings on each bead and felt substantial in his hand. "I'll get these. Smith, you want me to get you a set? To thank you for bringing me here?"

Smith eyed him, his mouth set in a smirk. "No, man. I'm good. Get them, and let's get going."

The girl stared at Casey, her face twisted in question. Casey smiled at her, holding the beads out. "Thanks. I'll take these ones."

She rang them up and handed them back to him, her green eyes twinkling. "Some people believe each strand is made for a particular person and will seek that person out."

Casey liked that idea. He slid the beads over his head, letting them rest against his heart. "I guess they found me."

CHAPTER TEN

The pressure on his chest was intense. Like someone was sitting on his heart and choking him. Casey punched toward his attacker, striking nothing but air. It was pitch black, and his hits were missing their mark. Where the fuck were they? Casey shoved himself up and fumbled for the light, waiting for the next blow to come. His fingers hit the light switch, and he clicked it on, his eyes scanning the room for who, or what, was coming at him.

He was alone.

Convinced someone was hiding, ready to take him by surprise, Casey jumped out of bed, his body tense and ready to fight. Taking deep breaths to calm his racing heart, he glared around the room. In the lamp's light, he could see his window was closed, his door shut. Nobody was in there with him.

Damn. Casey sat on the edge of his bed as his heart and body settled, realizing they weren't under attack. At least, not from the outside. It wasn't the first time Casey had been awoken like this. When he was little, he sleepwalked and was often found in random places in the house. Even outside, sometimes. Once he hit his teens, it transferred to secret attackers in the night who weren't there. He didn't tell his mother because part of him felt ashamed about it.

He took out his journal and began scribbling doodles and poetry. He never showed any of it to anyone. Well, since he was about thirteen and made the mistake of showing his journal to a therapist his mother insisted he go to after his grades dropped and he became withdrawn. The therapist told his mother she thought he was suicidal and wanted him to go on heavy anti-depressants. He'd resisted at first but, eventually, took them for about a month. It made him feel dead inside. After that, his mother agreed she didn't want him taking the medication when she found him staring at the wall for hours and refusing to talk to anyone.

He hadn't been suicidal before the meds, but he was after. Once he stopped taking the anti-depressants, he started experimenting with street drugs. Mostly just weed, sometimes mushrooms. A few times, he tried dropping acid, but it made him feel like he'd never find himself again, so he stopped. He smoked weed on the regular, and that helped keep the anxiety to a minimum.

However, Casey still felt like he was in the wrong time, the wrong existence most times. Until he tried ketamine at a party when he was sixteen. After the first dose, he discovered all the demons tormenting him faded away. Most of them, anyway. The ones who attacked him in his sleep still popped up unexpectedly. The ones that told him he was alone always were hanging about fucking with him.

Casey rooted around the bedside table drawer, his fingers landing on the shape he was looking for. He took out a ketamine pill and crushed it, snorting it rapidly. The effect was almost immediate, his knotted brain loosening. He lay back and stared at the ceiling, the journal slipping to the floor. That was better. As his thoughts untangled and the tension released from his body, a small smile played at his mouth.

Casey reached over and clicked off the lamp, letting the darkness envelop him. Instead of feeling like a claustrophobic abyss, it now covered him like a baby blanket. Casey rubbed his chest and relaxed, sending the demons back to their corners. He had the sensation of his body becoming one with his mattress and felt sleep overtaking him.

When he woke later, he could hear Aidan getting ready for school. It was now late August, and school had been back in session for a couple of weeks. Even so, Aidan hadn't gotten back into the swing of the morning routine and was thumping through the house, searching for his missing sneaker. Where Casey had been an overly organized child, setting his clothes and backpack out for the morning the night before, Aidan was consistently unprepared and chaotic. Casey chuckled as he heard Aidan running up and down the hall, calling out to his shoe like it was a pet.

He sat up and saw the journal on the floor. He picked it up and read the night's thoughts. He sighed and shut the journal, placing it on his nightstand. The poem was about his biological father, Mark Duncan. He didn't really know him but had snippets of memories from when he was a baby and later when his father had court-ordered visits. That all ended by the time Casey was five and his mother remarried.

He didn't know if the two were related, but that's when the visits stopped for good, as rare as they had been. The last time he'd heard from his father at all was a Christmas card when he was five.

Isaac was good to Casey. Treated him like a son. Yet, Casey always felt like he was on the outside looking in on their perfect little family. Even when he was completely immersed and included. He couldn't explain it. It was nothing they did or didn't do for him. They did their best as parents to both him and Aidan. It was all inside him.

Casey pulled a stack of photos out of the drawer, brushing the packet of ketamine. He was down to two pills. It had been a couple of months since the attack, and the pain was long gone, his ribs healed, but he was still taking a larger amount of ketamine. He needed to cut back. He didn't have the money to keep it up, even though Smith had helped him get a job with the town, cleaning trash off the beach and emptying garbage cans. It wasn't glorious, but it gave him cash and kept his parents off his back.

Casey flipped on his stomach and shuffled through the photos, finding the one he was searching for. A young man in military fatigues, holding a baby in his arms. Holding Casey. Casey peered at the man with Duncan stitched on the uniform. His father, Mark Duncan. The vivid blue eyes matched the baby's eyes.

Casey was almost the spitting image of his father, except he had his mother's raven hair. The curls were like his father's, though it was hard to tell as his father kept his blond hair cropped close to his scalp. The baby in the picture was open-mouthed, toothless, grinning without a care in the world. Or so it seemed. Like his memories, Casey wasn't sure what was real and what was created in his mind.

Casey sat up and slipped the photos back in the drawer. His mother was always willing to talk about his father, however, Casey stopped asking years prior. What was the point? Mark Duncan wanted nothing to do with him.

Casey considered taking another ketamine, then remembered he'd promised his mom he'd drop Aidan off at school on his way to work. He'd save it for later when he got home before the rest of them.

He slipped on his work slacks and gray, button-down uniform shirt. He hated the way they looked, but he needed the job until something better came along. Glancing in the mirror, he chuckled at his hair. It was frizzed out into a lion's man around his head. A little water and a comb, and he tamed it into curls that sometimes made ringlets. Girls always commented on his hair and his eyes. Products of a father who did little more than provide genetics.

Aidan was scarfing down a toaster waffle when Casey came into the kitchen, his hair sticking up all over the place. Like he did with his own hair, Casey wet his hands and smoothed Aidan's hair down to a more manageable shape, with a laugh.

Aidan grinned and stared up at Casey. "You're taking me to school, right?"

"You know it. You about ready?"

Their mother came in, holding a notepad in one hand. "He's never ready."

They chuckled, and Aidan grabbed his backpack. "I am, too. See, Mom?"

Casey shook his head and snagged Aidan's lunchbox off the counter. "Might need this if you plan to eat."

Aidan blushed and took the lunchbox. He headed for the door, his shoes still untied. Casey's mother turned to him, her face a cross of irritation and amusement.

"Are you packing lunch?" she asked Casey.

"Nah, I'm going by the restaurant. Wanted to see if Natalie could use some help. I'm only getting a couple days with the town and would like more work."

She nodded, somewhat distracted. "Alright. I'll pick Aidan up from school. Isaac has to work late."

Casey kissed her on the forehead and moved for the door where Aidan was struggling to put a notebook in his backpack. Casey helped him slide it in and zip the backpack shut, ruffling his brother's hair. "Got everything?"

Aidan shrugged. "I think so."

They went out and walked down the block in the direction of the school. The same school Casey went to. Isaac used to drive him most days on his way to work after Aidan came along, and their mother was home with the baby. They rounded the corner to the school, and Aidan took off, seeing his friend TJ on the playground. He barely looked back to give Casey a wave. Aidan was immediately absorbed into the group of children, making Casey think about his own school days.

He'd always been popular but quiet. The girls discovered him in middle school, however, he was less interested in them and more interested in surfing, skateboarding, and smoking weed. Until high school. By tenth grade, he returned their interest.

At least on the surface level.

He developed a sense of humor and became the class clown. Inside, though, he still felt like he was hovering on the outside, never quite understanding how they all seemed to connect to one another.

Casey turned and headed for the janitor shack, which was a block up from the beach. He had the keys and went in to grab tools for the day. It was a tiny room with a series of clipboards hanging on the wall and trash collecting supplies. It was depressing, and now he wished he'd brought ketamine with him to get through his shift. He'd swing by the lifeguard stand to see if Smith was there and had any on him. Grabbing the trash picker and some bags, Casey stepped out and closed the door behind him.

The lifeguard stand looked picturesque against the sky, and Casey paused for a moment, appreciating something he observed almost every day but never really saw. The pier was to the left, stretching like a woman's arm into the ocean. A lifeguard came out of the lifeguard shack, but it wasn't Smith. Damn. Casey would need to wait until later.

He spent the morning picking up trash, then paused for lunch, wandering into By the Sea. Natalie was behind the counter and raised her hand in a wave. Casey found a stool at the end of the counter and perused the menu, though he pretty much had it memorized. Natalie came over and leaned on the counter in front of him.

"Working for the town, now?" she asked, pointing at his uniform.

Casey grinned. "More or less. A couple of days a week. Still looking for more work to fill in the gaps, though. Are you hiring here?"

Natalie eyed him. "You looking?"

"I guess."

"You guess? Not a great way to apply for a job, Casey," she teased. Casey had known Natalie most of his life. She was a town fixture.

He shrugged, a smirk on his face. "It's been my life's dream to work in a restaurant. No, not a restaurant... *this* restaurant. Ever since I was a small child, I have hoped and prayed to work here. It would complete me."

Natalie laughed and winked. "That's better. I could use some evening help. Mostly bussing tables but behind the counter, too. Wednesday through Friday evenings from five til about ten. Can you do that?"

Casey only worked Thursdays and Saturdays for the town so he could swing it. "Yeah, that works. I get off at five on Thursday, though, so it might be like ten after five before I could get here."

Natalie frowned, considering, then smiled. "I think we could make that work. You can start next week. You ordering?"

Casey glanced at the laminated menu. "Yeah, uh, let me get the fish and chips basket with a sweet tea."

"You got it."

Natalie disappeared into the back as Casey glanced around the restaurant. Mostly locals now that school was back in session. Some older tourists in the corner. They were pointing out to the ocean with smiles on their face. His birthday was next month, and he was stuck in a town people from the outside thought was magical, while the locals knew it wasn't. Nineteen. He always thought by the time he was nineteen, he'd be long gone from the small-town life. Surfing on the West Coast, or at least traveling. That took money, and so did ketamine. It was all about choices.

Natalie brought out his food and waved her hand. "On the house, since you're an employee now."

"Thanks, Nat," Casey replied. He loved his family and people like Natalie, who seemed like family. It wasn't that he didn't appreciate the community he had. He felt like if he left, he might find himself. Find a place where the hole in him didn't drag him down constantly.

He let his thoughts wander while he ate, and a memory crossed his mind. It was of his biological father on one of their last visits. His father was in the Marines or had been back then. Casey didn't know if he still was. He picked up Casey in his uniform and took him to the beach. There was a carnival that day, and he bought Casey snacks and let him play games, but never seemed to connect to anything Casey was saying.

Casey remembered thinking it was weird his father came in uniform. Like he needed everyone to know he was in the military. Mark liked it when people fawned over his uniform and thanked him for his service. Meanwhile, Casey was an afterthought. Mark never seemed interested in Casey or his interests. Only being a military man.

That's how his parents met.

His father was stationed in North Carolina on the

coast, his mother was working on base at Camp Lejeune. They had a whirlwind romance and married too quickly. Casey came along around ten months after they tied the knot. Before they had the chance to discover they weren't right for each other. They'd moved to Crestview right after Casey was born. They divorced when Casey was too young to remember. His mother stayed in Crestview, and Mark apparently left for greener pastures.

Casey wondered how different life would have been had they stayed together, but then he wouldn't have Aidan as a little brother, and he wouldn't trade that for the world. He considered where Mark Duncan might be now, what he might be like. If he remarried. If Casey had other siblings. Would talking to Mark help Casey find himself? His place in the world? He set his mind to something he'd buried deep inside himself a long time ago.

He needed to find his father.

CHAPTER ELEVEN

C asey told Smith his plan to find his father a few weeks later. They were heading to a party, and Casey swung by the lifeguard stand before it started to meet up with Smith. They were sitting on the edge of the tower with their legs dangling over, smoking a joint.

Smith listened intently, then shook his head. "You sure that's a good idea? I mean, you're dad may be a raging asshole for all you know. Will your mom freak?"

Casey shrugged. "Probably not and probably. I'm going to be nineteen next week, so it's now or never."

Smith took a long drag of the joint, holding it in. Finally, he coughed and let it out, a huge plume of smoke filling the air. He handed it to Casey. "Oh, yeah. Your birthday is coming up. Any plans? Other than finding your father?"

"Nah. My mom wants to take me out to dinner, and they offered to help with a down payment on a car."

Smith's eyebrows shot up. "No shit?"

Smith had a beater he'd paid for with his own money. It drove, but was a piece of junk. His parents were loaded, however, they were stingy with their money. They refused to help Smith out unless it was something they wanted him to do. So, basically, they didn't help him at all.

Casey chewed his lip. "Yeah. Now that I'm working two jobs, they said they were willing to help out. I don't know, though. I don't want to feel like I owe them anything, you know?"

Smith shook his head. "I don't. I could be bleeding in the middle of the road, and my parents wouldn't even stop to check on me. Let them help if they want to."

Casey understood where Smith was coming from, but he didn't want the commitment. He'd started working at By the Sea and still had the job with the town, but he was already growing bored with them. Yet, a car *would* give him a way out of the town. That was the ultimate goal in the end. He took a hit and handed the joint back to Smith.

"I'll think about it. You have any K we can take before the party? I left mine at home."

Smith got up and went inside the lifeguard shack. He came back out and handed Casey a pill. "I'm waiting, but here you go. Is one enough?"

Casey peered up at him, suspecting something else behind his words. "Yeah, why?"Smith sat back down. "You've been buying a shit ton. Ever since that night with Tucker, you've been out using me. You still in a lot of pain?"

Casey wasn't anymore, but he'd become accustomed to the amount he'd been using for the pain. He sighed, staring out at the ocean. "Nah. You're right, man. I do need to cut back. I guess it just became a habit. That'll be my birthday resolution. Cutting back."

Smith chuckled, brushing his shaggy, golden hair out of his eyes. "Birthday resolution? Is that a thing?"

"Sure, why not? Maybe it will make me stick to it. Your birthday's in November, right?"

"Indeed it is, but I'm *not* making a fucking resolution. Unless it's to stay alive another year," Smith joked.

Considering he'd already once needed Casey to make sure that happened, Casey didn't think it was such a bad idea. Casey stood up. "Twenty-three, right?"

"Yep. Becoming old men, aren't we?" Smith said as he stood, towering over Casey. They were five inches different in height, but it never seemed to matter.

"You are, at least. I'm still spry," Casey teased and popped the ketamine pill. It would kick in by the time they got to the party.

"Fuck you," Smith replied and began climbing down the ladder. "I can out-surf you any day of the week."

That much was true. Casey was a good surfer, but Smith became one with the waves. Casey climbed down after him, and they started strolling down the beach to the pier. The party was under the structure to keep it out of sight.

The police didn't want anyone on the beach after dark, but the locals knew how to avoid them. The cops circled through the parking lot for By the Sea, which had public beach access parking at certain times, then not again until after By the Sea closed up for the night. The locals planned their parties accordingly.

By the time they made it to the pier, the ketamine was kicking in, and Casey was feeling alright. A group had gathered and were building a fire. Casey saw Miranda and scanned the crowd for Tucker. He wasn't there. At least, not yet. Casey let out a breath and made his way to the keg on the other side of the fire pit. A girl he didn't recognize was trying to figure the keg out, so he stepped up to help. She was cute. Petite with large, gray eyes and strawberry-blond hair. He grabbed the pump and showed her how to fill her cup without making a ton of foam.

She smiled shyly and stuck out her hand. "I'm Brittany. Miranda's cousin. Do you know her?" she asked.

Casey's eyes flitted from Brittany to Miranda, and he nodded. "Yeah, we're acquainted. I'm Casey. You visiting?"

"Sort of. I'm staying with Miranda's family for a bit. My uh... my mom is indisposed."

Casey frowned. "Indisposed?"

Brittany blushed and glanced away. "Rehab."

"Oh, shit. I'm sorry. I'm friends with Smith, who is friends with Miranda, so I guess I know her by association." Casey pointed to where Smith was talking with a couple of guys in a huddle.

Clearly, making a deal.

"Oh, yeah. She told me about him. Casey. Nice to meet you. If you don't mind me saying, you have the most beautiful blue eyes. Like water."

Casey had heard that a lot from the local girls. He chuckled. "It's cause I have no soul."

She stared at him, then laughed nervously. "So, how old are you, Casey?"

"Nineteen." Casey figured he'd round up since it was only a week away. "You?"

"Sixteen."

He took a step back. "Should you be here?"

"When did you start coming to these parties, Casey?" She emphasized his name a little more than necessary.

She had him there. He'd been sixteen the first time and became a regular. "Fair enough. Just watch yourself. Not everyone will respect your, uh, like, body."

That was not what he was trying to say, and he blushed furiously. She put her hand on his arm with a smirk. "My body? Well, then. I'll make sure to be aware of my body, so no one disrespects my body."

She was fucking with him. He kinda liked it but reminded himself she was only sixteen. "So, when do you turn seventeen?"

She raised an eyebrow. "Why are you asking?"

Fuck, he was digging a hole he couldn't get out of. "Legalities and all."

Brittany burst out laughing at that, causing others in the group to look over. She leaned in close. "Legalities. That's the best you got? Not because, I don't know, you might be interested in me?"

Casey didn't know how he'd gotten himself into this situation and shook his head. "You seem like a nice girl and all, but I'm not looking."

She tipped her head, her eyes reading his face. "Okay, are you at least looking for friends? 'Cause you seem kinda cool. I only know Miranda here, which is getting old fast. She doesn't want me hanging around with her all the time."

"I can do friends," Casey agreed. It wasn't that she

wasn't pretty.

She was.

So were most of the girls from school that chased him. He'd never found the desire to take it further than hooking up. He didn't want a girlfriend; that would tie him further to the town. He'd always made it clear, he was not the commitment kind. Not until he got out of there, anyway.

Well, that wasn't entirely true. He did find himself drawn to older women. Women twenty-five and older, who seemed to have their shit together. Hell, even ones that didn't. They just always seemed so much more self-assured. They, however, never looked at him the same. They only looked at him with hungry eyes. Fucking eyes. He'd hooked up with a few here and there, but they disappeared as soon as they were done. Boys were for a good time, not relationships.

Brittany wandered off and began talking to Smith, who'd finished his deal and was standing by the burgeoning fire. He smiled down at her, but like Casey, he wasn't interested. That was one thing they had in common, except Smith was even more removed from relationships. Miranda had been after him since high school, and he always kept her at arm's length. Like he was doing with Brittany.

Seeing she wasn't getting anywhere, Brittany found Miranda and followed her around like a puppy dog the rest of the night. Casey got bored around midnight and wandered up to the pier. It was one of his favorite places. He walked to the end and stared out at the world out of his reach. He had a few drinks, more joints, and ketamine. He was flying high. This was when he felt perfect. Like his limbs matched his brain.

Getting an itch, he took a running start toward the end of the pier, leaping over the rail at the last second. He plummeted down to the rough water, letting it drag him under. He loved the feeling of being tossed around like a rag doll. He surfaced after a minute, laughing and out of breath. A few of the party-goers were watching from the beach. As he swam in, he saw Smith standing at the edge of the water, waiting for him.

"You're fucking crazy, Casey. One of these days, that water is going to get you," he said as Casey came stumbling out of the surf.

"Maybe I want it to," Casey countered.

Smith took his arm and helped him up the beach. "Shut the hell up. You're an adrenaline junkie."

That much was true. Casey was drawn to anything that kept him on the edge of fear and made his veins course with excitement. But this was different. Sometimes, when he jumped off the pier, it was as if the water was calling to him. To bring him home. He couldn't tell anyone that, though. They'd think he was off his rocker.

They made their way back to the party, and Casey scanned around the scene. Tucker hadn't shown. Maybe he'd learned his lesson from Smith, however, Casey doubted it. Tucker didn't seem like the type to learn a lesson. As he was looking, he saw Brittany sitting on a log. She was wavering and didn't look too good. He thought about Aidan and wouldn't want him out there without someone looking out for him.

Casey nudged Smith and pointed at the inebriated girl. Miranda was nowhere to be seen, and a much older guy they didn't recognize was hovering around

Brittany, trying to move in on her. She didn't seem to understand what was happening or even much about her surroundings. They needed to intercede as quickly as possible.

Smith nodded, understanding.

They headed over to where she was and put themselves between Brittany and the guy. He looked pissed but Smith reached down and pulled her up, leaning her against him. "Gotta get my sister home."

The guy's eyes widened, and he moved away. He didn't want beef with her older brother. Smith motioned to Casey to help. They guided her away from the party, and she began vomiting. The stench of pure alcohol hit Casey's nose, and he winced. "Damn. She's shit-faced. I can't believe Miranda left her alone like this."

Smith grunted. "I can."

Casey peered around. "Let's get her to the parking lot. I'll sit with her if you can go grab your car. We need to get her back to Miranda's."

Smith bobbed his head, and they dragged her up to the parking lot. She was slipping in and out of consciousness. Had they not intervened, that guy might have taken advantage of her. They made it to a bench outside the restaurant and got her into a sitting position. Smith looked none too happy about being in the presence of a drunk minor.

He glanced around the parking lot and sighed. "I'll be back in a few. Keep talking to her. Try to keep her on this side of reality. Fucking Miranda," he muttered as he hurried away to get his car.

Casey propped Brittany against him to keep her upright. She wobbled, her head not staying upright. He kept talking to her about nothing to keep her mind from slipping away or passing out. She leaned forward and vomited again, her body shaking violently.

When she sat back, she met Casey's eyes with startling clarity. She seemed to comprehend how drunk she was and braced herself against the bench for support. Her mouth opened and closed a few times before she spoke.

"I want my mom."

CHAPTER TWELVE

By the time Smith came back with his car, Brittany was more aware of her surroundings but still slurring and wavering from side to side. Smith parked and got out, taking long strides to Casey and the drunk girl. Casey braced her from pitching forward and motioned for Smith to help. Smith leaned in and placed his hands on her shoulders.

He glanced back at the parking lot. "We gotta go. Cops are making their rounds already."

Casey stood up, still holding onto Brittany so she didn't hit the ground. Smith came to her other side, and the three of them made a staggering race to the car. Smith got Brittany into the back seat, propping her up. Casey climbed in next to her, and Smith practically threw himself in the front seat and started the car. He peeled out of the parking lot just as the police were pulling in the other side. Casey gazed back, his heart racing.

He didn't want to get in trouble with the cops.

"Have you seen Miranda?" he asked, trying to keep Brittany upright. He reached across and pulled the seatbelt over her, clipping her in.

Smith shook his head, flipping his headlights on. "Nope. She took off with some guy. I don't know if we should take Brittany back to her house or not. Miranda's mother might be pissed about the state of her." He jerked his thumb toward Brittany, who was now sobbing softly to herself in the back seat.

Casey agreed. The last thing they needed was to bring a drunk, underage girl to her family's house. Her aunt's house. She'd mentioned Miranda's mother was her mother's sister and agreed to let Brittany stay while her mother went through rehab. "So, what do we do?"

"Fuck if I know. Let's take a drive through town and see if we spy Miranda anywhere. That girl is trouble, sometimes," Smith muttered in reference to Miranda.

"She's your friend. Why do you even hang out with her?" Casey countered. He didn't trust Miranda as far as he could throw her.

"We went to school together. I guess it just stuck. She's actually a really funny and caring person, believe it or not."

Casey didn't.

They circled around town a few times, avoiding the cruising police. There wasn't a curfew, however, they didn't need extra eyes on the situation they were in. If they were caught with Brittany in her current state, they could risk going to jail. Not to mention, they were both a bit fucked up still.

After the third time around, Smith punched the steering wheel. "Goddamn it!"

Casey leaned forward, placing his hand on Smith's shoulder. "Chill, man. We'll figure it out."

Just as he said that, they noticed a red sports car parked in the gas station parking lot. It wasn't local, and they could make out two head shapes in the front. Smith jerked into the parking lot and pulled up beside the car. Miranda was in the front seat with some guy, smoking what looked like meth. Smith climbed out and banged on the window. This would have startled anyone else, but Miranda just peered up at him with a half smile and rolled down the window.

"Smith. Fancy seeing you here."

Smith was about done, his face flushed in anger. "We have your cousin in the back seat. You left her at the party completely fucked up and some guy was all over her. What the hell, Miranda?"

She glanced at Smith's car and spied Brittany in the back seat. She shrugged. "Seems like you have it handled."

Smith yanked her door open and dragged her out, pointing at Brittany. "Get your cousin out of my car now, and get her home. She's underage and beyond drunk. You'll have to fuck that guy later."

His words were so sharp, Casey felt the hair on his arms rise. Smith generally was easy-going most of the time, but he'd been pushed to the edge that night. Miranda's eyes widened with fear for a brief second, then her face set back into its not giving a shit mode.

She tipped her head with a smirk. "Yeah, whatever.

You know, Smith, you have become a real dick lately."

Casey got out and went around to Brittany's side, opening the door. Brittany's makeup had run, and she looked like pure misery. She was going to feel it in the morning. Casey helped her out, then stood, confused. Was she going into the other car?

Miranda sighed, crawling out of the red car, and took Brittany's arm. She pushed the front seat forward and began shoe-horning Brittany into the tiny back seat. The guy in the car started to protest, but one look from Miranda shut him up. She smiled coyly at Casey.

"Hey, gorgeous," she murmured, clearly trying to piss off Smith and her current companion.

Casey turned away, not answering. He was not getting in the middle of that mess. Smith moved close to her and whispered something in her ear. Miranda's eyes flashed in anger, then she pushed him away and climbed back into the red car, flipping him off. The car sped out of the parking lot, and Casey questioned if going with them was Brittany's best bet. Then again, Smith couldn't risk having her in his car. They did what they could, she was Miranda's problem now.

Casey sat in the passenger's seat as Smith folded himself back into the driver's seat. He took a moment to light a cigarette, taking a long drag, then blew the smoke out the open door. He slammed the door shut and sighed. "I'd better watch my back."

Casey frowned. "Why?"

"I told Miranda I'd uncover her bullshit if she didn't get her cousin home safely."

"Her bullshit?"

Smith turned to Casey, his hazel eyes tired. "It's not

only Tucker who is trying to make a name here. Miranda has been bringing in some outside people to try and take ground. She's even roped some of the local girls into prostitution. I assume she has ideas like that for Brittany."

Casey's stomach knotted. Fuck. He thought of that sweet girl and her saying she wanted her mother. "Damn. Are you in danger?"

Smith shrugged and flicked his cigarette butt out of the door. "When I started dealing, it was only to make sure I had enough for myself. I'm cool with that. They have other plans. They think they're going to be drug lords. I don't want anything to do with that."

"Your guy... uh... Ernesto? Do they work with him, too?" Casey asked, trying to piece it all together. He liked to party but never saw the other side of it.

"Not as far as I know, however, Ernesto wants what's going to make him the most money in the long run. He never fucked with prostitution that I know of, but that's not to say he wouldn't."

Casey sat silent, his mind racing over what Smith told him. He was just having fun taking ketamine and smoking weed. He knew Smith was providing to most of the other locals, but never thought it went beyond that. He chewed his lip. "Why don't you get out?"

Smith started the car, putting it in gear. He shrugged. "I really don't know. I've thought about it, but that doesn't make the problem go away. I know what I'm providing is at least clean, not cut with anything else. If they get involved, greed will make them want to do whatever it takes to line their pockets."

"Is this, like, what you plan to do forever?" Casey asked, regretting it instantly.

Smith's eyes blazed as he drove out of the parking lot. "What the fuck, Casey? You should know me better than that. I want out as much as you do, but I don't have the money or ability to do so. I'm working on it. I don't have anyone to fall back on like you do."

Casey stared at the road. They were all trapped, but at least his parents wanted him to have a better future. They supported him in whatever he tried to do. "Sorry, man. I know you're doing your best."

Smith laughed harshly. "No, I'm not. I'm doing what it takes to make it through each day. I hate this place, I hate what Miranda's doing, and all the crap dealing drugs brings. This isn't me. You understand that? This isn't me."

Casey had only known Smith as an adult since they were young kids, so he couldn't say he knew any other side of him. Smith had always been the party guy when they'd reconnected a few years prior. The supplier. He and Casey hit it off, however, Casey couldn't say he really knew Smith deep down. A wave of exhaustion came over Casey, and he wanted nothing more than to climb into his bed.

His bed. He turned to Smith. "You have a place to sleep tonight, dude?"

Smith eyed Casey, lighting another cigarette. "You wanting to have a slumber party?"

Casey laughed. "Fuck you, Smith. But you can crash on my floor. My mom won't care."

They were pulling up to Casey's house, and he could see Smith was considering it. He cut off the car, and they sat staring at the tidy house. Casey pushed his door open. "Seriously. I'll make waffles in the morning."

Smith shook his head. "You're on a whole other level,

Casey. Yeah, waffles sound good. I could use a shower, too."

Casey climbed out, snickering. "Yeah, you could."

They went in the back door to avoid waking anyone up. Casey pulled out extra pillows and blankets for Smith to use. He slipped down to the kitchen and smiled when he saw his mother had left him a couple of BLTs with chips. She was always thinking of him, even though he needed to be living his life as the adult he was. He snagged bottles of lemonade out of the refrigerator and balanced the sandwiches and chips in his other hand.

Smith was kicked back in a pile of pillows and blankets when Casey came to give him the food. He looked impossibly long, splayed out like that. When Smith saw the food, though, he sat up and grinned. "Damn, food, too? I could get used to this life."

Casey laughed and tossed him a lemonade. "My mom. She may be over-protective, but it comes with perks."

"No shit," Smith replied and took one of the sandwiches from Casey. He ate it in a few bites and chugged the lemonade.

Casey cut on the radio and flopped on his bed to eat his food. He fished in his drawer for ketamine and popped it so he could rest. It wasn't too long before the sun would be up, but he was off work, so he could sleep in. "You want one?"

Smith smiled and shook his head. "Nah, I'm good. I have plenty, anyway. Thanks for offering."

Casey shut the drawer and faced Smith. "You have to work in the morning?"

"Nope."

"Cool. Me either. I did promise Aidan I'd take him surfing. You want to go with us?"

Smith closed his eyes and nodded, his face slack in relaxation. "Dude, that sounds awesome. I'm down."

Casey watched Smith and wondered if his life would have been different if he'd had any siblings. As an only child, Smith seemed to be on an island most of the time. He'd become accustomed to it being only him and not needing anyone. Or at least, that's what it appeared like from the outside.

Casey had Aidan, and that gave him purpose. He always wanted Aidan to know how much he meant to him. After Aidan came along, Casey felt like he had something special, something other people could never understand.

He'd die for his little brother.

CHAPTER THIRTEEN

C asey's mother acted like he suspected she would when he told her he was looking for his biological father. He waited until the night of his birthday when they were all out to dinner in a public place. Her normal caramel skin turned a pale, almost green, color when he said it, and she clasped Isaac's hand on the table. Isaac comforted her but didn't speak. This wasn't his area to intercede. It was between Casey and his mother, Isaac respected that.

"I understand you want to know more about him, Casey, but there are things you don't understand. Things you don't remember," she whispered, trying to not draw attention to her distress from nearby patrons.

"Like what?" Casey asked, determined to move

forward with his plan. "I know he walked out on us. What else is there to know?"

She nodded, meeting his eyes. "Yes, there was that. However, there was more to it. To our marriage."

This piqued Casey's interest, and he leaned forward. "What do you mean, Mom?"

His mother looked at Isaac, who bit his lip. He didn't want to come between Casey and his mother, but clearly, there was more to the story than Casey was told before. Information Casey now needed to understand.

Isaac cleared his throat. "I'm not sure this is the time or place to discuss this, Casey. Please trust your mother on this. We love you very much."

Casey knew they did, but he felt if he didn't press now, he might never get the answers he was seeking. Plus, he had a decent dose of K in his system, which was giving him the courage to push on. "I need to know, Mom. Now. It's my right since he's my father."

Aidan shifted awkwardly in his seat, Casey's birthday dinner quickly degrading into family drama. Drama he wasn't part of. His eyes darted between his family members, hoping they would move away from the subject.

They didn't.

Their mother bent her head closer to Casey's. "Your father had a temper. He could be very cruel. I didn't see it until after you were born, but the stress of the military and a new baby brought it out. He became..."

Her voice trailed off, and Isaac took over. "This isn't my place, I am only relaying what your mother told me. What the police report told me about what happened. Your father took his stress out on Eva."

It was always odd to hear his mother called by her

first name, but Casey needed to know the rest. "What do you mean? He hit you?" he asked his mother.

She sighed, wiping her eyes with a napkin. "Can we finish the conversation at home? I don't need people out here hearing our business."

Casey glanced around. No one seemed to be paying them any mind. He shook his head. "I'm hanging out with Smith tonight. No one cares about our family shit."

Isaac's eyes grew wide. "I know you are frustrated, Casey, but please respect your mother and Aidan."

Casey looked at Aidan, who appeared like he wanted to climb out of his skin. This made him feel genuinely bad. "Fine. Please, just answer my question, then."

They were all taken aback by Casey's demeanor as he usually took things with a grain of salt. Adrenaline and ketamine were making him edgy. His mother put the napkin down and placed her hands on the table. "Yes, he hit me. Sometimes, he would lash out at you, but I would put myself between you and him. One time, when you were around a year and a half old, I didn't move fast enough. He got to you before I could. We were fighting when you woke up in your crib. He grabbed you out of the crib and shook you violently. When I tried to stop him, he began choking me. A neighbor heard and called the police."

"He was arrested?" All of this was news to Casey.

She stared at her hands. "No."

"Why not?"

Isaac jumped in, his voice calm. "With him being in the military, they turned it over to the base police. They pretty much brushed it under the rug. Your mother tried to block him from having visitation with you, but the court sided with Mark and forced her to comply. Allowing him to have unsupervised visits with you against her wishes. So, you can see why she doesn't want you looking for him now. She's only worried about you, Casey."

If Casey had any fantasies about his father coming back into his life and filling some void, they were being dashed over linguini. He nodded and pushed his chair back, his chest tight. "I need some air."

"Wait, Casey," his mother pleaded. "I want you to know, I made him leave. I couldn't trust him around you. He threatened to take you away, but his commanding officer convinced him it was a bad idea. I didn't tell you because I didn't want you to get hurt. I'm truly sorry."

Casey stood up and shoved his chair a little too hard against the table, causing the water glasses to spill over. He glared at his mother. "Well, you failed, Mom. I *am* hurt. And I *am* going to find him."

Aidan spoke for the first time since the conversation started. "Casey, don't."

Casey turned on the little brother he loved more than life itself. "Aidan, stay out of this. You have a complete family. I never had one, and now I'm finding out my own father probably would've preferred me dead."

He stormed out of the restaurant, not sure where he was going. He wandered the streets until he could feel the effects of the ketamine wearing off. He didn't want to go back home and didn't have any on him. He was supposed to meet up with Smith, but not for a couple of hours.

Casey made his way to the beach and walked straight into the water up to his knees, standing to face the horizon. He shouldn't have brought it up. Now, he knew more than he could handle. Mark Duncan was an abuser.

At first, Casey hoped he had siblings he didn't know about to give him more family. Now, he didn't. God knows what they would have gone through.

Hot tears slid down his cheeks, and he was glad for the cover of darkness to hide them. He should've known Mark was a bad man. His mom was a good mother. A good wife. A good person. She did everything she could to keep Casey safe. She would never do anything to knowingly hurt him.

A voice in the distance caught his ear, and he turned. He could see the lifeguard stand up the beach in the distance and a tall, lanky silhouette waving at him. Smith. At least Casey could bury his sorrows now. He stepped out of the water and ran up the beach, his shoes squishing out water with each step. He made it to the lifeguard stand and peered up.

Smith leaned over. "Thought that was you. What the fuck are you doing out here? I thought you were having dinner with your folks."

"I was. Didn't go as planned," Casey replied, scaling the ladder. His shoes were wet and kept slipping off the rungs.

Smith reached down and gave him a hand up. "Why were you in the ocean with your shoes on?"

Casey shrugged, not sure what he was thinking. "Seemed like a good idea at the time."

"You want a beer?"

"You have anything stronger? I was planning to go home before I got here and change first. Grab some K, but, well, here I am."

"Yeah, man, I got you. I have some flip-flops inside if you want to take off your wet shoes. Hold on a sec." Smith went into the shack and came out with the flip-flops and a baggie of pills.

Casey took off his shoes and tipped them against the shack wall to drain. It was still warm out, so he slipped on the flip-flops and rolled up his wet pants. "Thanks."

"Happy birthday, dude. You get anything good?" Smith asked as they sat down on the deck.

"A new skateboard, some clothes, down payment on a car. Oh, and found out my biological father is a wife beater... so there's that."

Smith stared at him, his mouth hanging slightly open. He snapped it shut. "I guess you told them you are looking for him, then?"

"Yup, I did. Didn't unfold quite how I was expecting, that's for fucking sure," Casey replied, sarcasm lacing each word. He crushed and snorted a pill, hoping it would numb him quickly.

"Damn. I don't even know what to say. I suppose it's good you found out so you don't waste your time on that piece of shit," Smith offered.

Casey laughed. "Oh, were it that simple."

"What do you mean?"

"I'm still going to find him. Make sure he didn't have more children and put them through hell. Make him answer for what he did to my mother. To me."

Smith cocked his head. "To you?"

Casey sighed, anger seizing his chest. The ketamine was kicking in, but so was the rage. "Apparently, Mark Duncan likes to knock around children, too. My mother had to stop him from killing me."

Smith lit a cigarette and glanced out at the dark water. He turned to Casey. "He go to jail?"

"Nope, seems like the military has a good old boy network where wife and child beaters don't pay for what they do. He went on with his life like nothing happened."

"Your mother tell you that?" Smith asked.

"Yeah, at dinner."

"Do you believe her?"

Casey considered that. What would she have to gain by lying to him? He'd pressed for answers about Mark. "I do. She didn't want to tell me at first, but when I told her I was looking for him, she said I didn't know everything. Damn, was she ever right."

"So, that's probably why you haven't heard from him all these years. Do you think he's ashamed of what he did to you and your mom?"

Casey laughed without humor. "I don't fucking know, dude. Can we stop talking about this? I just want to get obliterated and forget about all of it. You down?"

Smith smiled. "I'm always down. I got you a packet of K for your birthday. On the house."

That sounded pretty good to Casey. He crushed and snorted another pill, then chugged a beer. Then smoked some weed, then chugged another beer. Pill, beer, weed, beer, pill, until he didn't give a crap about Mark Duncan, their shit town, or anything besides staring up at the stars in the sky. He didn't even remember the rest of the night as it blurred into glorious oblivion.

When he woke up, he was at the lifeguard shack, but he could see he'd been elsewhere as he was barefoot, and the flip-flops were nowhere to be found. His shoes were still wet, and he had cuts on his arms and feet. He had no clue where they came from. Smith was curled up in the corner, sleeping. He, too, had abrasions.

DONE.

What the fuck had they done the night before?

Casey closed his eyes and tried to think. He remembered snippets of being around a bonfire, kissing some random girl, stumbling and falling in the sand. Staring at the night sky, wondering if the aliens were staring back at him.

Then one more memory surfaced, and he groaned. It explained the cuts and abrasions on both of them.

Casey and Smith had surfed between the pilings under the pier in the dead of night.

CHAPTER FOURTEEN

Weeks passed, and Casey was getting nowhere in his search for his father. He used the library's computers since they were connected to the internet and free. They had a computer at home, but it was in Isaac's home office, and Casey didn't want anyone looking over his shoulder. They'd dropped the issue of Casey searching for his father, but the tensions around it were still there. He didn't want to hurt his mother, despite his reaction at his birthday dinner.

When he found any sort of trail on his father, nothing was current. It almost seemed as if his father was purposefully trying to not be found. Maybe he wasn't. Casey considered the possibility his father had died, but obituary searches brought up nothing. Casey was about ready to give up when he thought of someone who might know more.

On his way into work one night, Casey knocked on Natalie's office door. He stuck his head in. "Nat, you have a minute to talk?"

She was pouring over a stack of receipts and nodded, leaning back in her chair. "Please, come in. Someone needs to save me from myself."

"That bad?"

She chuckled and motioned to a chair covered in stacks of paper. "Clear that off and have a seat. I need a break. Running the front end of the restaurant I've got, doing the paperwork... not so much. Still learning all this shit since I bought the place earlier this year. The previous owners were breaking all kinds of laws. I should have stayed only an employee like I was and left this shit for the birds. Anyway, what can I do for you?"

Casey moved the paper stacks to the floor and sat down. "I, uh, I've been trying to find my biological father. I know he lived here with my mother and me when I was a baby. He was stationed at Camp Lejeune and commuted to work from here before he left for good. Do you remember him at all? His name is Mark Duncan."

From the look on Natalie's face, she most certainly did. She gave a curt nod. "I do."

Casey couldn't get a read on her face and stammered on. "I keep hitting walls in my search. It's like he disappeared off the face of the Earth, but he's not dead. I know he was only briefly here in town, but do you know anyone who might know him or where he went after he left?"

Natalie shifted forward, her face lined with concern.

"Did your mother tell you what happened?"

Did everyone know except him? Casey bobbed his head, his cheeks flushing. "About him hitting her and me? She did. Not until recently, though."

"Alright, so you know. There are things your mother didn't know. Mark Duncan was up to no good on the side. Cheating, gambling. He fell in with a guy here in town who was getting into some illegal shit, as well. He and Mark had plans to make some money."

"Money. Doing what?" Casey asked, the picture of his father growing even darker.

Natalie shrugged. "I wasn't privy to the details, however, it seems they were wanting to run drugs, open strip clubs, things like that."

Seems like things hadn't changed much since then. Someone was always trying to make quick money off the people of the town. A sharp feeling formed in the bottom of his gut. "Who was the other guy?"

"Oh, he's still around and probably up to no good. Johnny Mason. You know him?" Natalie asked.

Casey knew of him but didn't know him personally. When he was thirteen, he did a paper route and remembered Mr. Mason was on his route. He always paid Casey on time but seemed to keep to himself. "I mean, sort of. I used to deliver his newspaper."

"That right? Well, anyway, they had a falling out one night. Mark wanted to take things farther than Johnny was willing to. Johnny liked to play things close to the vest. Mark wanted to run the show. They got into a fistfight one evening here, and Johnny whooped Mark real good. I was a waitress back then, and it was a pretty wild place as it was. That was the end of their partnership.

Maybe a week or two later is when the cops were called to your house for Mark abusing you and your mom. He left right after. Good riddance, I say," Natalie said with honesty and waved her hand in the air like she was swatting away flies.

Casey listened, taking it all in. Mark sounded like a total piece of shit to everyone who knew him. He wondered if Johnny Mason would have any idea where Mark was now. It didn't sound like it, but it was at least something to go off of. "Thanks, Natalie."

She watched him, her eyes unblinking. "Casey, it's none of my business, but why do you want to find him? You are better off without him in your life."

Casey could agree with that, but something in him kept insisting. "I don't know. I'm not looking for a father-son reunion or anything like that. Maybe I'm just searching for answers from him. About me. About... fuck if I know. Resolution, maybe."

"I get that. I really do. I came from a broken home. I used to imagine what it would've been like had my parents stopped beating on each other long enough to appreciate what they had. But they didn't. When I realized things were what they were, I was able to let go and get on with my life. I'm sure your mother doesn't want you finding him," Natalie replied, her voice softening.

"She doesn't. She's afraid I'll get hurt."

"Are you? Afraid you'll get hurt?"

Casey laughed painfully. "Any more than I am? Sure. It's probably a huge mistake. I know that, but I'll always wonder if I don't do this."

"Wonder what?"

That was the question, wasn't it? Casey sometimes

caught a glimpse of himself in the mirror and saw someone he didn't recognize. Someone distant and lost. When he was little, he referred to his reflection as the boy in the mirror. He shrugged. "If I'm like him."

He got up and headed for the door, pausing with his hand on the knob. "Thanks for the talk, Nat. I was hoping you might be able to give me some info on Mark."

She smiled but didn't speak, her eyes fixed on him as he moved to the door. Casey could tell she wanted to say something but was stuck.

He nudged her. "What?"

Natalie pushed a few strands of hair out of her face. "Casey, I've known you since you were a baby. You're a sensitive boy with a big heart. Maybe too big, so you're likely to feel things more than other people. I've seen you change a lot lately, and not in a good way. I suspect you're experimenting with shit you shouldn't be, and I'm not here to lecture on it, even though I want to. However, there's one thing I know without a shadow of a doubt."

Casey stared at her, his heart racing in his chest. "What's that?" "You are *nothing* like Mark Duncan. He would sacrifice anyone and anything to get what he wanted. You'd give up your soul for those you love. Make sure you don't, but never doubt who you are."

Casey wanted to cry hearing that, but wouldn't let his poker face break. He smiled at Natalie. "I appreciate you saying that, Natalie. I better get to work before the boss calls me out for slacking and fires me."

Natalie chuckled, her face still serious. "Nah, she likes having you around."

Casey slipped out and got to work, his brain thinking over what she'd told him. He hated that his biological father was such a horrible person, but it didn't change his determination to find him. If anything, it made the drive even higher. He didn't know much about Johnny, but he knew that needed to be his next stop. If Johnny could tell him anything, he'd be willing to face it.

Casey wiped tables and thought about his mother and Mark. She admitted she hardly knew him but was enamored by his looks and fast talking. However, she couldn't tell Casey much about his history before they met. He'd been a military brat, as well, so didn't have a hometown that she knew of. His parents were dead, or that's what he'd told her, and she believed him. At first. She said occasionally, he'd slip up and mention a sister, but when she pressed for more information, he'd change the subject. She wasn't sure what was the truth.

Casey got off after the dinner shift and retraced his paper route, looking for Johnny's house. At last, he found it and stood on the sidewalk, staring at the dark house. It didn't appear like anyone was home. Still, he stood there, trying to remember more about Johnny from when he'd go to collect money for the papers. All adults seemed about the same back then, however, Johnny was around his parents' age, Casey figured. He remembered him wearing glasses and having short hair. A little paunchy. Nerdy, even. Nothing special and certainly not a drug kingpin.

Casey walked up to the door and knocked, listening for movement inside. A calico cat jumped up onto the window sill to the left of the door, meowing silently through the pane of glass. Casey tried to peer in but couldn't see anything. He knocked again. After a few minutes, he headed back down the sidewalk. He'd try again tomorrow.

As he hit the end of Johnny's sidewalk, a car pulled up. Casey was lost in his thoughts and didn't notice it at first until the window rolled down and a familiar voice called his name. He glanced over to see Smith waving at him from his car. Casey wandered over.

Smith leaned to the window. "Hey, Casey. What are you up to?"

Casey glanced back at the house and shrugged. "Not much. You want to hang out?"

"Sure, get in. I'm starving, you want to grab something to eat?" Smith asked.

"As long as it isn't By the Sea. I'm about sick of that food," Casey joked.

"I bet. I was thinking of taking a ride to Banner. I heard they got a good burger joint over there. You want to go?"

Casey climbed in the passenger's seat. "I'm down. I need to get out of town, even if it's just for a burger."

Smith pulled away from the curb, handing Casey a joint he'd been smoking. Casey took a drag and held it in, letting it blur his thoughts.

Smith took a hit, then blew smoke out through the rolled-down window, his mouth set in a straight line. He seemed agitated about something and eyed Casey. "So, man, why were you there?"

Casey frowned, not understanding what Smith was asking him. "Why was I where?"

"Seriously? What's going on? I saw you leave his house when I drove up."

Casey wasn't sure if it was the weed or if he was missing something. It was like they jumped into the middle of a conversation he wasn't in on. He stared at

Smith, trying to make sense of what he was asking him. Was Smith talking about Johnny's house?

"Wait. You know Johnny Mason?"

Smith watched Casey, his eyes analyzing what Casey was saying to him. Searching for truth. His face relaxed when he realized Casey wasn't trying to put one over on him. "Do you not know, for real?"

"I have no fucking clue what you are talking about, Smith. Do I not know what?" Casey asked, shaking his head.

"Yeah, so, I wasn't totally honest with you when I said I didn't know Ernesto's real name," Smith confessed.

"How's that?"

"Johnny Mason is Ernesto."

CHAPTER FIFTEEN

C asey felt like the air had been knocked out of him. Johnny Mason was Ernesto? He shook his head, the words not making total sense, yet coming together like a puzzle. Smith's dealer had been Mark Duncan's partner.

He stared at Smith. "Christ. I guess I should've put that together at some point. Sounds like Johnny and my biological father were business partners."

"Business partners? Doing what?" Smith asked. Then, his face changed as he realized. "Oh, shit. I didn't know your father was into that stuff."

"That's what Natalie told me. It's why I went there. I thought maybe he'd know how I could find my father, or where he might be," Casey explained.

Smith rubbed his forehead, letting it all sink in. "Do

you think they're still in touch?"

"No. Natalie said they had a huge falling out, and Mark left town shortly after. Well, after he tried to kill me."

"Damn, man, that's some heavy shit. So, why do you think Ernesto would know where he is now?" Smith questioned, slowing the car as they passed a cop.

Casey shrugged. "Since they were close, I thought Johnny, uh, Ernesto, would know more about him. About his family or something."

"Yeah, it's worth a shot. I can introduce you to him. He usually doesn't answer the door anymore, unless he knows who the person knocking is."

"You know, I used to deliver papers to him when I was younger. He always seemed so benign. Boring even. I'd never have guessed he was a drug dealer."

Smith snickered and nodded. "He's really into Star Wars and shit. If you didn't know, you wouldn't know. That's why he goes by Ernesto. That's his dealer side. Johnny is his nerd side. He likes to keep aspects of his life separate."

They both laughed at that, Casey picturing him playing with action figures in his house. The conversation fizzled, and Smith turned up the radio. By the time they made it to Banner, Casey was deep in his thoughts about finding his father and was craving ketamine. He fished around his pocket and groaned. He'd only brought enough for work.

Smith saw him searching and shook his head. "I didn't bring any, either."

Smith never seemed to need it as much as Casey did. Then again, he was good with beer and weed, too.

Casey liked drinking and smoking, but it never got him to the same place. They only made him want ketamine even more. Casey was a consistent user now, Smith could use ketamine only to party and skip it other times.

Casey missed those days.

"Can we get the food to go? I really need to get some," Casey suggested.Smith frowned. "Damn, dude. Is it from pain?"

"It was, but now I feel fucking empty without it. I'm trying to cut back but shit keeps coming up, you know?" Casey answered, ashamed it was true.

Smith stared out the window, then bobbed his head. "Sure, we can get it to go. You want to go back to the lifeguard stand when we get back? I have some hidden in the wall there. We can hang out, and you can get to where you need to go."

"Yeah, that sounds good. Do you have any more weed on you right now?"

Smith reached over and popped the glove box. "I wasn't slowing near that cop for my health. There's a baggie in there. Roll a big one, we can share it."

Casey did exactly that, and by the time they got to the burger place, he was feeling alright. Not the same as ketamine did for him, but the weed had taken the edge off. They went in and ordered, standing off to the side while their food was being made. Sometimes, Casey felt like everyone could see right through him. See how messed up he was. He turned and leaned on the counter, focusing on a menu as a distraction. When their food came out, Smith nudged him, and they high-tailed it out of there.

They ate on the ride home, though Casey's appetite had disappeared with smoking weed. Even so, he picked at his food to make sure he put something in his body. His mother got on him when she noticed him dropping weight. Smith, on the other hand, scarfed his food down and was chugging his soda as he drove one-handed. He cranked up the radio and tapped his fingers on the steering wheel to the music.

A mixture of the weed, driving with one hand, and trying to get home made Smith slip up, so he was speeding when they passed the cop again. He realized it a second too late and took his foot off the gas, but lights flashed behind them. Casey glanced back, panicked when he saw the cop following them. He scanned the front seat area to see if there was any sign of the joint, but they'd smoked it all. There was, however, still a bag of pot in the glove box.

Smith gave him a short wave as he pulled over. "Keep cool. Quick, get my registration out of the glove box before he gets over here."

Casey fumbled through the glove box, shoving the weed behind some papers. He found the registration and handed it to Smith, slamming the flap shut just as the cop came up to the window.

He was actually a she and rather young. Smith rolled down the window and smiled real friendly-like. "Sorry, I caught myself and tried to slow down when I realized I was speeding."

She leaned down and peered at the both of them. "You were going ten miles over the speed limit. Can I please see your license and registration?"Her eyes lingered for a moment on Casey, and he smiled with a nod. He swore he saw her blush. Smith handed her the required documents, and she glanced at them. "Where are you heading?"

"Home, now. We heard about Mike's Burgers and came over to try them out. We live in Crestview." Smith held up his drink cup full of ice and shook it as if to show he was telling her the truth.

"I see. In a rush?" she asked.

"No, ma'am. I was eating and didn't realize I had my foot so hard on the gas. My mistake." Smith could talk his way out of a lot of things, but she seemed to keep looking at Casey.

"Your name?" she asked Casey.

"Casey Duncan." He did his best to make eye contact and smile. It seemed to be working. She probably wasn't much older than Smith and appeared new on the job.

"I'm going to let you go with a warning, Smith Sinclair, is it?"

"Yes, Ma'am." Smith calling her ma'am seemed out of place and even a little silly.

"Alright, then. Slow down." She handed him back his license and registration. "Be safe."

Casey gave a small wave and a boyish grin at her. "Thank you so much, Officer Vincent," he replied, reading her name tag.

"Kelly," she answered, meeting his eyes. She wanted him to know her full name.

"Kelly. Nice to meet you," Casey said, hoping her interest in him would let them move on their way.

She stepped back, clearly blushing this time. She was pretty in a plain kind of way, maybe because she was at work. Smith shoved the paperwork into the console between the seats, not wanting to open the glove box while she was standing there. She paused a moment as if she wanted to say something else to them, then turned and headed back to the police cruiser.

Smith got back on the road and let out a deep breath. "Fuck, Casey. I think she would've made an issue had you not flashed your baby blues."

Casey started laughing. "I was ready to piss myself. That definitely wore the weed off."

Smith agreed and glanced in the rearview mirror. She wasn't following them. "Let's get back home before we do anything else. Thank fuck you look like you do. Girls just can't help themselves around you."

Casey never really understood it, but he'd seen that reaction time and again. He put his head against the back of the seat. "I guess I'm good for something."

"Damn right, you are. She wasn't interested in my tall, skinny ass, that was for sure," Smith joked. Smith always had his fair share of girlfriends, but girls never fawned over him like they did Casey. "You're a friggin' movie star."

Casey chuckled and shook his head. "Only on the outside. On the inside, I'm a trainwreck."

They fell silent as they made their way into town and headed for the beach. Casey felt his hunger returning and chowed the rest of his food as they walked to the lifeguard stand. He knew once he took K, he wouldn't be hungry again for a while.

As promised, Smith pried open one of the wall panels and reached behind it, drawing out a large bag of pills hidden inside there. He tossed Casey a small packet. "On the house, for using your sexual charisma to get me out of a speeding ticket. Or worse."

Casey laughed and sat on a bench against the wall. He liked being in the shack. There wasn't much to it, but he felt like he was away from the world when he was in there. He crushed a pill, snorting it, then shoved the packet in his shorts pocket. The first wave hit him, and he knew he was home. He closed his eyes, allowing the feeling to wash over him. To set him free. He knew he needed to cut back, however, at that moment, all was right in the world.

When he opened his eyes, Smith was standing at the shack door, looking out. A cigarette in one hand, a beer in the other. He was so tall, his head brushed the top of the door frame, and he was slightly hunched. In one motion, he chugged the rest of the beer and turned around.

"You need a ride home... before I get too fucked up?" he asked Casey.

Casey shook his head. "Nah, I'll walk. Feeling good right now. You got another beer?"

Smith reached down into a small cooler and tossed him a can of beer. "Always. You want to sit outside?"

"Sure."

They moved out to a bench on the deck, facing the ocean. Casey sipped his beer while Smith crushed one after another. Casey glanced at his watch and groaned when he realized what time it was.

"Fuck, I'd better head home. I have to take Aidan to school in the morning. You alright here tonight?"

Smith grinned, which changed his whole face. His face was thin and long, but when he smiled, it all made sense. "Yeah, man. I'm golden."

Casey got up and set his beer bottle down, liquid still in it. "Thanks for the ride, Smith. Burgers were good, so was the company."

Smith peered up at him, his amber eyes slightly unfocused from the beer and weed. "I'll introduce you to Ernesto. Don't try going over there again, though. He won't answer the door. Next time I do a pick up from him, I'll bring you along."

Casey nodded. "That would be cool. He might not know anything, but it's worth a shot."

As he climbed down the ladder, he heard Smith singing softly to himself, his voice muted with drunkenness. It made Casey chuckle to himself. From the moment they'd started hanging out when they were kids, they'd been friends. Once they were teens and reconnected, they'd been inseparable. Almost brothers.

He knew Smith would always have his back.

CHAPTER SIXTEEN

By the time Smith's birthday rolled around the second week of November, Casey wondered if his friend had changed his mind about introducing him to Ernesto. Whenever he mentioned it, Smith either changed the subject or promised to do it soon. Casey stopped bringing it up and grew frustrated with the dead end in finding Mark.

On the night of Smith's twenty-third birthday, he came by the restaurant to pick Casey up for the party. Casey was securing the outside tables and watched as Smith strode across the sand toward him. Smith hopped the rope fence surrounding the patio with one movement, grinning as he walked in Casey's direction.

"Hey, you almost done?" he asked.

Casey gathered the trash bags out of the cans and nodded. "Let me toss these real quick and say goodnight to Natalie. You're early."

"Yeah, I thought we could make a stop first."

"Where?"

"I've got to pick some stuff up, so thought I should introduce you to Ernesto," Smith answered, brushing his shaggy, sun-bleached hair out of his face.

Casey wanted to say it was about time, but he knew better. "Cool, uh, be back out in a second."

He went inside, his heart pounding in his chest. He felt Ernesto was the key to finding Mark and didn't want to mess it up. He tossed the trash out back, then locked the door leading to the dumpster. Natalie was counting the till in her office.

Casey knocked. "Hey, trash is out, tables are secure. I wiped everything down. You need me for anything else before I leave for the night?"

She glanced up, clutching a stack of ones in her hand. "Nope, that should be it. I'm finishing the deposit and heading out myself. You need a ride?"

"No, it's Smith's birthday, so we are heading to a party. Thanks, though."

Natalie tipped her head, her eyes saying something her mouth wasn't, then she went back to counting cash. Casey paused a moment, and she glanced back up. "That all?"

Casey took a deep breath, considering if he should say anything or not. "Smith is taking me to talk to Erne-Johnny Mason. He knows him."

Her eyebrows shot up as she leaned back. "That so? I suppose I'm not all that surprised."

Casey felt his ears get hot. All of a sudden, he was back to being a schoolboy getting reprimanded by his teacher. "I'm hoping he might know something about where Mark went."

Natalie nodded. "Fair enough. Be careful."

"Why?"

"You know what he's into. Don't get wrapped up in that shit, Casey."

Casey didn't tell her he already was in deep. That he very well might be Johnny's best customer. Rather than cutting back, he found himself depending on ketamine more and more as weeks went by. He made sure to go light when he was at work, but there was never a time he didn't have it flowing in his system. Instead, he smiled and took a step back. "You got it. I'll see you Sunday."

Natalie eyed him, reading his face. They both knew there was more than was being said, but neither approached it. She bobbed her head. "See you Sunday."

Smith was smoking a cigarette when Casey came out, leaning against the wall by the door. Casey handed him a bag of fries and a burger. "Extras. Thought you might want some. Happy birthday."

Smith grinned, peering in the bag. "Hell, yeah. Thanks, man."

Being such a small town, the drive to Ernesto's was only a couple minutes, and Casey fought back butterflies. He could walk away with no more information or have a lead on his father. If Ernesto didn't know anything, Casey officially was at the end of the line in his search for Mark.

Smith parked a block up, shrugging at Casey. "Ernesto doesn't want me parking by his house to avoid drawing attention from neighbors. We'll cut around back and go through his garage."

Casey followed Smith's lead as they wound through a couple of backyards until they got to the rear of Ernesto's house. Casey considered he didn't know if he should call him Ernesto or Johnny and decided to let Smith do the talking. At least until Ernesto accepted him. *If* he accepted him. They slipped into Ernesto's garage and went up to the door.

Smith knocked a couple of times, then went in as he called out, "Hey, it's me."

"In the den," a response came.

Smith waved for Casey to follow him through the kitchen and down a hall to a cozy, dark living room. It was tidy and sparsely furnished. Casey let his eyes adjust to the dim room. He could make out the shape of a man sitting in a recliner. Just as his eyes adjusted, a small lamp flicked on. As he remembered from before, Johnny Mason was an unimpressive man. Slightly nerdy and very nondescript.

"Smith, this the kid you were talking about?" the figure in the chair asked.

"Yeah. This is Casey. Casey, meet Ernesto."

Casey didn't know if he should shake his hand or what, so he stammered, "I used to deliver your newspaper when I was a kid."

Ernesto stared for a second, then laughed. "Yes, you did. Do I still owe you money or something?"

Casey's face flamed. He didn't know what to say and began to wonder if this was a mistake when Smith nudged him. "He's just fucking with you, Casey. Ernesto is funnier than he looks. Come on, let's sit down."

They sat on a small couch across from Ernesto. Smith and Ernesto spoke in hushed tones and exchanged cash for a package. After they were done, Smith leaned back, motioning to Casey. "Hey, Ernesto, Casey is looking for his father. He thinks you might know him from back in the day. He doesn't live here anymore."

At this, Ernesto focused in on Casey, his eyes scanning Casey's face. He seemed to recognize Casey beyond being his paper boy, which threw Casey off. He didn't know Ernesto except for then. Ernesto sighed and rested back in his chair. "You're Mark's kid, right?"

"Yeah, I am. I haven't seen him since I was a child, so he's really just a picture in my head. People sometimes tell me I look like him."

Ernesto nodded. "That you do, but you have a nicer face. Mark always looked pissed. Mark always *was* pissed. Anyway, I used to know him, but we don't talk anymore. Haven't in about eighteen, or so, years. I can't tell you where he is if that's what you are asking."

Casey suspected as much, so he wasn't disappointed. "I heard you had a falling out with Mark. Natalie, my boss, said you two went at it one night in By the Sea."

Ernesto tipped his head back and laughed. "Damn right, we did. I set him straight that night. Last time we ever spoke. How's Nat?"

"Uh, good?" Casey didn't know what he was supposed to say about that. Small talk seemed out of place. "So, I was wondering when you did know Mark, did he ever talk about where he came from? Like his hometown or anything? Or about his family?"

Ernesto stroked his chin, then took off his glasses and rubbed his left eye. "Hmm, that was so long ago. Let me think.

Mark was a really private person, he didn't talk about

personal stuff much. He was in the military, I know that. Stationed at Lejeune. Other than that, I can't remember him saying much else about himself."

Casey's heart fell. He already knew all of that information. Smith nudged him and motioned his head toward the door. Casey was crushed. He didn't know what he was expecting, but Ernesto, Johnny Mason, may have actually known less about Mark than he did. Casey didn't want to let it go. There had to be more.

"Look, he must have said something at some point. Talked about his childhood, his parents, siblings... anything," Casey insisted. He felt Smith stiffen next to him. Ernesto was a nice guy but had his limits.

"Sorry, kid. Your father was a single-minded person. He wanted to be on top. To rule things. He never let anyone or anything get in the way of his goals. He didn't care about anyone except himself. I never could understand why your mother was with him."

"You knew my mother?" Casey asked, surprised.

"It's a small town. I more knew *of* your mother. Saw her in the grocery store, the post office, things like that. We chatted here and there in passing. She knew Mark and I were acquainted. She always seemed nice and took good care of you. You were better off without him. I don't know why you are looking for him now, to be honest. You dodged a bullet."

Casey wasn't sure, either, but that was none of Ernesto's business. He stood up, anger rising in him. He couldn't let it show, though. Smith had gone out of his way to arrange this meeting and Casey didn't want to fuck things up for him. He pushed his frustration down.

Another fucking dead end.

"Thanks for talking with me," he muttered and nodded at Smith that he was ready to leave. He wasn't getting any answers there.

Ernesto didn't speak, gazing at Casey with hard eyes. Maybe he was seeing more of Mark in Casey than he expected. Casey turned away, hiding his emotions. As Smith rose and tucked the package under his arm, Casey moved toward the door, signaling he wanted to get out of there.

Smith made arrangements with Ernesto for the next meet-up and joked with him about something Casey couldn't make out, but he was pretty sure he heard Tucker's name in the mix. Tucker had faded from the party scene, but Casey was sure it was only a matter of time before he resurfaced. It made Casey think of a saying Isaac liked to say.

A bad penny always turns up.

Smith met Casey at the door, and Ernesto had risen from the recliner to walk them out. Casey needed some air, time to think. Some ketamine to numb everything. As they hit the garage, Smith turned to thank Ernesto. Casey kept moving, letting them finish talking. He paused by the outside door to wait and turned around.

Ernesto was squinting at him, his eyes unfocused for a moment. He seemed caught in a memory. Even Smith stopped talking and stared at him. Ernesto's eyes widened, and he snapped his fingers. "Hold on, kiddo. I almost forgot, there was this song. Mark liked to play it all the time. County music from back in the day. Not my thing, but he insisted on putting it on the jukebox when we went out. He said it reminded him of home."

Casey frowned. "What was it?"

"By that sniper guy. Uh, John Denver. *Take Me Home, Country Roads.* Yeah, it went like, 'country roads, take me home to the place I belong. West Virginia, mountain mama'... something like that."

Casey absorbed the information, feeling like he finally had something to go off of to find Mark. Not just something, somewhere. A place.

West Virginia.

CHAPTER SEVENTEEN

O ver the next couple of months, Casey worked hard and saved whatever he could to buy a car. His parents gave him money for a down payment for his birthday, so he squirreled away anything extra from his paycheck. The town dropped him once it got cold as there wasn't much to do cleaning the beaches, promising to hire him back once spring break rolled around. However, the restaurant stayed busy, especially in the evenings, so Natalie made up the hours. Casey couldn't cook, but he did just about everything else at the restaurant. The tips were good... especially from middle-aged, tourist women who went on and on about his dark, curly hair and crystal blue eyes.

Having a focus helped Casey cut back on ketamine,

and he went back to only using at parties for the most part. At least, that's what he convinced himself of. As suspected, Tucker had started sniffing around again but made it a point to stay away from Smith.

Even so, Tucker seemed to be up to his old ways and was providing some of the younger kids in town with drugs. Where he was getting it, Smith had no idea. Ernesto insisted he wasn't selling to him.

One day, after the first of the year, Casey got to work and was surprised to see Brittany there. He hadn't seen her since the night of the party when he and Smith had gotten Miranda to take her home. She was standing behind the counter, holding a stack of papers.

She looked rough.

"Hey, long time no see," Casey said as he tied an apron around his waist and clocked in.

Brittany looked uncomfortable. "Casey, right?"

"One and the same. What are you doing here? Shouldn't you be in school?" Suddenly, he felt years older than her, instead of just a few.

"Dropped out. I'll get my GED," she responded, not meeting his eyes.

Casey stood watching her. Kids who dropped out rarely went back. They usually spiraled out and eventually disappeared. "Damn, I'm sorry. I gotta get to work, but it was nice seeing you again."

"You'll be seeing a lot more of her," Natalie said from behind him as she came out of the office.

Casey turned, cocking his head. "Yeah?"

"She's my new waitress. I'll have you show her the ropes today."

Casey glanced back at Brittany, who looked about

as thrilled as he was with them being paired up. Casey noticed dark circles around her eyes that hadn't been there before, and she'd dropped weight. Too much weight. He knew the signs all too well. "Got it. You have an apron?"

Brittany lifted an apron from behind the counter. "Sure do. Let's get this over with."

Natalie glanced between them, sensing the tension, then motioned for Casey to follow her into her office. She shut the door behind them and faced him. "Want to tell me what that's all about?"

Casey didn't want to betray Brittany's trust but knew Natalie would fish it out of him. "Yeah, so I met her at a party awhile back. She got super fucked up. Smith and I had to rescue her from some dude who was all over her and get her back to her cousin. Not sure she even remembers most of that night, though."

"Miranda," Natalie said it as a statement. "She's bad news, that one. Too big for her own britches. Did you and Brittany have any issues I need to know about?"

"Nope."

"Good. I need you two to work together without problems. I have a feeling she's going through some shit and would like her to feel at home here. You understand?" Natalie asked, not blinking.

Casey rubbed his neck. "I understand. I don't have any issues with Brittany. I think she's embarrassed about that night, is all."

Natalie nodded and opened the door, tipping her head. "She'll get over it. Run her through the process. She shouldn't be behind the bar at all. She can waitress, but I'll use her for day shifts. I have a feeling she's using, so don't want her around the night crowd."

Casey wondered if Natalie had been able to tell when he was using. "Sure thing. Better get to it."

Natalie reached out and put her hand on his arm. "You are looking better these days, Casey. I hope you've been able to come to a place of peace with your biological father situation."

So, she *had* known. Casey briefly met her eyes, then smiled. "More or less."

She dropped her arm. "Well, get on, then."

Casey spent the next couple of hours showing Brittany the different responsibilities. She caught on quickly but kept herself tucked away behind an emotional wall.

Finally, tired of talking to a statue, Casey pulled her aside. "What's the deal with you?"

Brittany stared at him, then dropped her eyes. "Nothing, just trying to learn this job."

"Come on. It's not rocket science, you have it. What's really going on? Is it about that night at the party?"

Her gray eyes met his, and she shook her head. "No. That was stupid, but whatever."

"Then, what?" Casey prodded.

She looked like she was going to say something about it, then her face shifted, and she was behind the wall again. "I just need to make some money to get out of here as fast as possible."

"Oh. Is your mom still in rehab?" Casey asked, thinking enough time had passed that she shouldn't be. Yet, Brittany was still here.

"Fuck no. She walked out about four weeks in and hasn't been seen since."

"Where will you go?"

Brittany looked tired of the questions and began scrubbing down a table. She turned her back to him and muttered, "Anywhere but here or there."

Casey watched her for a moment, realizing that the sweet girl he met the first night was long gone. She was still a teen but came across like a forty-year-old who'd been through the wringer. He could tell the conversation was over and went to clean glasses behind the bar. He gathered the trash in the kitchen, and when he came back, Brittany was gone. Her apron hung on a hook by the office door. He untied his and hung it next to hers.

On the way home, he thought about what Smith said about Miranda working with some of the local girls as prostitutes. The story around town was, she would get them using, get them hooked, and keep them using by selling sex for drugs. Smith said it wasn't like that, but he was friends with Miranda, so he might be biased. She wouldn't use her own family for that, either, right? Brittany looked ragged out, but she'd been through hell with her mother.

That was probably all it was. He hoped.

When he got home, Isaac was cooking in the kitchen, and his mother was helping Aidan with homework. Casey grabbed a soda out of the refrigerator and sat down across from Aidan and his mother. Aidan had his forehead resting on his upturned palm and looked miserable as his mother explained fractions. Casey felt for him; he struggled with math, as well, in school.

Casey kicked him playfully under the table. "You want to go surfing tomorrow?"

Aidan's face lit up. "Yeah!"

Their mother frowned. "It's too cold."

"It's never too cold to go surfing. We'll wear wet suits," Casey insisted.

Aidan glanced at his mother, hoping she'd agree. She sighed. "Fine. Wetsuits, but if you get cold, you need to get out and warm up."

"Deal," Casey replied, laughing. It had been a while since he and Aidan had gone surfing, so he was glad she didn't fight him on it. They both needed it.

Isaac came over, holding a dishtowel. "Aidan, you want to put away your homework and set the table?"

Aidan groaned dramatically. Casey chuckled. "I'll help, little dude."

Aidan stacked his homework on a sideboard as Casey gathered dishes and silverware. Their mother went to help Isaac serve the food.

Aidan turned to Casey. "You promise we can go surfing tomorrow?"

"I said I would, right?"

"Yeah, but sometimes you forget. Or don't come home," Aidan replied.

That was true. The more Casey had used, the less he'd been around. He was embarrassed to have his family see him like that, even though he wasn't sure they suspected. He also didn't want to influence Aidan to be like him. Aidan was so pure, so happy, Casey was afraid he'd fuck him up. It was a motivation to cut down using. He wanted to completely stop, but he couldn't. It was like dangling off a cliff, holding on to a tiny, thin rope.

If he stopped, he'd fall.

Casey smiled and winked at Aidan. "We'll go surfing, alright? I want to go."

Aidan tipped his head, his dark eyes reading Casey's

face. "Okay."

They finished setting the table as their parents came in with platters of steaming food and placed them in the center. Casey sat across from Aidan and grinned at him. Aidan was changing day by day. He was losing his baby face and becoming leaner, more gangly. Casey never wanted him to grow up and deal with the world. He wanted Aidan to always believe anything was possible.

After dinner, Casey went to his room and pulled out his journal. He tried to let the words roll out, but they were trapped inside. If he could simply express himself without doing drugs, maybe it wouldn't feel like a weight was holding him down.

He sketched a surfboard with a large bite taken out of it. Then he drew a grinning shark next to the board. For some reason, it made him think of Tucker, so he balled it up and threw it in the trash.

When he was Aidan's age, life in the town seemed idyllic. Living near the ocean. Skateboarding and surfing with friends. They'd ride their bikes all over town, seeing what they could get into. He still saw kids doing that but wondered about what went on behind closed doors. Drugs, sexual abuse, domestic violence?

Had it been going on then?

Clearly, it had since his biological father was involved in it. Hell, even Casey wasn't without fault. He bought into the culture that fed those things. He leaned back on his bed and closed his eyes as images of Brittany, Tucker, Miranda, and Ernesto filled his mind. Like Brittany, he wanted to get out of Crestview.

To leave and never come back.

Aidan. He'd never leave him to the wolves. As long

as his brother was stuck there, so was he. He needed to find Mark and resolve that part of himself. Put it behind him forever, so it couldn't haunt his waking and sleeping hours. It had controlled him long enough. He'd find Mark, face his demons, and end his own torment.

Then, he needed to save Aidan.

CHAPTER EIGHTEEN

"Casey, look!" Aidan yelled as he rode a wave without falling. His face was lit up, his raven hair in a wet, salty frame around his face. Where Casey's hair fell into ringlets in the ocean water, Aidan's was smoother with a little wave to it like their mother's hair.

Casey grinned, wanting to tell Aidan how much he meant to him. If only everything could be like that moment. Free. He remembered being Aidan's age, and hanging out with friends was all he needed. He thought back to then, the image of Aidan running after him, crying and calling out for him as he rode away with friends, came to mind.

Shame washed over him, and he tried to shake it off. He'd only been a kid then, too; he didn't mean to make

Aidan feel bad. He was trying to make up for it now. Though, sometimes, he could see the doubt in Aidan's eyes. Casey wished he could take that away.

Aidan wiped out and surfaced, laughing.

Casey paddled toward him, sliding up beside the board as Aidan climbed on. "You want to get out? I'm hungry."

Aidan groaned. "Come on, Casey. Just a little more."

Casey chuckled and shook his head. "Fine, like ten more minutes. We gotta eat."

Aidan paddled back out and tried to repeat the prior ride. It didn't happen, and eventually, he agreed to go back to shore. They got off their boards as the waves moved them to shallow water and carried them up the beach. Their mother had packed sodas and sandwiches, so they sat and ate, watching the seagulls maneuver around them for food. Casey chucked his crust away from them, and the seagulls followed the scraps of bread in a hoard.

Aidan did the same, then lay back on the beach towel he'd spread out. Casey could see him changing day by day. He'd be twelve soon, the teen years were coming faster than he was ready for them. Part of him wanted to keep Aidan young forever. Untouched by the darkness of the world.

Casey lay next to him and shielded the sun from his eyes with his hand. "Aidan, promise me something."

Aidan glanced over, his face open and trusting like only a child raised in a safe, loving home could have. He tipped his head. "What?"

"You're growing up. There are some things you need to understand once you're out from under Mom's wing in the world. Not everyone out there has your best interest in mind, you understand?"

Aidan watched him, but Casey could see he didn't. How could he? He'd only lived in that town, with both parents who protected him from the hard realities of life. Casey sighed, not wanting to say anything to change Aidan's belief that life was still good. That he was safe

He smiled. "Don't worry about it, but if anyone ever says or does anything to you that makes you uncomfortable or feel scared, you let me know, okay?"

Aidan frowned. "Okay. Like that guy on the street the day I went after the ice cream truck?"

Casey turned to him. "Tucker? Did he make you feel weird that day?"

"Kinda. He was being, like, creepily nice, but I felt like he meant something other than what he was saying to me. It was weird."

"Like what?" Casey was doing his best to keep cool, but the idea of Tucker being anywhere near his little brother was raising his anger.

"I don't know. Like a spooky clown. They are smiling but really want to eat you," Aidan replied with a chuckle, not understanding the danger he could have been in.

Casey forced a laugh so Aidan didn't suspect he was seething. He cleared his throat and sat up, glancing back down at Aidan. "Have you seen him again?"

Aidan sat up and shrugged. "I mean, yeah. He's around but doesn't talk to me or anything."

"He doesn't follow you, right?"

Aidan's face screwed into confusion. "No? Why would he follow me?"

Casey knew he needed to tread carefully. It was a small town, so Tucker being around sometimes when Aidan was out wasn't all that unusual. However, something in him told Casey there was more to it. Tucker had seen Casey with Aidan that day. He was still trying to push Smith out and had a personal vendetta against Casey.

Casey shook his head. "I'm not saying he would, but are you seeing him more now than before the day he asked you about Ernest?"

Aidan tipped his head to one side, considering. His eyes formed into dark slits. "I guess so."

Casey focused on the waves and considered his options. He needed to shut Tucker down once and for all, before he dragged Aidan into his bullshit. Casey tossed a rock toward the waves and stood up. "Let's head home. Mom wanted you to shower before dinner."

Aidan got up and shook his towel out. Casey was in his own head, gathering the rest of their things. They picked up their boards and walked toward the car Casey finally bought, with the intent of finding Mark. Aidan climbed in the passenger's seat, and Casey fastened the boards on top of the car. When Casey got in the car, Aidan looked like he might cry. Casey cocked his head.

"What's going on?" he asked.

"Are you mad at me, Casey?" Aidan asked softly, his voice quivering.

Casey felt like shit. He was pissed at Tucker, and Aidan misunderstood his anger. "Little dude, not at all. I'm sorry. I don't like that guy Tucker, and I don't want him anywhere near you. That's all."

"Why? Will he hurt me?"

Hearing that made the rage surge through Casey. He clenched his fists. "Fuck no. I'll beat him to death before

I'd ever let that happen."

Aidan's eyes grew wide, not used to seeing that side of Casey. He pulled away, chewing his lip. Casey did an about-face and reached out, ruffling Aidan's hair. "Sorry, that came out wrong. All I mean is, no matter what, I'll protect you. You're my favorite person in the world, Aidan."

"Except for Smith," Aidan said. He'd been doubting this more as he got older.

Casey laughed and started the car. "Even more than Smith. He's my friend, but you're my brother."

Aidan grinned, liking hearing that from Casey. "Am I your friend, too?"

Casey nodded. "My best friend."

That seemed to settle Aidan's worry, and they headed for home. Aidan went straight for the shower at their mother's insistence, as Casey went to his room to make a phone call. He only hoped Smith was at Jenny's house. He'd been seeing her lately and spending a lot of time at her home. The phone rang a few times, then Jenny picked up.

"Hello?"

"Hey, Jenny, it's Casey. Is Smith around?"

She sighed. "Yeah, hold on. Smith, phone!"

Casey could hear the irritation in her voice, but he didn't care at the moment. He needed to talk to Smith. It sounded like the phone was set not so gently on the counter, with a rustling sound in the background.

Finally, the phone picked up, and he could hear Smith whispering back at her, frustration lacing his words. They were bickering back and forth in hushed tones, then Smith came on the line.

"Hey, Casey. What's up?"

"Trouble in paradise?" Casey joked.

"Dude. Yeah. What's going on?"

"We need to talk as soon as you can break free. I can't say much here, but I have a feeling Tucker is around Aidan too much," Casey said.

"Really? Aidan tell you that?" Smith asked. Jenny was still bitching in the background.

"Kinda. Aidan mentioned he was seeing him around a lot. You got time to meet and talk? I think we need to nip this in the bud," Casey explained.

"If it gets me out of here, yeah. Where do you want to meet?" Smith sounded tired and more than agitated.

"How about the pier in like two hours? Dinner with the folks, but I'm free after."

"Sounds good. You want me to bring anything with me?" Smith inquired.

Anything meant K, and Casey was tempted. He pushed it away. "Let's stick to beers tonight. I need to be clear-headed on this. Tucker isn't going away unless we make him. We need a plan to deal with him."

Smith laughed. "You want to off him?"

Yes, but no. "I mean, I've thought about it. Seriously, though, we need to find a way to make him want to leave town. Or have to."

"I'm down, man. See you in a couple of hours. Meet me at the end of the pier," Smith said, then started arguing with Jenny again.

Casey suspected they were done and figured he'd offer Smith to crash at his house again. His mother didn't mind last time, especially when Smith had breakfast made for everyone the next morning. His family was nothing if not welcoming to everyone.

Aidan was especially chatty during dinner, recounting his wave ride. Casey was proud of him. That boy was fearless. Isaac had to keep reminding Aidan to eat bites between talking. Aidan's dark eyes flashed with excitement, and for a moment, Casey envied him. That feeling of the moment being enough without the heaviness of the world.

After dinner, Casey excused himself to meet up with Smith. His mother asked him to stay and watch a movie with them, but he needed to get the ball rolling on the Tucker situation. He begged off and headed out, wishing he could stay and be part of the family, instead of dealing with Tucker.

Smith was waiting for him at the end of the pier and was already a few beers in. There was a bench facing out over the water, and Smith was splayed out on it, his long legs stretching out in front of him. He didn't even look back as he handed Casey a beer with one hand when Casey came up behind him, drinking another beer with his other hand.

"Gotta catch up to me," Smith joked.

"Impossible," Casey replied and sat down next to him. For a few moments, they just watched the sun disappearing below the horizon.

Finally, Smith turned his golden eyes to Casey. "So, what's the plan?"

"I don't know. That's why I needed to talk to you. I was planning to go to West Virginia to find Mark, but I can't leave Tucker around Aidan when I do. I don't trust him, especially if I'm gone. One way or another, Tucker needs to go away," Casey answered.

Smith nodded, not a smidge of surprise crossing his face as he considered their options. He leaned forward and whispered, "We could set him up."

Casey frowned, taking a swig of beer. "What do you mean? Like with drugs?"

"Something like that. He's desperate to get in business with Ernesto, which means he both fears and respects Ernesto. We can use that."

"Yeah?"

Smith pulled his legs closer and sat up a bit, shifting his neck until it made a popping sound. "He doesn't want to end up on Ernesto's bad side if you get my meaning."

Casey sort of did. The only reason Tucker was around was to try and take Smith's place with Ernesto. If he didn't have that, he had nothing. "How do we do that?"

Smith grinned, his eyes glinting like a lion about to consume its prey. "We need to make Ernesto think Tucker is trying to double-cross him. If we pull it off, Tucker will be running for his life."

Casey let his brain run over the possibility, knowing Smith could do almost anything when he set his mind to it. If Ernesto thought Tucker was screwing him over, he'd make sure Tucker never stepped foot in town again. Casey smiled.

It was fucking brilliant.

CHAPTER NINETEEN

W hile Casey was ready to go find Mark and get some answers, he knew he couldn't leave the Tucker situation hanging. He needed to take care of that first. Smith laid out a simple plan. All it would take would be to make Ernesto think Tucker was moving in on him. Tucker had already done half the work for them. He'd been brash about making his presence known, going so far as showing up at Ernesto's house and trying to push Smith out. Ernesto hadn't answered the door but had seen Tucker banging and calling out to him. Ernesto asked Smith about Tucker and made it clear he didn't trust him or want him around.

All they needed to do was make it look like Tucker was taking matters into his own hands. Smith knew

Ernesto's patterns like clockwork, when he would and wouldn't be home. Since he rarely left, they needed to wait until he had a scheduled outing. The other part was a little more tricky. Casey asked Smith to go over it again so he understood.

Smith was happy to oblige. "We need to leave evidence of Tucker behind. Nothing obvious. Something that requires a little detective work. If it's too obvious, Ernesto will suspect something is up."

"How do we get that?" Casey inquired.

"That girl, Brittany, Miranda's cousin? I've seen her with Tucker a lot. I don't know if she's his girlfriend or what, but he seems to have her on a short leash."

Casey frowned. Tucker was older than Smith, and Brittany was sixteen. The thought sickened him. That dude was predatory. "Okay? So, we need to ask her?"

"Not we, you," Smith replied with a smirk.

"Me? Why me?"

"Well, one, you are closer to her age and work with her at the restaurant. Two, she likes you."

Casey shook his head. "Nah, we just hung out that one time. Besides, she quit showing up for work. She only lasted like two weeks there. She isn't interested in me, dude."

Smith laughed, his voice full. "Man, I saw the way she was looking at you. Like all the girls look at you. She asked Miranda about you after that night, too."

"Oh. What do I need to do?" Casey really didn't want any part of involving some underage girl, but if she was the key to taking Tucker down, he was willing to do what needed to be done. When she was working at the restaurant, she was nice but didn't seem overly friendly.

Then, she just quit showing up for work. Now, he understood why.

"I'll tell Miranda you were asking about how she was doing. Why she stopped coming to work. See if we can't arrange a little meet-up. It's going to be hard because Tucker is always around her, but she doesn't appear happy about the situation. If we can get her away from him for a bit, we might convince her to help us out."

Casey nodded, thinking about the plan. That would be the hardest part. He wasn't a liar and didn't want to drag Brittany into their mess. However, it was the smartest way. Besides, he wanted to know if she was okay. Getting sucked in with Tucker could only lead to bad things. "Alright."

Smith grinned. "Alright. I'll get the ball rolling and let you know when and where."

"Thanks, man."

"Trust me, I want to take out his ass much as you do. He's been a thorn in my side ever since he showed up here in town. It's time to take him down a notch. Or all of the notches."

Casey stared across the water and sighed. Life used to be so much simpler. He didn't want any of this, but it was here. He needed to do something about it.

Later that night, he sat on his bed and meditated, the mala beads hanging on his chest. He'd been focusing more on going inward to resist using ketamine, but tonight, he couldn't settle. His mind kept running over finding Mark and dealing with Tucker. The two weren't connected, yet he couldn't help feeling like they were. Giving up, he opened his eyes and got off the bed. The house was quiet as he walked to Aidan's room and peered in. His brother was sound asleep, his mouth slightly open in rest.

Casey paused and remembered when Aidan was little, how he'd climb into Casey's bed when he was scared. Casey always let him because it comforted him, as well. They were connected by more than blood. He and Aidan were the same. They believed things were better than they probably were. He was feeling less of that nowadays but didn't want Aidan to ever lose that innocence.

Casey went over and sat on the edge of Aidan's bed, watching his brother sleep. Aidan's dark, thick eyebrows made him look much older than he was. He faced the world with such honesty, Casey forgot he was still only a kid. Casey lay next to Aidan. He rested on his back, staring up at Aidan's ceiling. As if he sensed Casey in his sleep, Aidan rolled over, throwing his arm across Casey's chest. Casey placed his hand on Aidan's arm and smiled.

His mind finally rested.

He woke up around midnight and slipped out of Aidan's bed, reaching back to tuck his little brother in. Aidan shifted in his sleep, and a small smile played on his lips. Casey leaned down and kissed Aidan on the forehead and crept out of the room. He set his mind to taking Tucker down and making sure Aidan got to live the childhood he deserved.

Casey went back to his room and slid on a pair of headphones, playing music until he drifted off to sleep. When he woke again, the house was in full swing. Aidan was getting ready for school, darting through the house looking for his items in a disorganized fashion. Aidan never got the concept of placing things where he could find them later.

Casey checked the clock, sitting up and running his

hands through his wild hair. He needed to move if he was going to make it in time. He dressed quickly and made it to the kitchen just as Aidan was grabbing his lunch box.

"Hey, Isaac, I'll take Aidan to school this morning," Casey offered.

Isaac had his briefcase and coffee as he was moving toward the door. He paused to look at Casey. "You sure? It would really help me out this morning. I have a client I'm already late for."

"Yeah, I'm sure. Some brother time, you know?" Casey replied, winking at Aidan.

Isaac nodded and hurried out the door before Casey changed his mind. Aidan dropped his lunch on the floor and muttered, "Damnit."

Casey laughed. "What did you say?"

Aidan's ears turned red as he scooped up the bag. "Uh, nothing."

Casey helped him gather his things. "Don't worry, I won't tell. Where'd you learn language like that?"

Aidan rolled his eyes. "I'm not eight. All the kids cuss now, Casey."

Casey fought back a grin and tipped his head. His baby brother was growing up. "Fair enough. Don't let Mom hear, though. The first time I cussed in front of her, I thought she was going to burst into tears."

Aidan shrugged. "Duh."

Casey shuffled him out the door, then stopped. "Walk or ride?"

Aidan looked at Casey's car, then down the sidewalk. "If we ride, can we go by the store?"

"For what?"

"Beer." Aidan said it so straight-faced, Casey did a

double take to make sure he hadn't heard what he thought he did. Then, Aidan began cracking up. "You should see your face, Casey. Not going to cry, are you?"

Casey picked him up and threw his brother over his shoulder. "Little shit."

Aidan was yelling and laughing as Casey carried him to the car. When Casey set Aidan down, they both were out of breath and bending over from laughter. Casey stared at his brother for a moment and thought how cool it would be when they were both adults and could hang out. He looked forward to that time.

They stopped by the store on the way to Aidan's school and grabbed snacks their mother most definitely didn't want Aidan to have. Casey paid for it and swore his brother to secrecy. Aidan carried the bag of junk food to the car, grinning from ear to ear. He was going to be a very popular kid at school that day.

Even if he didn't have beer.

As they were nearing the car, Casey heard his name being called and saw Smith loping across the parking lot toward them. Aidan climbed in the passenger's seat with his prize as Casey met Smith halfway.

"Hey! Surprised to see you up so early. What's up?" Casey said to Smith.

"Early shift. I was going to come by your house before work when I saw your car here. You got a sec to talk?" Smith said, his eyes darting to the car where Aidan was sitting, sifting through the bag of contraband.

Casey glanced in at the time on the dashboard. "Shit, no. I'm late getting Aidan to school. You want me to come by the lifeguard stand after I drop him off?"

Smith bobbed his head, his eyes hiding something.

"Yeah, do that. I'm on my way there now. Don't forget, okay?"

Casey cocked his head, hearing the seriousness in Smith's voice. What was going on? "I won't. Give me like fifteen minutes."

Smith turned and left as Casey got in the car. Aidan was watching him, his almost black eyes reading Casey's face. "What was that all about?"

Casey shrugged. "I honestly don't know. Probably nothing to worry about. Just Smith being Smith. I'll find out, though. Let's get you to school."

When Aidan got out of the car carrying his bag of snacks, his friends swarmed around him, clapping him on the back. Casey grinned, happy to help his brother have a good day. He drove out of the school parking lot to head for the lifeguard stand. He pulled into the lot near By the Sea and got out. Natalie was opening the restaurant and raised her hand in a wave as he crossed the boardwalk to the lifeguard stand. Casey waved back and kept moving.

Smith was setting out equipment for the day when Casey came to the bottom of the ladder. Being so tall and thin, Smith almost hit the overhang of the roof as he prepared for his shift. He was wearing his lifeguard uniform, a t-shirt and shorts, his whistle dangling from a cord as he moved around the tight space.

Casey climbed up. "You need any help?"

"Nah, I got this. Like driving a car. I'm glad you came by, we have a problem."

Casey frowned as he ascended the ladder. "Why? What's up?"

Smith motioned to step inside the shack so they could talk. Casey followed him in and shut the door behind them. Smith turned, his face twisted in concern. He shook his head. "I talked to Miranda last night after you went home. Casey, man, this is bad."

Smith wasn't one to overreact, so Casey knew he was about to hear some dark shit. He wasn't sure he was ready for what Smith had to tell him. "What did she say?"

"Tucker isn't Brittany's boyfriend."

"Okay?" Casey felt like the temperature in the shack dropped twenty degrees. Not her boyfriend, so his intent was something more sinister. "What is he always doing hanging around her, then?"

Smith rubbed his nose, his face looking older than his years. He took a deep, shuddering breath as if to steady himself with what he was about to say. He met Casey dead in the eyes, his own telling Casey the truth before his words did.

"He's her pimp."

CHAPTER TWENTY

"He's her fucking what?" Casey asked, his chest squeezing tightly in horror.

"Remember how I told you Miranda was working with a few girls in town? You know, prostituting?" Smith replied, turning his face away.

"Yeah?"

"Well, in that scenario, the girls were willing participants. They all agreed to it so they could make some money. Miranda made a small percentage, but the girls made more," Smith explained.

"So? It's still fucking wrong," Casey spat. "She whored out her own cousin?"

Smith shook his head. "It's not that clear."

"Did she tell you that? Miranda? She's such a bitch.

Brittany needed someone to protect her, not treat her like a piece of meat." Casey could feel his blood boiling and knew what followed after was usually something he couldn't control.

"Like I said, it's not that simple. Miranda didn't get Brittany involved." Smith's voice softened as he saw Casey getting pissed.

"Then, who did?"

Smith sighed and rubbed his bottom lip. "From what I was told, Tucker beat Miranda up one night and told her he was taking over the girls. I guess he roughed them up, too. He cut himself in and Miranda out. Instead of them working to make money, he's locked them in, and he's taking the bigger cut," Smith explained.

Casey felt like his head was going to explode. He clenched his fists, wanting to strike out at someone. No, not someone. Tucker. "And Brittany?"

"This is where it gets a little cloudy. It sounds like he took her under his wing and got her hooked on drugs. From there, he forced her to feed the habit by prostituting."

Casey turned and punched the shack wall as hard as he could, his knuckles splitting wide open. This couldn't be happening in their small town. "I'll call the fucking police."

Smith stood still, watching Casey. "To say what?"

Casey turned, eyes blazing. Then he realized what Smith was saying. If he said anything, it would take them all down. Ernesto, Smith, Miranda, the girls, maybe even Casey. Anyone involved in the party scene would be at risk.

He shook his head, his brain scattered. "What do we

do now?"

Smith stepped forward, placing his hand on Casey's shoulder. He met Casey's eyes, his own determined. "We stick to the plan, but we need to move faster. I don't think we'll be able to get Brittany's help at this point."

"Okay, so how do we frame Tucker?"

"I think Miranda might be willing to help. She never did sex work for anyone else, but Tucker has now forced her into it. She seems pretty on board with whatever it takes to get rid of him," Smith answered, dropping his hand.

"How soon can we do this?" Casey asked, ready to do it at the moment if that's what it took. Even though he wasn't thrilled about bringing Miranda into it as he saw her as the catalyst to most of the problem.

"Alright, so Ernesto is out of town visiting his mother tomorrow. I asked Miranda to meet us tonight. If she can get something personal of Tucker's by tomorrow morning, we can get in when Ernesto leaves and plant it."

Casey listened, no longer afraid to do it. Now, he was willing to put himself at risk to fuck up that piece of shit Tucker once and for all. "Let's do it."

Smith nodded. "Look, meet me back here around eight this evening. The other lifeguard will be gone by then. What time do you work?"

"I have a shift from three to seven at By the Sea," Casey replied, wondering how he'd be able to focus all day. Natalie could read him like a book and he sucked at hiding his emotions.

"Perfect. I'll tell Miranda to meet us here, then. Kill some time after work to make sure the lifeguard stand is empty. Once it is, head on over."

DONE.

Casey did a quick bob of the head and opened the door. "Tell Miranda to bring Brittany with her."

"To do what? You going to hide her at your house?" Smith asked, pointing out the flaw in that plan.

"I fucking don't know, Smith, but I can't let a kid be treated like that. Jesus Christ, she was sent here to have support while he mother was in rehab. Instead, she's been stripped of everything!" Casey yelled.

Smith flinched slightly, then set his face back into its usual calm demeanor. "Alright, I'll tell her. Miranda may not be able to get Brittany away from Tucker that easily. She's his prized possession."

Casey could only imagine why. He threw the door open and went down the ladder, his body shaking with rage. He glared up at Smith. "Make it happen."

Casey didn't look back as he went down. He began walking down the beach, wanting ketamine more than ever. He couldn't do this sober. He couldn't think straight. By the time he realized he'd been moving for a bit, he was far from the lifeguard stand and had passed the outskirts of town. He sat down in the sand and fought back angry tears. He bowed his head, the mala beads swinging forward. He wanted to rip them off his neck and chuck them into the ocean.

As his fingers wrapped around the carved wooden beads, Aidan's face came to mind. He thought about Brittany being that age, and he couldn't fight the tears anymore. He wept silently, thinking about how she probably never had a good home or a safe family. Now, even if she got out, she'd carry that damage forever. He hated Tucker for robbing her of a chance at a supportive environment.

165

The tears stopped, and Casey sat for a long time, staring out at the rhythmic water. From the outside, their town looked idyllic. Tourists loved to visit, saying how they wished they lived there. From the inside, it wasn't so pretty. Most teens ended up using some sort of substance regularly by the time they graduated high school.

If they graduated. Teen pregnancy was common enough that each class had at least one. Very few teens broke the cycle and got out. No one changed anything inside the borders of the town.

Casey wondered why his mother stayed. After she met Isaac, they could have moved anywhere. He asked her once, and she said she didn't want to uproot him. Then, Aidan came along, and the cycle continued. They were trapped by an idea of stability. The idea that security was more important than taking a risk.

He wanted that risk.

Casey got up and wandered home. No one was there when he arrived. He rummaged through his drawers and prayed he'd find at least one pill. He'd made a point to only use at parties and not bring anything home, but he thought maybe a stray pill might have found its way into his nightstand.

After ripping everything out and throwing it on the floor, Casey finally accepted there were no hidden drugs. He sat on the edge of his bed and took out his journal. He was always careful to never write anything that could tell what he'd been doing. Only poems and random thoughts. Today, he held the pen to the paper, but nothing came. He was empty. He threw the book across the room and paced the floor.

When it was time for work, Casey was moving

through the motions. He put on his work clothes and went to the bathroom. A glance in the mirror showed someone he couldn't relate to. It was like he was watching a different version of himself from the outside.

Unreachable and lost.

Work was a blur. Natalie was busy getting ready for a private event, so she didn't interact with Casey enough to realize something was going on with him. When he got off, he wandered by the lifeguard stand. It appeared empty, but as he was about to climb the ladder, the other lifeguard came out of the shack, so Casey ducked under the platform and waited until the guy left. He knew his name but couldn't bring it to mind. They rarely crossed paths.

Once the guy was gone, Casey went up the ladder, heading straight for Smith's hiding spot. He moved the board and put his hand in, finding the stash spot empty. Fuck.

Smith showed up shortly after, eyeing the board, which was still moved out of place. He didn't say anything but watched Casey. He pulled a packet out of his pants, tossing it to Casey. "On the house."

Casey took a pill out immediately and crushed it on the bench, leaning over to snort it. He needed it to talk to Miranda. "Thanks, man."

Smith bobbed his head. "You ready for this?"

He wasn't. He was. He didn't know. "Yeah."

Miranda showed up about an hour later, without Brittany. Casey bit back anger but waited to see what she had to say about Tucker. She looked rough. Not the polished girl who came to the parties. Her hair looked unwashed, she'd lost weight, and had a fading bruise under her left eye.

Smith helped her up the ladder, and the three moved back into the shack, closing the door behind them for privacy. They stood awkwardly staring at each other for a moment, not sure where to start the conversation.

Miranda looked at Casey, her eyes tired. "Hey, Casey."

"Miranda."

Smith, sensing the tension, cut in. "Let's do this quickly. I know Tucker has eyes on you. We could use your help, Miranda."

She stood stone-faced, so Smith continued. "We need something of Tucker's. Something that could be dropped fairly easily. Nothing too big or obvious. Does he have anything he carries on him on the regular? Something that would tie back to him?"

Miranda stared at him, her face blank. About the time they thought she didn't understand what they were asking, she nodded. "He wears a metal bracelet. It has 'Player' inscribed on it. He's such a dick."

"Can you get it off him?" Smith asked.

"He always takes it off and sets it on the counter when he showers," she replied, her voice so monotone, it didn't even sound like her.

"We need it for tomorrow. Can you do that?" Casey grumbled, his voice not hiding his irritation.

Miranda gazed at him, her eyes lacking the fire they once held. "Yeah. He showers every morning."

"How do you know that?"

"'Cause I'm staying with him."

"Why? How can we trust you?" Casey asked with an accusatory tone.

"Brittany. He has her. Like a prisoner. I moved in so

I could look out for her."

Casey fought back a bitter laugh and shook his head in disbelief. "Great job."

Miranda's eyes flashed, showing some of her old energy. "Fuck you, Casey. Not all of us have a safety net like you do. My mother isn't much better than Brittany's. I was trying to get enough money to get out of here. To get us both out. How about come down from your high horse? I'm trying to help you."

Casey turned away, not wanting to get dragged into her sob story. The ketamine was kicking in, and he wanted to disappear. He shrugged. "What's in this for you?"

Miranda glanced at Smith. "Trust me, I want Tucker gone as much as you do. It's the only way any of us girls are getting out of this alive."

"Look," Smith interjected, "we can piss and moan about this all night, but we're on a timeline. Miranda, if you can get that bracelet, I'll be staying here tonight. Bring it by in the morning as soon as you can."

"Sure thing. I do need something from you, too, though," she whispered.

Casey felt the hair on his neck prickle, but a glance from Smith told him to chill out. Smith tipped his head. "What can I do for you?"

"Once he finds the bracelet and me gone, he's going to suspect I took it. I can't go back there, Smith. I need you to hide me. Please. He'll kill me."

"What about Brittany?" Casey asked. "You're a package deal. You want us to hide you, you'll need to bring her along, as well."

Smith and Casey met eyes, having no idea how they could hide two girls in a tiny town. Casey jingled the keys to the restaurant.

"I can let them hide at least for a couple of hours in the morning at By the Sea. We don't open until lunch tomorrow. As long as they are out by ten, we should be fine."

"Then, what?" Smith inquired. "I got nothing."

"Then, my family will be gone from the house until Aidan gets out of school. He has an afterschool program until five o'clock. They won't be back until five thirty at the earliest."

"Okay, that gives us time to get to Ernesto's and leave Tucker's bracelet. Miranda, do you have your car?"

She shook her head. "No. Tucker sold it for drugs."

Casey had an idea that combined two of his goals together. "I'm leaving town to find my father. Do you have any place you can go?"

Miranda nodded. "Brittany's house. Her mother isn't at the house, but we can stay there. It's a few hours from here."

The three looked at each other and knew there was no going back now. Their only path forward was set.

Miranda got up to leave and gave Smith a hug. "Tomorrow."

Tomorrow.

CHAPTER TWENTY-ONE

The moonlight shining through his window was the first thing Casey noticed when he found himself standing in the middle of his bedroom. He was drenched in sweat and naked. He'd gone to bed with his clothes on. His heart was pounding in his chest as if he'd come back from a run. However, the prickles on his skin let him know this workout was mental. He reached back and grabbed a blanket off his bed, wrapping it around him as he shivered in the dark.

It had been hard to fall asleep in the first place, thinking about their plan. It couldn't fail. As soon as Smith and Casey planted Tucker's bracelet at Ernesto's and took some of Ernesto's stash, Casey was high-tailing it out of town. He'd tell his mother in the morning he was leaving for West Virginia to find Mark. He expected she'd be upset. On his last shift, he'd let Natalie know he'd be gone for a week or so.

He honestly didn't know how long it would take. First, he needed to get Miranda and Brittany to Brittany's house. It made him nervous. He was no fan of Miranda and feared what had become of Brittany. She'd be different, that much he knew. He wasn't ready to face any of it.

Casey slipped back into bed. He was trying to save the rest of his ketamine for what they were about to do. But, man, did he want to take some. Instead, he slipped on his headphones and clicked on music. That usually calmed him enough to sleep. It took a couple of hours, but he finally drifted off into a deep sleep, peppered with images of surfing surrounded by a school of sharks. Aidan was on the other side of them, but Casey kept them focused on him so they didn't go after his little brother. The sharks were bearing down on Casey, and he was trapped with no escape.

He woke with a start, realizing he was still in the nude. He fumbled around for his clothes on the floor and slipped them on. His mind was playing over the different scenarios of what could happen later, however, he needed to talk to his mother first. That was scarier than breaking into Ernesto's house. Drawing up courage, Casey went downstairs in search of his mother.

She was reading in a chair and smiled when he came in, her deep brown eyes watching him. "Good morning, Casey. There are waffles in the kitchen."

Casey sat across from her, calming his breath. "I'll have some in a minute. Can we talk?"

She set her book down, her mouth drawing in a

grimace of worry. "Yes. Is everything alright?"

"You know how I said I wanted to find my father? I have been looking for him for a while with no luck. However, I have a lead in West Virginia I want to follow."

She was silent, tears brimming in her eyes. She rubbed her nose and sighed. "Casey, I wish you wouldn't. I understand your reasons, but he is not a good man."

"I know, Mom. I don't have any illusions of a happy reunion. I need to do this to put some things in me to rest. It's probably a bad idea, but I need to face him. Otherwise, it will always hang over me," Casey explained, making his voice as gentle as possible. His mother had risked her life to save him, and he didn't want to hurt her.

She fidgeted with the book in her lap. "You are my son and everything to me. You and Aidan. I can't bear the thought that someone could hurt you. I know you'll do what you feel you need to, but it breaks my heart."

It broke Casey's, too. He got up and slipped his mala beads over her head as he kissed her on the forehead. "You are the best mom. I have your strength to take with me. Keep my beads while I'm gone, so you know I'm still here. I'll be back in a week or so. If I don't find him, I'll let it go. If I do, it's only to confront who he is. I won't let him hurt me."

She placed her hand on the beads, meeting his eyes. They both knew Casey couldn't stop Mark from hurting him. At least, not emotionally. She reached out and took Casey's hand. "Please be careful."

"I will. I promise." Casey knew he needed to break off the conversation before he wavered. He turned to walk out of the room when he saw Aidan at the door.

Aidan appeared hurt and spun on his heel to leave.

Casey caught up to him, grabbing his brother in a hug. Aidan cried into Casey's chest. He hiccupped and peered up at Casey. "Don't go, I don't want you to."

"Aidan, I need to. I won't be gone long, I swear. I have to put this to rest."

Aidan looked up at him, his black eyebrows knitted in concern. "Aren't we enough?"

Casey fought back tears. Aidan didn't know what it was like to carry a hole in him he couldn't fill. Casey didn't want to be the one to make him feel that way. "You are enough. This has nothing to do with you or Mom. You mean the world to me, little dude. I just... I have to. I'm sorry."

Aidan hugged him tight. "Come home."

"Of course, I will. This is where I belong." Casey wasn't sure why, but something in that felt untrue even though he believed it. He hugged Aidan back, lifting him off the ground.

When he set Aidan down, his little brother took a step back. "Bring me something."

Casey laughed. "From West Virginia?"

"Yeah."

"Okay. Not sure what I'll find there; might be socks," Casey teased.

Aidan grinned and rubbed his nose. "Fine."

Casey checked the time and realized he needed to go over to the lifeguard stand since he had the keys to the restaurant. Hopefully, Miranda got the bracelet and Brittany, and they were on their way to meet up with Smith. He slipped on his shoes at the door and headed out, his skin feeling like bugs were crawling on it. He needed to take ketamine to get through this.

Casey drove through the streets, working out the details of the plan in his head. Worrying about getting caught. Smith was at the lifeguard stand, but Miranda and Brittany hadn't shown up yet. Casey took ketamine and paced inside the small structure. Smith finally put his hand on Casey's arm.

"Dude, you're making me nervous."

Casey stopped and stared out the door. "Where the hell are they?"

"They're coming. Miranda has as much at stake here as we do. More," Smith reasoned. He sat on the wooden bench, his lanky legs stretched out in front of him.

Casey plopped down next to him. "Yeah, I guess you're right. I just want to get this over with."

Casey glanced at the time. They needed to hurry. About the time he'd convinced himself they weren't coming, a voice called out from the ladder. Smith jumped up and went out, helping Miranda into the shack. She was shaking and looked like she might vomit. Smith guided her to the bench, glancing behind her.

"Did you get it?" he asked.

Miranda fished the bracelet out of her bag, holding it out to Smith. Casey frowned and peered outside. She'd come alone. He turned to her. "Where's Brittany?"

Miranda shook her head. "She wasn't there this morning. I looked in her room, but she wasn't in it. Her bed wasn't slept in."

"Where the fuck is she?" Casey asked. Getting Brittany out was part of the deal.

"I don't know. Sometimes she stays over at..." She didn't have to finish. She sometimes got stuck at the john's house.

"How do we get her?" Casey asked, not letting it drop.

"She should be home by lunchtime. Tucker makes that rule for the girls. We'll have to go by there, then, to get her."

This was falling apart. Brittany was at risk for Tucker's wrath once he noticed his bracelet missing. Casey glared at Smith, who nodded in response. They needed to move either way. Smith slipped the bracelet in his pocket and motioned toward the door.

"Let's go. Miranda, you'll stay in the restaurant until right before they open. After that, we'll get you to Casey's house. I need to run a couple of errands first."

Miranda nodded and followed them out. They went down the ladder, and Casey let her into By the Sea. He locked the door behind her. They had an hour before Natalie came to open up for lunch. By then, his family would have left the house for the day.

He and Smith went to the hardware store so Smith could get some tools to pick Ernesto's locks. They needed to get into the door, into a locked room, and into a lockbox. They didn't want to make it too clean, so it was clear to Ernesto he'd been robbed, but they needed to do it quickly before he came back home and caught them.

After the hardware store, Casey swung into the grocery store for travel supplies. He didn't want to have to stop until Miranda and Brittany were safely to Brittany's house. He grabbed drinks, chips, and candy, not sure what they'd want. After he checked out, he saw Smith come out of an electronics store. Casey wondered what Smith was doing in there. He came over and helped Casey load the food into the car.

Smith handed him a small cell phone. "It's a burner. Pay as you go. I got one, too, and programmed our numbers into each other's phones. Let me know when you get the girls home. I'll let you know what happens with Ernesto. Don't come back to town until I tell you it's clear."

"Clear?" Casey asked.

Smith shrugged. "Maybe Tucker will simply leave town. If not, all hell is going down. Ernesto won't be crossed, he'll make sure of that. Trust me, wait until I give you the heads up to come back."

That was fine by Casey, he was heading to West Virginia, anyway. He slipped the phone in his pocket and looked at Smith. "My family should be gone by now. Let's get Miranda to my house. We need to do this before they get home, though. Would be fucking weird if they came home and she was in there alone."

Smith laughed. "Yeah. Now or never."

They headed back to the restaurant and got Miranda. She lay in the back seat so no one could see her as they drove to Casey's house. As soon as he saw everyone was gone, he let Miranda in, eyeing her. Could he trust her?

"Stay here, but don't touch anything."

She glared at him. "I'm not a fucking thief, Casey."

"I didn't say you were," he spat. He didn't say she wasn't, either.

She went and sat on the couch, her hands in her lap. She sighed. "Hurry. Being here is strange as hell."

Casey shook his head, wondering how he'd be able to sit in a car with her for hours. They took Smith's car over near Ernesto's but not too close. Smith circled around once to make sure Ernesto's car wasn't there. Once Smith was sure he was gone, he parked a block over. He grabbed his bag of tools.

"We'll go the back way. Here, take this beach towel and throw it over your shoulder, so it looks like we are walking to the beach," he instructed.

Casey took the towel and followed Smith through the alleys that led to backyards. When they got to Ernesto's place, Smith opened the gate, glancing around. They went through the yard and to the back door. Smith dropped the bag and knocked. Once he was sure Ernesto was gone, he picked the lock. As he got it unlocked, he opened the door and stuck his head in to be sure.

"Hey, Ernesto, you here? I need to get some for a party," he called out, listening for any sign of life.

The house was quiet, so they slipped inside. Smith knew exactly what he was doing as he made his way through the house. He went to a bedroom door and picked the lock. The door opened easily. Casey stood awkwardly as Smith worked his magic. He wasn't sure why Smith had him come along until Smith motioned him over.

"Come here. We need to push open the false ceiling. This shit is heavy, so I need to hand it down to you. It's a large lockbox." Smith climbed up on the bed and shoved what looked like a normal ceiling tile away, revealing the hiding spot for Ernesto's stash.

He reached in and tugged a large metal box across to him. Casey moved underneath as Smith shifted the box through the opening, sliding the awkward container down to Casey's waiting hands.

He wasn't kidding; Casey almost dropped it when a thought came to him. "Wait, how would Tucker even know this box was in here?"

Smith grinned. "I wasn't the only one Ernesto used to move this shit. The last guy got caught using more than he was selling, so Ernesto sent him packing."

"Yeah?"

"I had Miranda introduce that guy to Tucker at a party. Remember the guy in the red car at the gas station?"

Casey frowned. "You knew then? About all of this?"

Smith ran his hand through his unkempt hair. "Not this necessarily, but I figured it wouldn't hurt to connect them. I knew I needed to get rid of Tucker. This all kinda came together when you mentioned worrying about Aidan."

Casey appreciated that Smith was always thinking and planning. He helped set the box on the bed as Smith jumped down. Casey watched in admiration as Smith popped the lock like he'd been breaking into shit his whole life. It was all coming together.

Tucker was done.

CHAPTER TWENTY-TWO

A few minutes later, the sound of a car door slamming outside let them know they needed to move and fast. Casey froze, not sure what to do.

Smith peered out the window, his eyes growing wide. "Fuck. Here, grab these." He tossed a couple of bags filled with packets to Casey. "Ernesto's outside checking the mail but will be in shortly. I thought he'd be gone visiting his mother longer. We gotta get going now before he gets inside."

Casey shoved the bags in his backpack and went to help Smith put the lockbox back up into the ceiling. He lifted the box and started climbing onto the bed, struggling with the clumsiness of the large box. He almost dropped it and couldn't get the right angle to get it into the ceiling tile opening. Smith put his hand out to stop Casey, his mind ticking away at the situation. Casey paused and stared at Smith, waiting for guidance on what to do.

Smith shook his head. "Don't worry about it."

Casey frowned. "Won't he notice right away? We'll barely have time to get down the alley."

Smith nodded. "All about the risks. It will take us too long to shove this back up there and get out the door. Just leave it; we don't have time. Let's go."

Smith bolted out of the room, then down the hall, Casey on his heels. He stopped, almost causing Casey to ram into him. Smith whipped around, his eyes in a panic.

Casey put his hand up in confusion. "What?"

"The bracelet. Uh... shit, let me think. It needs to be discoverable but not so much that it looks planted. I have an idea." Smith took the bracelet and hurried back down the hall. He jumped onto the bed and bent the metal band of the bracelet open. He stuck it in the ceiling and wrapped it around a nail sticking up.

Casey watched, his heart pounding in his chest. He could hear Ernesto pulling the car into the garage and the door closing behind the vehicle as the engine cut off. "Smith? Come on, we're going to get caught."

Smith hopped down and peered around. "Okay, it looks like the bracelet got pulled off when Tucker took the box out. It will have to do. Shit, shit, shit..." he trailed off, gazing around. "Alright, follow me. New escape plan. We can go out through the basement."

Smith crept into the hallway as they heard the inner door from the garage open into the kitchen. Smith waved at Casey to follow him, and they went down to the other end of the hall. It ended and turned left into the front foyer. Smith glanced back at Casey and nodded, his finger to his lips to let him know to stay quiet.

Casey knew better than to say anything and wondered why they didn't just go out the front door. Then it dawned on him, it would be obvious to neighbors if they did. Two guys running out the front door was sure to set off alarms. Smith ducked through the foyer to a door at the side. He opened the door with a grin.

Casey never understood how Smith stayed so calm all the time. It was like he got a fix from putting himself in danger. Taking unnecessary risks. Smith went through the door as Casey trailed behind, praying Ernesto wouldn't catch them. They slipped down the basement stairs, closing the door quietly behind them. Casey couldn't see, however, Smith had no problem leading the way.

They made it to the bottom, and Smith flicked a lighter, scanning the space. He extinguished it. "Over here. These stairs go out to the back."

They went to a set of four concrete stairs leading to a flat, wooden door. Smith tested it, relieved to find it was only fastened with a barrel lock from the inside. He slid the lock, careful not to make any noise, and pushed on the door to see if it would open.

It creaked when he did, and Casey held his breath, sure Ernesto would come raging down the stairs any second. Smith held the door still and paused. After a few seconds, he pushed it a little more. Light streamed in, illuminating the two of them in the basement.

Casey felt panic rising in him and stared at Smith for assurance. Smith shrugged with a half smile and opened the door enough for them to slip out. He motioned to Casey with his head to go first.

Casey crawled through the opening, trying to get his bearings. The door opened to the backside of the house. It was overgrown, unlike the front, and he tripped in the weeds trying to stay out of sight. A hand grabbed him, and he whipped around, sure he was caught by Ernesto. Instead, Smith was holding onto Casey to keep him from falling. To get to the alley, they'd have to cross the open backyard in broad daylight, so Smith gestured to the side fence as he sidled along the house wall.

"We can scale that fence and cut through the neighbor's yard," he whispered.

Casey's mind raced. What if there were dogs? What if they were seen? He froze, his thoughts keeping him from moving toward the fence. Smith turned and looked at him, shaking his head.

"Old lady. She can't hear and can barely see. Ernesto helps her out sometimes, has me get her groceries, and mows her yard. Come on."

Casey followed, still unsure. As they scaled the fence, he thought he heard Ernesto yell inside the house. This motivated him to move faster, and he hustled over the top and dropped into the neighboring yard in a crouch. No dogs. That was good. The house looked unlived in, so he hoped Smith had his facts straight.

They crept through the yard and made it to the back gate leading to the alley. Smith eased the gate open and squeezed through, Casey on his heels. They went the opposite way of Ernesto's, out toward the ocean. Casey felt like they were being watched the whole time, bile rising in his throat. His palms were sweaty, and his breath came in short gasps. Smith, on the other hand, walked like he was on a stroll to the beach without a care in the world.

They made it out to the main road and headed for Casey's house. Smith would get his car after Casey picked up Miranda and Brittany. Casey had packed a bag and stuck it in his car for traveling and was anxious to get on the road out of town. When they got to his house, he was relieved to see none of his family had unexpectedly come home and discovered Miranda in there.

Inside, they found Miranda asleep on the couch, her knees drawn up to her chest. Casey pulled the drugs out of his bag for Smith, then headed to his room. He wrote a quick note for Aidan, letting him know he'd be back soon. When he came back down, Smith had woken Miranda up and was telling her what happened. She eyed Casey warily as he came in, still listening to Smith.

Smith turned to Casey, his eyebrows raised. "You have that phone I gave you?"

"Yeah, it's in my bag. We better get going before my parents come home."

Smith stood up, his lanky frame seeming too tall for the low ceilings. "Alright. I'm going to go back over for my car. You and Miranda are heading to pick up Brittany?"

Casey nodded. "That's the plan. Hopefully, she's home. If not, we're fucked."

Miranda sighed and got up. "No time like the present, right? Let's go."

The three went out of Casey's home and paused on the porch for a moment. Smith hugged Miranda and slipped her a wad of bills. She took it and shoved it in her shorts pocket. They were like family. A fucked up family, but they depended on one another. Casey watched, wondering what it was like when they were in school together. It was a world he wasn't part of, being over three years younger.

Smith ducked into the alley across the street to cut over to his car. He stopped and gave them a wave as he disappeared out of sight. Casey turned to Miranda, still not loving the idea of being stuck with her for the drive.

"You think Brittany is there by now?" he asked, stepping off the porch.

Miranda shrugged. "I hope so."

This pissed Casey off. They were risking everything to take Tucker down and get Brittany away from him. Miranda was acting like it was just another day. He breathed out slowly and walked to his car. Miranda got in the passenger side as Casey threw his backpack in the rear seat. He climbed in, glancing at her. "Where to?"

She guided him through the streets, then put her hand on his arm. "Stop here. Pull over. If Tucker sees your car, he'll know something is up."

Casey didn't trust her but didn't have much choice. He put the car in gear and let it idle. "Hurry. If you aren't back in ten minutes, I'm leaving without you."

She faced him, a wry smile on her lips. "Brittany?"

She had him there. He wanted to get Brittany out of there so she had a chance at a normal life. He glared at Miranda. "Just fucking hurry."

She shut the door and sashayed down the sidewalk. He wanted to wring her neck for not taking this seriously. He closed his eyes to steady his breathing and release the anger building up inside him. He went to place his hands on his beads, then remembered he had given them to his mother until he came home.

It was better that way.

After about ten minutes, Casey began to worry Miranda wasn't coming back. Maybe she was playing him. He chewed his thumbnail and considered how long he should actually wait. Too long, and he'd draw attention to himself. He cursed under his breath and put the car in drive.

He slowly moved in the direction he saw Miranda go when something caught his eye. A hunched figure making its way down the sidewalk. He peered closer, and his stomach clenched as he realized what he was seeing.

It was Miranda, and she was trying to get a very weak and wobbly Brittany to the car. Casey sped up and threw the car into park. He jumped out as Brittany fell to her knees. Miranda tried to get her up on her feet, but she was losing the battle. Casey put his arm around Brittany and lifted with all his might. She came up but couldn't stand, so he threw her like a sack of potatoes over his shoulder, rushing for the car.

Miranda yanked the back door open, and Casey unceremoniously dumped the disoriented girl into the back seat. He heard Miranda gasp, and he whipped around to see where she was looking.

Tucker was coming out of a house, brandishing a gun and yelling at them. Casey and Miranda locked eyes for a second, then bolted into the car.

Casey put the car in drive and pressed the gas pedal to the floor, squealing recklessly away from the curb. He righted the steering wheel and glanced in the rearview mirror in a panic. Tucker had the gun pointed directly at them and went to fire it. Something went wrong, however, and the gun misfired, causing Tucker to drop it as he cradled his hand to his chest in pain.

Casey hauled ass out of town, not looking back. A peek at Brittany in the backseat showed him she was passed out, her body pressed into a ball. She was pale, bruised, and sickly looking. It was better if she rested as he drove; she had a long road ahead of her. No matter what, though, they got her away from Tucker and the abuse he was inflicting on her. Casey took a deep breath and focused on the road.

As they passed the town limit signs, Miranda began to laugh hysterically. Casey looked at her, wondering if she'd lost her mind. She kept laughing, her body shaking like she was vibrating. After a minute, she fell silent and gazed out the window.

Casey focused back on the road, his hands shaking from the day. He cracked the window for fresh air and stared at the painted lines on the road whizzing past them. They were on their way. He thought he heard Miranda laughing again and was about to tell her to knock it off when the words got caught in his throat.

She was curled up in the seat, bawling her eyes out.

CHAPTER TWENTY-THREE

T hey rode in silence toward Brittany's hometown a few hours away. Casey kept checking on Brittany, but she remained sound asleep. It was like a death sleep. She didn't move and he had to look hard to see any sign of life. Miranda stared out the window, clenching her fists in her lap. She'd stopped crying but had fallen into a frozen stare.

Casey knew she'd been through some shit, too, but didn't know what to say. Now that they were out of their town, she seemed smaller, more vulnerable. She'd always been loud and brash at parties, but this was a different side of her. He watched her, feeling sorry for her for the first time.

He wracked his brain, thinking of a way to bridge

the gap between them. "So, do you think you'll stay at Brittany's for good?"

Miranda faced him, her eyes tired and hollow. "I don't know. I don't want to. It's not my home. I want to go back to Crestview, eventually."

Casey nodded, keeping his eyes on the road. "You want to stay there? I can't wait to leave."

"Where would you go?" Miranda asked.

Casey laughed, his voice dry. "I'm not sure. I suppose I need to figure that out first, huh?"

Miranda shrugged. "Who am I to say? I fucked things up pretty good for myself and Brittany."

"Will your mother wonder where you went?"

Miranda shrugged. "I doubt it. Since Britt and I moved into Tucker's, she hasn't thought much about us. I think she was ready for us to leave so she could get on with her life, to be honest."

Casey thought about everything. He was careful in how he worded his next question so as to not offend her. "How did you end up, uh... you know?"

"Prostituting? Honestly, a few girls and I were talking after high school about how we felt we were expected to put out anyway, so why not make some money off it? It was stupid, but it worked for a while. We were in control of who we slept with and where the money went. No one was forced to do anything they didn't want to. Then, Tucker came along. I should have paid attention to the red flags."

"Why didn't you? He's a piece of shit and doesn't try to hide it," Casey replied.

Miranda shook her head. "You're right. He didn't play that at first, though. He was funny and, I thought, harmless. However, once he set his sights on taking Smith out of the picture, I became aware there was more to him than he'd shown me before. I knew Smith could hold his own with him, but didn't know Tucker would come after me."

Casey listened, trying to understand. Miranda always seemed to act like she was too big for their small town, but now wasn't the time to say so. He took the next exit to get gas and glanced back at Brittany again. She was still out cold, not aware of her surroundings. He couldn't imagine what she'd been through. Miranda, either. They didn't deserve what happened to them.

"Was it because of Brittany? I mean, what happened first? Did he rope Brittany in or take over your business initially?"

"Brittany. I'm sure you noticed, but she's kind of a mess. Her mom really fucked her up. She's been looking for a family of sorts, I guess. Tucker saw that and took advantage of that fact. He acted like a big brother, then turned on her."

Casey thought back to the night he met Brittany and how she latched onto anyone who gave her the time of day. He felt bad now, he hadn't been more protective of her. Even though he and Smith rescued her from that guy and got her back to Miranda, they should've watched her better that night. Or Miranda should have.

"Did they date?"

Miranda sighed. "I suppose, or something like that. Tucker took an interest in her and I was too wrapped up in my own shit to notice. She started hanging out with him all the time. She has a habit of clinging to anyone who gives her attention. The next thing I knew, she was hooked on meth."

"Meth?" Casey's brows shot up. He liked to party with K but he never fucked with that shit. He turned into the gas station and pulled up to the pump, leaving the car idling for a moment. "Fuck. I didn't know."

"Yeah. After that, they were sleeping together, and he manipulated her into having sex with other people for money. Well, she did it for the drugs, he took the money for himself. Then, he got greedy and came after my operation. He pulled a gun on me."

"Was he always carrying, or is that new?"

"He is now. After Smith beat his ass for going after you. I don't think he was before. He always has it on him, so the girls are afraid to challenge him or try to get away."

Casey cut off the car and got out, knowing he needed to warn Smith about the gun. He pumped gas as he mulled over if this would screw up their plan. He heard the passenger door creak and saw Miranda get out and open the back door where Brittany was. She crouched down and was murmuring to her cousin.

Casey bent down and peered in, seeing Brittany finally stir. Miranda helped her sit up and get out of the car. She braced Brittany around the waist as they made their way slowly to the gas station.

Miranda glanced back at Casey. "I'm taking her to the bathroom. She's going to start detoxing soon. How much longer until we get there, do you think?"

Casey chewed his lip. "About an hour?"

Miranda nodded and turned to take Brittany inside. Brittany moved like she was an old lady, and Casey could only imagine the amount of pain she was in. He fucking wanted to kill Tucker for what he did to her. He finished pumping gas and sat in the car to call Smith.

Smith answered on the first ring. "Hey, Casey, what's up? You good?"

"Yeah, we're about an hour from Brittany's house. She's seriously fucked up. Tucker did a number on her. I don't think she'll be the same ever again. Anything yet?"

"Nah, Ernesto asked me if I had seen anyone around his house, but I told him I'd been at work. I don't think he found the bracelet yet. He's pissed, though, and ready to take someone out over this."

"I bet. Hey, speaking of. Miranda told me Tucker is carrying now."

"That right? Pussy," Smith replied. "Thanks for the heads up. How is Miranda doing?"

Casey could hear the concern in Smith's voice. He and Miranda had been friends for years, and he saw her as a sister. Casey respected their relationship, even though he didn't understand it. "Not great. Seeing a different side of her for sure. She seems broken."

"Damn," Smith whispered. "I can't wait to take that motherfucker down."

"Just be careful, man. He always has the gun on him, Miranda said. He likes to pull it on people."

"I will. I may nudge this along."

"How?" Casey asked.

"I know people. I may start floating word that Tucker wanted to take me out and was trying to find Ernesto to take over. All of which is true. It will get back to Ernesto quickly, especially with him asking around about what happened at his house," Smith answered.

Casey saw Miranda come out of the gas station holding a bag and helping Brittany walk. Brittany was cleaned up and seemed a little more aware of her surroundings. She'd been wearing a long-sleeved hoodie over a tank top but had taken it off. Casey saw multiple bruises and track marks running down her arms as they drew closer. He wasn't sure she'd be able to detox on her own.

It was going to be hell.

Miranda helped her get in the back seat. Brittany wouldn't meet Casey's eyes, and he couldn't blame her. She'd been through more than anyone could understand. Miranda got in the passenger's seat, her eyebrows raised, then gestured to the phone. "That Smith?"

Casey nodded, handing her the phone. She put it to her ear. "Hey, Smith."

Casey started the car as she talked to Smith, driving out of the parking lot and back onto the highway. She talked so softly, he couldn't make out what she was saying to Smith. He heard her sniff a few times, then she handed the phone back with tears in her eyes.

Casey put it to his ear. "Hey, we're back on the road. Let me know what happens there. I'm going to stay the night when I drop them off, then get on the road to West Virginia first thing in the morning."

"Sounds good, man. Be safe. Thanks for getting them somewhere far away from here. I'll take care of it on my end. Good luck finding your father," Smith said.

Casey grimaced, not wanting to think about that at the moment. "Thanks, bro. Talk to you soon."

They made it to Brittany's house before dark. Casey pulled up in front of the two-story, rundown house. Brittany stared at the structure, her face unreadable. Miranda got out and guided Brittany up the cracked sidewalk. They took a key from under the doormat and opened the front door. Casey followed, feeling out of place. Once inside, Brittany began to cry, being surrounded by her previous life. His heart broke for her, knowing how many people had let her down. Miranda whispered to her, rubbing her back.

She turned to Casey. "Make yourself at home. I'm going to run a bath for Brittany. I bought some groceries at the gas station. Frozen pizzas, soda, beer. Feel free to have some."

Casey glanced around. "Do you need my help?"

Miranda's eyes flashed with humor for the first time since before all the shit went down. "You mean, like giving Brittany a bath?"

Casey blushed, putting his hand up in front of him. "No, I meant, cooking or anything."

"Yeah, throw those pizzas in. I'll be down shortly."

Casey grabbed the bag of food out of the car and went to the kitchen. The house was dirty and in disrepair. Brittany's mother obviously had other priorities. He washed the dishes in the sink that had been there for who knows how long and threw the pizzas in the oven. He was surprised the power was still on, considering Brittany's mom was nowhere to be found. Clearly, someone was still taking care of the place.

Miranda came down a bit later in fresh clothes. Casey pulled the pizzas out and searched for a knife to cut them. He finally found one shoved in a drawer of receipts and rubber bands. Miranda took plates out and set them on a small round Formica table.

"Is Brittany eating?" Casey asked.

"Maybe in a bit. She's out of the bath and resting. I

think she's glad to be home."

Casey looked around, not sure why. The place was a dump. Better than being trapped by Tucker, though, he surmised. "Alright. You hungry?"

"Famished." Miranda sat and peered around the kitchen. "Jesus, Aunt Lisa really let this place go to shit. Not that she was much of a housekeeper, but this is way worse than the last time I saw it."

"Was it only the two of them?" Casey inquired.

"Sometimes. Aunt Lisa always had a selection of dudes coming in and out. No one steady, though. She loves Brittany, don't get me wrong. She's an addict and makes bad life choices. But she's trying."

"I see," Casey said, even though he didn't. "How's the power still on?"

"Oh. Brittany's grandparents on her dad's side own the house. They keep up on the bills."

"Where's her dad?"

"Dead. He OD'd like ten years ago."

"Fuck, I'm sorry." Casey was seeing a different side of life and he felt like shit for making his mother feel like she wasn't enough for him. She was. Isaac and Aidan, too. He owed them everything. Once he got home, he'd make sure to let them know how much they all meant to him.

They ate in silence and drank a couple of beers each. They moved to the living room after eating. Miranda turned on the radio and plopped down on the couch. "I know we aren't friends, Casey, but I appreciate you helping us out. Smith thinks the world of you."

Casey sat down next to her on the couch, sipping his beer. "Thanks."

Miranda watched him, then put her feet in his lap

and lay back on the cushions. "I'm not a bitch, you know. You may think I am, but I'm trying to work things out. I made bad decisions, however, I'm doing my best."

Casey could see that she was. The Miranda he thought he knew had been replaced with a girl who'd been dealt a rough hand in life. "Your mom and Brittany's mom are sisters?"

"Yeah. Pretty much cut from the same cloth, too. My mother said their father was super abusive and molested both of them. They grew up here in this town, but my mother wanted nothing to do with it and met a guy from Crestview when she was a teenager. My father."

"Where's he now?"

"With his new family. I have, like, a shit ton of siblings I don't even know. They are a lot younger than me, too. My father isn't interested in me and didn't seem to want them to know I existed."

Casey could relate to that. "I'm sorry."

Miranda yawned. "Look, I get wanting to find your father, but don't have any expectations. He's probably a piece of shit. I made the mistake of reaching out to my father to have him tell me basically he only wanted his new family and didn't have time for me. Protect your heart, Casey."

"I don't have any expectations from this," Casey lied. "Just looking for answers to put this behind me. I'm not hoping for him to want me around. He didn't back then, so I doubt he will now, either. Even if he did, that ship has sailed now that I know what he did to my mom and me. To be honest, I'm not entirely sure why I'm doing this. I suppose it's simply to know one way or another and get on with my life."

"I understand that. I guess it's better to get it over with now than to wonder your whole life if he is out there wanting to be part of your life," Miranda replied, closing her eyes with a sigh.

Casey chuckled dryly. "Trust me, he isn't."

That much he knew was true.

CHAPTER TWENTY-FOUR

C asey felt bad as he slipped out into the cool morning air before anyone else was awake. He and Miranda stayed up talking until after midnight. He learned more about her in that time than he had in the years they'd gone to the same parties. She was a survivor. All her bravado and coolness were simply walls protecting the young girl she'd been.

Let down by everyone around her.

Around midnight, they heard something fall upstairs and went to check on Brittany. She'd woken up thinking she was still at Tucker's and ran into a dresser, knocking everything off. Miranda immediately went to her side while Casey cleaned up the spilled items. Makeup containers, perfume bottles, knickknacks. The room of a typical teenage girl interested in clothes, boys, and music.

Except that was robbed from Brittany. She was still a teenager, but she was also an addict and a victim of sexual abuse. The days of being an optimistic teen were long gone.

Miranda clicked on the light and talked softly to Brittany, reminding her that they were back at her house and she was safe. Brittany was disoriented and in the early throes of detox. Her body trembled uncontrollably, and she slurred everything she said. Casey pulled Miranda aside when Brittany went to the bathroom.

"Do you think she should be in rehab?" he asked.

Miranda frowned. "With what money, Casey? Her mother's rehab has drained everything they had, and she's nowhere to be found. I have nothing to offer."

"What about her grandparents?"

With a snort, Miranda waved her hand dramatically in the air. "They didn't even want her here when her mother was sent away, which is why she came to us. They might pay for the house, but they have no interest in dealing with another addict. Trust me, it's better if they stay away."

Casey considered this and understood how truly alone Brittany and Miranda were. "I'm sorry, Miranda, for everything. For not understanding what you were dealing with. I wish I could help."

"You have. You got us here. She won't be the first detox I've sat through. I got this."

Brittany stumbled back into the room, staring at Casey like she'd never seen him before. Her eyes flicked to Miranda, and she skirted away from where Casey was standing as if he might harm her. He felt like an outsider and moved toward the door to give them space.

Miranda stopped him. "Brittany, do you remember Casey? You met him at that first party in Crestview. He and Smith brought you to me that night. You worked together at the restaurant By the Sea for a bit. He also helped get us back to your home."

Brittany glanced at Casey, no ounce of recognition in her eyes. She shook her head slowly. Casey understood to a degree. Whoever she'd been back then was gone. The Brittany he'd met was not the girl in front of him. She was still in flesh and blood, but her soul was different. He smiled, meeting her eyes. She dropped hers and turned away from him.

Miranda winced, then faced Casey. "It's not personal. Her brain is scrambled. Give it time."

Casey stepped out into the hall, and Miranda followed. He placed his hand on her shoulder. "I'm heading out in the morning. Will you be all right when I leave?"

She chuckled dryly. "As much as we can. You're welcome to stay longer if you want."

He could hear almost a desperation in her words. She didn't want him to go. He needed to, though. He had his own shit to face. He'd also promised his mother he'd be back in a week, and time was ticking. He shook his head, about to speak when Miranda smiled, understanding. She leaned up and kissed him gently on the lips.

Even though Casey had never been attracted to Miranda, that moment stirred something in him. Well, on him. He felt the blood rush to his groin and took a step back, putting his hand up to let her know to stop.

Miranda glanced down and laughed. "Sorry. You

know, if you want... I'm not opposed to taking this farther," she offered.

Casey seriously considered it, needing a physical release, but then thought better of it. It wouldn't be fair to Miranda, even if she was willing. She was still dealing with the after-effects of Tucker's bullshit. Casey had no intention of sticking around, either, and she had a lot on her plate already.

He ran his thumb down her cheek, realizing how pretty she truly was. Once her walls came down, she showed a vulnerable, beautiful side. He could now see the family resemblance between her and Brittany, finding himself very attracted to her.

He shook his head. "Trust me, I'm tempted... but I have to get on the road in the morning and probably need to grab some sleep."

If she was offended, she didn't show it. "You can crash on the couch. There's a blanket and pillow in the trunk on the far wall in there. If you need more, check the closet in the hallway. I'm going to sleep in there with Brittany, so she doesn't wake up alone and freak out."

Casey smiled, his body beginning to cool. "Thanks. If I don't see you in the morning, I appreciate you letting me stay tonight. I'm glad we got to talk."

Miranda batted her eyes at him, showing some of her old self. Her eyes flashed with humor. "I couldn't rightly throw you out after you drove us here. Maybe on your way back, you can swing through?"

"Maybe." Casey knew he wouldn't and suspected Miranda knew that, as well. He could imagine them naked, sweating on each other, and became aware he wouldn't be able to resist again. "Good night, Miranda."

"Good night, Casey." She watched him go down the hall and to the stairs. "Hey. Thank you again."

Casey waved his hand with a half smile.

Part of him wanted to turn around and drag her to one of the bedrooms so they could tear each other's clothes off. The other part of him didn't want to add any more entanglement. He went down the stairs and lay on the couch until his eyes felt heavy. After a few hours, he woke up anxious and ready to get on the road to West Virginia.

He went to the bathroom and listened for any sounds or movement from upstairs. At one point, he thought he heard crying, but it fell silent. He crept through the house, scooping his wallet and keys off the coffee table. He almost wished Miranda would come down the stairs and stop him, but the house remained still. It was time for him to go on to the next leg of his journey.

Slipping out into the morning air, Casey stretched and instinctively reached for his beads. His hands touched his shirt, and he smiled, imagining his mother wearing them, thinking about him. He thought about just driving home, but the need to face Mark was too strong, so he got in the driver's seat with the atlas open on the steering wheel.

Taking Brittany home was out of the way, but he could still make good time and get to West Virginia by lunchtime. He shoved the atlas between the seats and started the car. Glancing one more time at the house, he thought he saw someone standing in the window, but when he peered closer, the figure was gone.

It was just him, now.

Getting onto the highway, Casey cranked the radio and bobbed his head to the music. After an hour, he pulled off for coffee. He found a small gas station, but the coffee looked like it had been reheated from the day before. He poured a cup, anyway. He pressed the lid on and peered around for something edible.

Dusty donuts it was.

He placed the coffee and donuts on the counter as a hunched, old man came over to ring him up.

The man's hand shook as he took Casey's money. "Don't see too many people this early. You visiting?" he inquired, his eyes large and watery.

Casey slipped the change in his pocket, shaking his head. "Passing through."

"Where you heading?"

"To be honest, not entirely positive yet. West Virginia. After that, not sure."

"That right? What's in West Virginia?" the man asked, lighting a cigarette. The same kind Smith smoked. This made Casey homesick.

"My father, I guess. Answers, hopefully," Casey responded, more to himself than anything.

"Ah, I see. Well, best of luck to ya."

Casey took the coffee and nodded at the man as he left. Doubt continually nagged at him. West Virginia, though small, was still a big enough state. He'd researched and found a few Mark Duncans, but they were all in different cities. If any of them were even his father. It was a shot in the dark finding the man who gave him life, then tried to take it away.

Best and worst-case scenarios, he found Mark. It could be a lose-lose situation either way. It was all a gamble, but even winning could mean losing. Casey took a swig of the gas station coffee and winced, considering dumping it out the window. It was terrible, yet he kept sipping it as he drove, his mind lost in thought. The donuts weren't much better, but kept the coffee from ruining his stomach.

Sort of.

By the time he crossed into West Virginia, Casey was jittery and nauseous. Maybe from the coffee, likely more so from the impending task at hand. He pulled off at the welcome center and threw up everything in his stomach onto the parking lot. An older lady walking a tiny, fluffy, white dog grimaced at him in disgust but kept moving. The dog seemed overly interested in the vomit, so she yanked the leash and whispered harshly at the dog to move along.

Casey went to clean up in the restroom, rinsing his mouth with tepid, metallic-tasting tap water. He glanced in the mirror, not connecting with his image at first. The mirror was dirty and bent, giving Casey a strange reflection. He wet his hair down, helping the curls form to his shoulders. He could see Aidan staring back at him and had another pang of homesickness.

What was he doing so far from home?

As he was walking back to the car, the phone Smith gave him started buzzing and he took it out of his pocket. Smith was calling. Casey got to the car and climbed in before answering. "Hey, man."

"Hey, Casey. You alright?" Smith's voice only added to his homesickness.

"Yeah, yeah. In West Virginia, now."

"That's good. Miranda and Brittany home?"

Casey thought about Miranda's kiss and flushed, glad Smith couldn't see him. "They are. I headed out this morning before they woke up."

"Well, I hope you find what you are looking for. I have some news," Smith replied, changing gears.

"What's that?" Casey's heart fluttered in his chest, and he pressed his hand against his leg.

Smith paused and, from what it sounded like, took a drag off his cigarette. "So, I did a little work. The guy Miranda was hanging out with that night? The one I told you about? Seth's his name. I bent his ear at a party last night when he was good and drunk. Mentioned that Tucker told me that he was the one that got Seth in trouble with Ernesto. That he took Seth out so he could move in on Ernesto."

"Did he buy it?"

"I think so, he seemed pretty hot about it when I was done. Everyone knows Ernesto got robbed, so this may help get word back to Ernesto about Tucker. With that, and the bracelet, should be the nail in the coffin."

"Has Ernesto said anything else about it?" Casey asked.

Smith started laughing. "Yeah, he asked me to try and find out who it was. Like cat and mouse, except I'm feeding the mouse to him."

"I guess he hasn't found the bracelet yet?"

"Not yet. However, I'm going over tomorrow to help him secure the product in a different place and will nudge that along, you know what I mean?"

Casey knew exactly what he meant and had no doubt Smith would do just that. "Anything else?"

Smith was quiet for a moment, his voice more serious when he came back on. "I didn't want to tell you this, but you need to know. Tucker knows it was you who got

Miranda and Brittany out of there. He's telling people he's going to give you payback for hurting his business and taking his girls. He knows you're out of town at the moment, so he's searching for a target close to you to attack."

Aidan.

"What the fuck, Smith? He knows Aidan is my brother."

"Don't worry, I got you, Casey. I'm keeping an eye out on Aidan. Watching to make sure he makes it to school and back safely. Not that I really have to, though. Your mom's overprotectiveness is definitely helping right now. That woman is like a hawk with him. She never lets him out of her sight, huh?"

Casey was grateful for his mother's need to know where Aidan was at all times. Especially now. "Yeah, she's always aware. Look, you need to make sure Aidan is alright, though. I'm holding you to it, man."

"Dude, he's my little brother, too. Like you, you know? I won't let anything happen to him. I promise on my life."

Casey prayed that was true.

CHAPTER TWENTY-FIVE

C asey sat in the car at the visitor's center for some time after he hung up with Smith. He trusted Smith to look out for Aidan, however, all it took was a minute of Aidan being alone for Tucker to try something. Casey didn't want to worry his mother for no reason but couldn't risk Aidan's safety, either.

He considered how to tell his mother to be aware of what was going on with Tucker without setting off any unnecessary alarms.

Due to why he had the burner phone in the first place, Casey didn't want to use it to call his mother, so he went to the pay phone at the rest area and placed a collect call.

Isaac picked up and accepted the call without question. "Casey, is that you?"

"Hey, Isaac. It is. I made it to West Virginia and am at the visitor's center to stretch before I get back on the road. Is my mom around?" Casey asked.

"Yeah, hold on. She went to check the mail. I'll let her know you're calling. We miss you already, kiddo," Isaac said, his voice kind and supportive.

Casey felt like shit putting his family through all of this, but it had to be done. "Thanks, Isaac. One day, I'll be gone for good and out of your hair."

It sounded weird when he said it, and from Isaac's silence, he figured it did on his stepfather's end, as well. He only meant he'd be moving out at some point. Isaac cleared his throat. "You have a home as long as you need it, Casey. We want you here."

The phone exchanged hands, and his mother came on the line. "Casey! Is everything alright?"

"Hey, Mom. Yeah, nothing big. I made it to West Virginia. About to go to the first Mark Duncan listed."

"Oh, I see. Please be careful," she said, not hiding the concern in her voice.

"I will. Hey, do you have a minute to talk?" Casey considered his words, worried she might freak out.

"Of course, Casey. What's going on?"

"Look, I just wanted to give you a heads up about something I heard through the grapevine." His throat tightened with the partial lie he was about to say. "Um, word has it someone is trying to sell drugs to kids in town. Hanging out around the schools, offering them stuff."

"Oh! That's horrible. Where did you hear this?" his mother asked, aghast.

Figuring it was safe to say since she was out of town, Casey went with the first name that popped into his head.

"Miranda. She's a friend of Smith's from high school. She said some guy has been showing up outside the school, luring kids over. Can you make sure someone is there to pick up Aidan and drop him off?"

"Yes, yes, we will. Did she say what he looked like?"

Casey went on to describe Tucker, sticking as close to the truth as possible. That way, if they saw Tucker, they'd know to keep Aidan away from him. After he told his mother what he could without telling her the actual truth, Casey felt a little better. He asked to speak to Aidan.

After some murmuring and crackling of the phone being handed off, Casey was thrilled to hear his little brother's voice come on the line. "Hey, Casey."

"What's up, little dude?"

"Not much. Homework, blah. Where are you?"

"In West Virginia."

"That was fast," Aidan replied.

"I'll be home soon. Hey, I need you to watch out for anyone trying to talk to you away from Mom or Isaac. Like that guy the day you went after the ice cream truck. Alright?" Casey warned, attempting to play it cool.

"Okay? Why?"

Why? *Because that guy could seriously hurt you.* Casey shook his head. "Trust me, he's bad news. Unless it's Smith or Mom and Isaac, don't go up to anyone's car. I told Smith to keep an eye on you while I was out of town, too."

"I won't talk to anyone. Am I in trouble?"

"You? No! There are some dicks roaming around town and you'd be better off staying away from them. They are the trouble." Casey wanted to stress this but didn't want to freak his brother out, either.

"Yeah, okay. You want to talk to Mom again?"

"Nah, I'm good. About to get back on the road. Hey, Aidan?"

"What?"

"I love you."

"Duh. Love you too, Casey."

The line cut, and Casey sat a moment, hoping he'd done enough to protect his family. He started the car and headed back onto the highway, driving to the town of the first Mark Duncan. There were three total in the state he could find information on. He accepted none of them might be his father, as well. Mark could have moved anywhere.

When he got to the first town and found the address, Casey parked across the street from the home. Looking at the yard and decorations, he doubted it was the right Mark Duncan. Flowers lined the path, and garden flags decorated the yard. A colorful windsock hung on the front porch, and a wooden bear holding a welcome sign sat by the front door. Nothing that matched the description of the angry man who fathered him.

After about fifteen minutes, Casey confirmed it was not the Mark Duncan he was searching for. An elderly couple came out to sit on the porch, and they were at least seventy years old. He considered they might be Mark's parents when a neighbor walking by greeted the old man as Mark and he waved back.

Mark had kept his parents a secret from Casey's mother, saying they were deceased and nothing more, but Casey was pretty positive these people weren't them. Even if Mark's parents were still alive, these old folks didn't seem to share any of Mark's traits. Casey felt in his gut this was a dead end, but had expected as much.

He pulled out and looked at the paper with the next town and address written on it. It was an hour away, so he grabbed food at a drive-thru before getting back on the road, heading in that direction. His nerves were rattled, and he wished he had some ketamine with him. He'd made it a point not to bring any for just that reason. He needed to be sober and clear-headed to confront Mark.

A decision he was currently regretting.

By the time he got to the next town, it was starting to get dark. He thought about holding off until the morning but knew he might chicken out if he did. He wound through the town until he came to a shitty trailer park.

Driving slowly through the rows of trailers, Casey looked for the number on his paper. Children scattered from playing basketball and riding scooters as he came through. A young boy about Aidan's age smiled shyly and waved as Casey passed by. Casey waved back, then spied the trailer he was searching for.

If the trailer park was run down, the trailer was even worse. Weeds grew up around the outside, and an abandoned car with three wheels sat out front. Casey frowned, figuring he'd hit another dead end, when a shirtless man stepped out of the trailer. Casey parked a few trailers down and cut his lights. He watched the man smoke a cigarette, then flick the butt into the weeds.

Casey peered closer at the man. He didn't remember what his father looked like exactly but had the pictures of a fit military man with short curly hair. This man wasn't that.

The man he was staring at had a paunch and long,

curly, graying, blond hair. Casey cocked his head, trying to put the two images together. If that was his father, he'd taken a turn for the worse. The man grabbed a bottle of whiskey off the window sill and chugged it.

Casey observed from a distance, coming to grips with his feelings as he realized this was, in fact, the man who fathered him. The man ran his hand through his matted curls, his hand getting stuck about halfway. He finished off the bottle and threw that, too, into the overgrown weeds.

The man turned and glanced at Casey's car. Casey felt like a deer in the headlights. The man kept watching, and Casey could see his own blue eyes staring back at him. He dropped his eyes, acting like he was looking at the atlas. When he glanced back up, the man had gone inside the trailer.

None of this is what Casey expected. He imagined coming face to face with a formidable military man. Not a washed-out drunk. He chewed his thumbnail and considered driving back home. Mark had clearly gotten what he deserved in life... living in a shit home, in a shit trailer park, drinking himself to death.

However, Casey still had to know for sure. To know if Mark had any more children. If Mark had a wife. If Mark ever thought about him. If Mark was remorseful for what he did to Casey and his mother. Casey needed answers to questions he couldn't push aside.

Not tonight, though. Tonight, he needed to regroup.

Casey drove out of the trailer park and looked for the closest motel. He found a dive motel a couple of miles from the trailer park, paid for the night, and went into a room that smelled like a dirty ashtray. He flopped back on the bed and thought about Aidan.

Aidan had won the parent lottery. Not only with their mother. Isaac was a good father, a good man. Even to Casey. He'd always treated Casey like his own son. Casey was raised in a home of love and respect.

He appreciated that, but Isaac wasn't his father. Not biologically.

Instead, Casey got a drunk abuser. He closed his eyes and wondered how much of his father's blood in him would impact the rest of his life. He didn't want to end up like Mark. Yet, he couldn't deny seeing his biological father made him see parts of himself he didn't want to accept. The addiction, running from himself.

The spiral into emptiness.

Casey had never felt so alone as he did at that moment. He pictured his family watching television and joking around, oblivious to his absence. He could see Aidan sitting between his mother and Isaac, surrounded by everything he needed. He didn't need Casey. Like Casey had said to Isaac, one day he'd be gone from the house.

Aidan's life would go on.

Casey dozed off to the sounds of a game show on the television and woke with a start hours later. He sat up and peered around the dingy room. The television was still going, and he could hear the sounds of people arguing a few rooms down. After a few minutes, it fell silent.

He got up and hopped into the shower to distract his mind, the water coming out in little more than a trickle. Even so, he stood under the stream until it ran cold.

After the shower, Casey climbed back into bed and closed his eyes, thinking about what he would say to Mark when he confronted him. Everything sounded stupid.

Like a child begging for attention.

Casey switched his thoughts to Tucker, and his chest tightened. No matter which direction he looked, someone had control over his thoughts and his future.

Something had to give.

The next morning, Casey gathered his belongings and headed back over to the trailer park. In the light of day, it was even more run down, and Casey felt bad for the kids growing up there. He parked a block away and went the rest of the way to Mark's trailer on foot. It was early, but he was afraid if he waited too long, Mark might leave.

A school bus passed him as he walked, and he glanced up to see the boy from the day before watching him from the small, rectangular window of the bus. Casey waved again, but this time, the boy didn't wave back. He looked absolutely miserable, gazing out the window. Casey considered if his mother had stayed with Mark, that would have been his own fate, as well. Or worse.

He cut through the dense weeds and climbed the rickety steps to the trailer. His heart was pounding, and he wanted to run away. To forget Mark Duncan and all the unanswered questions. It was the smarter decision, Casey told himself as he stared at the chipped and bowed metal door. He should just leave and cut his losses.

Instead, he raised his hand and knocked.

CHAPTER TWENTY-SIX

C asey dropped his hand and waited. After about a minute, he considered the possibility Mark wasn't home. It was hard to tell as the only vehicle near the trailer was the three-wheeled car, and that wasn't going anywhere. He raised his hand to knock again when he heard movement from inside the trailer. The door lock in the trailer rattled as it was shifted to a different position. The door swung open, shedding the only light that the inside of the trailer probably saw. It was dark and smelled like cigarette smoke.

It reeked of stale liquor, as well.

"What do you want?" Mark asked Casey, not recognizing his own son.

Casey stared at the shell of the man before him. If

Mark had ever had his shit together, he sure as fuck didn't anymore. Casey cleared his throat. "Mark Duncan?"

Mark's eyes narrowed, and he went to shut the door. Casey stuck his hand forward, stopping the door from shutting. Mark grunted in response. "I ain't got no money. Take me to court."

Casey tipped his head in confusion, then realized Mark thought he was a bill collector coming about a debt. "No, uh, I'm not here for any money."

"What the fuck do you want, then?" Mark asked, irritated.

"Can we talk inside? I don't think you want the whole neighborhood knowing your personal business," Casey replied, shocking himself with how calm he sounded.

Mark eyed him, a flicker of recognition crossing his face. He stared at Casey for a few seconds, then sighed. "Come on in, I guess."

Casey followed Mark into the cave-like trailer. Mark motioned to a couch that dipped in the center. "Coffee?"

Casey nodded, feeling out of place and out of sorts. "Sure. Do you know who I am?"

Mark turned and eyed Casey. "I reckon. I wondered if you'd ever show up. Clearly, not for the family inheritance." Mark laughed and poured two cups of coffee from a cloudy, worn coffee pot.

His laugh was jovial, not what Casey was expecting. Casey watched as Mark came closer, handing him a cup of black coffee. Mark sat down across from him and poured a shot of whiskey into his coffee. He didn't bother offering Casey any, nor would Casey have accepted if he did. Casey sipped the coffee, surprised it was good.

"I don't want anything from you," he said, his voice

shaking more than he wanted it to.

"Why are you here, Casey?" Mark asked.

Now that he was sitting in front of his father, Casey had no clue what he was there for. He told himself it was answers, but he didn't have any specific questions to ask. Maybe he needed to see Mark, to connect the biological part of himself he could never resolve. He could see himself in Mark's features. The bright blue eyes, the curly hair. Even the curve of Mark's weathered smile.

"I don't know. I guess I just needed to see for myself."

"See what? This shithole? The complete fucking wreck I made of my life?"

Casey shrugged. "Yeah. I suppose."

Mark chuckled, his eyes crinkling at the corners. "You feel better now?"

"Actually, I do," Casey responded, not caring if it hurt Mark's feelings.

"Ah, you're like me when I was young and brash," Mark said, splashing more whiskey in his coffee.

This made Casey angry. He didn't want to be like Mark. He didn't want to end up like Mark. "Minus the wife and child-beating."

Mark's cup paused halfway to his mouth, and his eyes narrowed. "Give it time."

"I'll never be like you. Everyone talks about what a dick you were. My mother is a kind person, she didn't deserve what you did to her. To us."

If Casey was ready for a fight, Mark wasn't giving it to him. He shook his head. "You're right there. I loved your mother. At least, I thought I did. However, I didn't want children or the home life. I liked being in the military because we were always on the go, onto the next

217

adventure. Then, your mother ended up pregnant, so we got married out of obligation. I was hoping once you came along, I'd feel something different about being a father, but I didn't. I didn't feel anything for you except resentment. You took away my freedom. I hated you for it. I hated her for it."

Casey felt his face flush and stared at the coffee in his cup. It was a punch in the gut to hear he was hated for simply existing. He wasn't expecting a happy reunion, but he thought Mark might at least want to know more about him. Clearly, he didn't. "Do you have any other kids? A wife? Family?"

Mark laughed, this time with bitterness. "I wasn't making that fucking mistake twice. I despise children and wives just bitch and moan. You seem like a nice kid, but I'm glad you weren't around."

Casey continued, undeterred by Mark's vitriol. "Do you have siblings? Do I have grandparents?"

"My parents are dead, you were named after my father. I have a sister who doesn't talk to me. Betty. Well, Elizabeth, but we called her Betty," Mark didn't seem bothered he literally had no one in his life.

"What's her last name?" Casey was grasping at straws, but he didn't want to end up like Mark, alone with no family. A waste of air.

"Carter. Or, at least, it was if she's still married. She lives in South Carolina. Like I said, we don't talk anymore. Anything else, or are we done here?"

Casey gripped his cup, resisting the urge to throw it at Mark. He really wanted to, though. Fifteen minutes into meeting his father, he understood why his mother fought so hard for him not to come.

He should have listened to her.

He met Mark's eyes. "Why did you try to hurt me the night you left? What did I ever do to you? Other than 'take your freedom'?"

Mark set his cup down, his face serious. "I'm sorry for that. I didn't want you, but didn't want to hurt you, either. I had a hell of a temper back then. Plus, I was taking uppers. I was all over the place. I didn't do that because of my freedom. I flipped out when your mother told me she was pregnant again. I saw red. You were in the line of fire."

Casey almost dropped his cup. "I'm sorry, what?"

Mark frowned, tipping his head. "That night. Your mother told me she was expecting another baby. I flew into a rage. I don't remember much else until the cops took me away. I have issues. Not an excuse, but I can't control my anger sometimes. I can't hold a job without flipping out on my boss, can't be in a relationship without wanting to bash their face in. It's why I live here, like this."

Casey couldn't catch his breath. If his mother had been pregnant, where was the baby? He looked at Mark for answers but could see Mark had none. What had his mother said? Mark had beaten her, then went after him. She'd gotten between them. What else had she told him?

"That night... I know you said you didn't remember, but did she end up in the hospital?"

"Look, kid. I don't know. I was arrested and taken away that night. I never went back, per your mother's request. I regret what I did to you both, but I should never have been there in the first place. I wasn't meant to be a family man. I can't tell you anything else."

Casey stood up, the need to get the hell out of that trailer becoming pressure in his head. "I have to go."

Mark followed him to the door, watching Casey rush outside. He stood at the opening as Casey almost fell down the stairs. "Casey?"

Casey turned, the world spinning around him as he tried to process what Mark told him. "What?"

"I may not have wanted to be a father, but you seem to have turned out okay." For a split second, Mark appeared regretful.

Sad even.

"Despite you. My mother and stepfather loved me and made sure I knew I was wanted. You know what, Mark? You fucking suck. I hate you."

Mark laughed and waved his hand in the air. "Tell me something I don't know."

He disappeared inside, and Casey knew that was the end of it. He'd never see Mark again. He began the tangled trek through the weeds when the sound of a gunshot rattled the walls of the trailer. Casey jerked around, his eyes wide. Too afraid to go back to see what happened, Casey ran to his car and climbed in. He bawled the tears of a child who had time and again lost his father.

Sirens filled the air after a few minutes. Casey sat in a trance as police cars and an ambulance sped up to the trailer. The police went in first, then came out and waved to the paramedics. Casey didn't want to stick around to see anymore and drove out of the trailer park. Had Mark killed himself in there?

Either way, Mark was dead to him.

Casey drove for a few miles, then pulled off on the side of the road, not fighting the tears rolling down his cheeks. He punched the steering wheel until his knuckles bled. All he could think about was home and his family.

The people who loved and raised him. His phone began to ring, and he answered it, needing to hear a familiar voice.

"Hey, Casey, how's it going?" Smith asked.

"Not good, man. Not good."

"Damn, you sound shaken up. You find your dad?"

"My father, he was never my dad. I found him. In a shithole trailer park. He's a worthless drunk." Casey left out the rest of what transpired.

"You coming home, then?"

"Yeah. There's nothing for me here. Never was," Casey said, defeated and empty.

"Dude, you have all the family you need here. Your mom, Isaac, Aidan... and me. It's not been the same without you around."

"Thanks, Smith. This was all a fucking waste."

"Never a waste to find out the truth. He ever have any other kids?"

Not that lived. Casey was still reeling from that unexpected news. "No. Good thing because he would have fucked them up, too, just like me."

"Nah, you are one of the most compassionate people I know, Casey. You're nothing like him, believe that. I don't know him, but I know you. Shake it off and come home. You did what you needed to; put it behind you."

Casey cleared his throat, wiping his face. "I am. Should be there sometime tomorrow."

"Cool, cool. Oh shit, I called for a reason," Smith replied, his voice sounding excited. "What's that?"

"Ernesto found the bracelet. He knows it's Tucker's," Smith answered.

"How did he figure it out?"

"That guy, Seth, ID'd it. Ernesto is on the lookout for

Tucker. He's out for blood."

"Did you tell him Tucker is carrying?"

"Yeah. I told Ernesto I saw Tucker flashing a gun at a party recently," Smith answered.

Casey pulled back onto the road. He was ready to go home. He'd only been gone a few days, but he felt like it had been months since he'd seen his family. Now, he knew without a shadow of a doubt that Mark had never been his family. It hurt, but he had people who wanted him home. He'd drive halfway, then stay in a hotel for the night. The next morning, he'd push the rest of the way home.

He sighed. "So, what do we do now?"

"Now, we let karma take effect."

CHAPTER TWENTY-SEVEN

That night in the hotel room, as he lay in the bed playing over the events of the day in his mind, the truth of it all hit Casey like a ton of bricks. The denial he'd been in about why he was searching for Mark, what he was hoping to get out of the encounter with his biological father. He thought it was to put everything behind him or get answers to questions even he didn't know to ask. However, as he lay in bed, staring at the water-stained ceiling, the reality came crashing down on him.

From his first breath of life to that very moment, he was a throwaway in someone's eyes. Unwanted to the point of being disposed of. His mother loved him, and he knew that, but that only made up half of who he was. Even Isaac and Aidan were part of that same half. The other half was a child wandering lost in the desert unprotected, vultures ready to pick his bones clean.

Discarded.

That realization shattered Casey. It broke him down through all of the years of his life, tainting every memory. From when he was a baby to the exact place he sat, in a worn-down hotel room, isolated and aching. Casey rolled over in the bed and cried from the very depths of his soul. He never felt as alone as he did then, and something shifted deep inside him. Part of him gave up. His hopes, his plan for the future, his reason for being.

None of it mattered.

When he couldn't cry anymore, he stared at the faded, peeling wallpaper and emptied everything in his mind. Like meditating before mental suicide. He stayed like that for hours, the fight gone from his body. He was numb to the bone. Like how he felt on ketamine, but without any of the good feelings. Just staring into a vast nothingness.

Barren.

By morning, Casey was running on autopilot. He dressed and grabbed his belongings, ready to make the rest of the drive home. He didn't bother putting on the radio and drove in silence for hours, his mind blank, his body worn. He didn't remember stopping for gas, but he must have, as he made it all the way home.

He sat outside his mother's house, not ready to go in. He didn't want to talk to anyone about anything. He knew she'd have questions, and she should. She was right, Mark was toxic. Casey never should have gone to find him. Now, he was pretty sure Mark was dead. Did he kill himself because Casey had shown up? Or was it just bad timing? Obviously, Mark had nothing left in his life to live for.

Casey related to that at the moment.

Casey cut the car off and got out, staring at the house for a second before walking slowly up the path. He wished he could be invisible and slip in unnoticed. However, as soon as he opened the door, Aidan came barreling down the stairs and grabbed Casey in a big hug, his energy bouncing off the walls.

"Casey, you're home!" he hollered, his face shining with delight.

Casey hugged him tight to his chest, the sensation of his arms around his little brother giving him a little spark of hope. At least someone wanted him around.

"I'm back."

Home. The word seemed foreign to Casey now. This was their home, he was a guest. Or, at least, that's how it felt at the time. It was as if he wasn't really there. Not all of him, anyway. Part of him disappeared the moment Mark pulled the trigger. There was a segment of him that ceased to exist as the bullet ended Mark's life.

Casey couldn't explain why, but even though Mark had never been a father to him, he still removed a piece of Casey with his actions.

What was done was done.

"Did you bring me socks?" Aidan asked, dancing around Casey with excitement.

"Oh shit, I forgot. I'll get you something somewhere else. I'm sorry, Aidan."

"I'm so glad you are home!"

"Even without the socks?"

"Yeah. I have plenty of socks. I only have one brother," Aidan said, grabbing Casey by the hand and dragging him to the living room. "Mom, Casey's home!"

His mother was folding laundry and turned to look at Casey, her eyes searching his for answers. She dropped the shirt she was holding and came over to him, placing her hand on the side of his face, tears in her eyes. "Are you alright?"

Casey couldn't answer. If he did, he was afraid he'd break down. He shook his head. She nodded, understanding, and led him to the couch. "Aidan, go grab your brother a drink. He's had a long trip."

As soon as Aidan left, Casey felt tears forcing their way up. "I'm sorry, Mom. You were right. Mark was a bad person. He didn't want to see me. I shouldn't have gone."

"What did he say?"

"He told me he never wanted me. He resented me. He... he..." Casey couldn't go on, as his chest seized with unnamed grief.

"Shh, it's okay, honey. We want you. We love you, Casey. Isaac sees you as his other son. Not his stepson, his son. Do you see that?" she asked, stroking his hand.

Casey did, but it still didn't fill the hole in him. "Mom. I know. It's just..."

He couldn't form the words. Aidan came back in the room, staring at both of them. The anguish must have been apparent on Casey's face because Aidan hovered by the door, his face worried. Their mother smiled at Aidan and motioned for him to give them a minute. Aidan glanced at Casey, his dark eyes filled with concern. He left, glancing back for a moment. Casey smiled at him to let him know he was alright.

After Aidan left, Casey turned to his mother. "Can you tell me the truth about what happened that night? The night Mark hurt us and had to leave for good?"

She looked uncomfortable but nodded. "I will. It's time for you to know everything."

"Did you have to go to the hospital? Did, did he do something to someone else other than you and me?"

"Casey, I have tried to protect you all these years. I knew Mark was bad. I am glad I have you, and for that, I was willing to go through what I did. You were worth everything," she replied, not answering his questions.

"Mom, tell me the truth. Was there a reason he attacked us that night?" Casey needed her to say it, to stop hiding behind time and memory.

She sighed and got up, pacing the floor like Casey often did. "I assume Mark told you, then. Our marriage was already bad when that happened. I was young and naive and thought if I simply tried harder, gave it time, he would come around. By the time I knew that wasn't possible, something happened that froze me in place. I didn't know what to do."

"Which was?"

Come on, Mom, say it.

"I found out I was pregnant again. It wasn't planned, and it wasn't something I thought I could face on my own. I decided to talk to Mark and see if we could come to a place of peace to move forward. If I could convince him our family was worth fighting for. It was stupid, I know, but I didn't know what else to do."

"What did he say when you told him?" Casey asked, needing her to fill in the blanks. To see if what she said matched what Mark told him.

"He was furious at me. He accused me of becoming pregnant to trap him. I pointed out we were already married, so there was nothing to trap. I begged him to try and see the positive side of it. That set him off, and I knew I'd made a mistake in telling him. You were in bed, so I tried to keep the situation calm, but he exploded." She paused and sat back down, not meeting Casey's eyes as she worked through the painful memory.

"What happened next?" Casey coaxed.

"He came at me and started beating me. I attempted to block my stomach, which only made him angrier. He pinned my hands above my head with one hand as he forced me to the floor and trapped me between his legs. He punched me in the stomach over and over, saying he wouldn't let me control him anymore. I couldn't get away." She sobbed into her hands, her shoulders shaking violently.

Casey wanted to comfort her, but something held him in place. "Mom, why did he go after me? If I was asleep in my crib, how did he get to me?"

She wiped her nose with the back of her hand. "You heard me screaming and woke up. You began crying from your crib, which shifted his attention to you. He was in a blind rage and went to your room. I ran after him, begging him to leave you alone. He grabbed you out of the crib and began shaking you. I shoved him to get him to stop, then he started hitting you. I threw myself at him repeatedly, and he dropped you. I covered you with my body, so he kicked and choked me. The neighbors must have heard us and called the police because they showed up right after that."

Casey dug his fingernails into his hands and stared at her. "Had they not come in time, do you think he would have killed us both?"

She nodded. "Yes."

"After the police showed up, what happened?"

"He answered the door and tried to deflect them, but they asked to talk to me. I was holding you, and they could see what he did to us. They called an ambulance and took him away. The ambulance took us to the hospital. You were bruised and traumatized but otherwise alright. I had broken ribs, a concussion, a fractured sternum, a broken arm, and..." She stopped as tears rolled down her face, her hands floating to her womb protectively to shield the child who was no longer in there but still in her soul.

"You lost the baby," Casey said it out loud, so she didn't have to.

She met his eyes. "I wanted that child so much. Just like you and Aidan. Sometimes, I like to think the soul of that baby came back as Aidan because it was meant to be with us. I was devastated. I didn't want you to go see Mark because he was a dangerous man, but I knew you needed to see for yourself, or you would never believe me."

Casey went over and put his arm over his mother's shoulder. He was devastated, too. Maybe if that child had lived, he wouldn't feel so alone in the world. He closed his eyes and tried to picture his sibling. He pictured a baby with curly, dark hair and his mother's almost black eyes. A perfect cross between him and Aidan.

Tears slipped between his lashes, and for that moment, he and his mother were back to when it was only the two of them. He understood now why she was so worried about him and Aidan all of the time. Always watching, always hovering. She was also guarding that child in her mind.

Aidan came back into the room and whispered, "Is everything okay?"

Casey looked at his little brother and wanted nothing more than to wrap him in his arms and protect him from the world. He put his hand out to Aidan, who came and took it. Casey pulled him in close and murmured in Aidan's ear, "I love you, little dude."

Aidan hugged him hard, seeming to comprehend what they'd been through on a deeper level. Maybe he was Casey's other sibling. Casey hoped so; he couldn't bear the thought of his sibling's soul lost somewhere out in the cosmos. Aidan sat as close to Casey as he could get and rested his head on Casey's shoulder. Casey peered down at his baby brother and pushed away the sensation of how fragile he was. He couldn't handle the possibility of losing him, too.

He thought about Tucker and the threat he presented to Casey's family. Smith was convinced Ernesto would take care of the problem once and for all, however, Casey didn't know if he could wait for that to happen. Ernesto believed it was Tucker who robbed him and was out for blood, but who knew how long that could take? In the meantime, Tucker was still out there, fucking up people's lives.

Casey knew he needed to find Tucker and deal with him before anything happened to Aidan or anyone else he cared about. He had nothing to lose.

No... he had *everything* to lose. Mark showed him that Casey was nothing without his family. His mother had thrown herself on top of Casey to save him, even though it cost her the life growing inside her. Casey would never allow another person to come in and rip his family apart.

No one would hurt Aidan as long as Casey had breath

left in his body.

That was enough for Casey to decide to track Tucker down and put an end to his bullshit, once and for all. He couldn't wait for Ernesto to find Tucker. Casey didn't know where or how he'd do it, but he would confront that monster and remove him permanently from their lives.

Even if it cost him his own.

CHAPTER TWENTY-EIGHT

For the next few weeks, Casey tried to track Tucker down, but it was as if he'd disappeared into thin air. Casey didn't tell Smith his intentions, however, he asked Smith if he had seen Tucker anywhere around as they were sitting on the deck of the lifeguard stand smoking weed after Casey came home.

Smith shook his head. "Nah. I think he's lying low because Ernesto is looking for him."

"Okay, well, let me know if he resurfaces," Casey insisted. His voice sounded harsh, even to him.

"You planning to confront him?" Smith asked, trying to read Casey's face.

Casey shrugged, not meeting Smith's eyes. Smith always had a way of reading between the lines, and Casey wasn't ready to show his hand yet. He knew Smith would try and talk him out of confronting Tucker. "Something like that. I need to know where he is to keep him away from my family."

"Fair enough. I don't think we'll see much of him, though. Word is out Ernesto is after him."

That makes two of us, Casey thought. He stood up and leaned on the railing, crossing his arms in front of him. Smith put out the joint and joined him. He stared at Casey for a moment, sensing the change in Casey.

"Hey, man. Are you alright? You seem different since you got home."

Casey nodded slightly, then shrugged. "I guess so. Just worn out from everything, I think."

"You want to tell me what happened when you met your father in West Virginia? You've been pretty tight-lipped about it," Smith urged.

Tell him that his father pretty much said Casey was an unwanted piece of shit, that he murdered Casey's sibling, then blew out his brains? "Not much. My mother was right. He wasn't worth the visit. That chapter is closed."

Smith lit a cigarette and eyed Casey like he often did. "Okay. You don't have to tell me. I'm glad you're back."

Casey laughed; there was no pulling anything over on Smith. After all, he had his own family shit to deal with. "I appreciate it, man. It was a mistake to go. I should've listened to my mom. I'm glad to be home, too."

It was starting to get dark, and Casey wanted to spend some time with his family. He turned to Smith. "You want to come over for dinner? I'm sure my mom would like to see you again. She has a soft spot for you."

Smith shook his head with a grin. "Thanks, but I can't. Have a date."

"Oh yeah? With who?"

"You don't know her. She's not local."

"How'd you meet her?" Casey asked.

Smith winked. "Tourist. I was on lifeguard duty when her dog got loose. I helped her wrangle it."

Casey could picture Smith with his long legs and arms tackling the dog. "That's one way to meet girls."

"Women, dude. This one has a few years on me."

Casey's eyebrows went up. "Like how many?"

"Ten."

"She's thirty-three? Damn, Smith. Chasing the old broads, now?"

"Thirty-three is hardly old, and I'm tired of these young girls and their drama. Jenny wore me the fuck out. Besides, it's a date, maybe a hook-up. That's all. She leaving tomorrow and made it clear she's just looking for a fun time while she is here. Works for me."

Casey tipped his head and laughed. "Only you can find these situations."

Smith chuckled. "It's cause I'm so tall, seems to have a power over them. Then, they find out I'm an asshole and send me packing."

It was a joke, but it was true. The girls, women, who went after Smith seemed to be drawn in by his height and lifeguard uniform but quickly discovered he was a mess and not relationship material. They tried to change him but figured out Smith was set in his ways. He'd yet to find anyone who made him want to do better.

Casey climbed down the ladder and glanced back up at Smith. "You know the offer for dinner or a place to crash always stands. You're practically family."

"I know, man. It's much appreciated," Smith replied with sincerity.

Casey waved and headed across the boardwalk. He popped into By the Sea to see if Natalie was still around. He was ready to get back to work and back to some semblance of normality. He was still struggling with feeling he belonged anywhere, so making things normal was a priority. Starting with work and a routine.

Natalie was mopping the floor when he came in and paused to look up. "Casey! I thought I saw you over at the lifeguard stand."

"Yeah, I'm back. Got any shifts for me?"

Natalie stood up straight and rested the mop against the counter. "Let me look."

She disappeared into the back to grab the schedule, and Casey sat at the end of the bar on his favorite stool. The restaurant was still open but quiet. A couple of locals were sitting in the corner, drinking a pitcher of beer, but otherwise, the restaurant was empty.

Natalie came back out and set the schedule down between the two of them on the bar. "As you can see, it's pretty slow right now. I'm working most shifts with just me and one other person. But looks like I can use you next Friday and Saturday night?"

Jobs in town when it wasn't tourist season were scarce, and he couldn't be picky. "I'll take it. I appreciate you keeping me on, Nat."

"As long as I can. So, did you go find your father?" Natalie asked bluntly.

"Yeah. It was stupid. He's a dick."

Natalie laughed and bobbed her head. "Tell me

something I don't know."

Did you know he beat my mother so badly that she lost the baby?

"I guess it was good I saw for myself. Hard-headed," Casey replied, tapping his knuckles against his head.

Natalie did something surprising and reached out, placing her hand on the side of Casey's head. "No, honey, you have a big heart and think everyone else does, as well."

Casey dropped his eyes, feeling vulnerable and supported at the same time. "Thanks, Nat."

Casey waited until she was distracted by the customers in the corner to take his leave. She'd seen through him like Smith had, and he was afraid they'd see what he was trying to hide. His shame and feeling lost. Once she went to refill their pitcher, Casey ducked out. The sun had set, and a coolness rolled in. The lifeguard stand was empty, so Smith must have left for his date.

Casey drove the long way home, through town, and down back streets. He even drove by Tucker's house, but it was pitch black and deserted. Maybe Tucker had gotten scared and left town. Part of Casey hoped so, but the darker part of him wouldn't rest until he made Tucker pay for what he did. What he intended to do.

As Casey was leaving the street Tucker's house was on, he caught a glimpse of something down the next street. A flash-like light hitting metal. He turned his car down the road and drove slowly, trying to see what it was. It was a dead end, and when he got to the end of the road, he didn't see what made the light, so he turned around in the last driveway.

He drove past Ernesto's house and was surprised to see Ernesto standing on the porch. Ernesto recognized

Casey and waved at him to stop. Casey pulled over and rolled his window down. "Hey, Ernesto."

"Hey, kid. Have you seen that asshole Tucker around?"

"Nope, but I hope I do."

"Why's that?"

Casey considered how much he could safely tell Ernesto. "He's threatened my family in a way."

"In a way?"

Casey surprised himself by letting it all out. "I helped rescue some girls from him. A couple of girls he was forcing into some bad shit. He saw me and pulled a gun on us as we were driving away. It misfired. Anyway, he made threats against me and my little brother."

Ernesto listened, his face emotionless. "That so? Not surprised since he's a thieving, little shit. You know who he reminds me of?"

He didn't have to say it; Casey had come to the same conclusion. Mark. Maybe that's why Casey kept feeling there was a connection between the two. They were both sadistic, selfish assholes. "Yeah. I do. Now that I've met my father in person, I can understand why he was pretty despised by people around here."

"You did? In West Virginia?"

"Yeah, there weren't too many Mark Duncans up there. I tracked him down, but now I wish I hadn't found him," Casey confessed.

"You think he'll come back around or something?" Ernesto asked, staring past Casey down the street.

Always looking for his target.

"Nah. I think he's done with this place," Casey sort of lied. He a hundred percent knew Mark was done with their town, done with any place.

"That's good. This town doesn't need that fucker back again," Ernesto whispered as if he was speaking only to himself.

Casey waited to see if Ernesto would say anything else, then, realizing the conversation was over, began rolling the window back up. He paused and cleared his throat. "Hey, Ernesto?"

"What's that, kid?"

"Can you let me know if you see Tucker? I have a score to settle with him."

Ernesto met Casey's eyes and nodded. "Don't we all? I can't promise he'll still be alive if I do, but I'll give you the heads up either way."

"Thanks, Ernesto. See ya around."

Ernesto waved his hand and disappeared back into his house. Casey drove down the street, lost in thought. He was glad to have Ernesto on his side, but he hoped he came across Tucker first. He wanted to be the one to make Tucker pay. To make him suffer for what he did to Brittany. To Miranda. To all the girls Miranda was working with. Tucker needed to suffer for his actions.

As he was thinking about that, his mind drifted back to seeing the flash of light on the other street. Something told him to go back over there to check it out, so he turned that way, instead of heading home. He wasn't sure what he was looking for, but knew he'd know once he saw it. He cut his car lights and crept down the road slowly, scanning each house and driveway as he went by them.

As he drew close to where he saw the flash before, he turned off the car and let it ease to stop on the side of the road. In the dark, he peered around, looking for the source of the flash when he saw it again.

One of the tourist rental homes at the end of the road was empty for the season. Or should have been empty, but something was catching a reflection from a neighboring light inside the dwelling.

Casey waited in the dark, his eyes fixed on where he'd seen it. The house stayed dark, and he rested his head against the back of the seat. He didn't see anything else and went to turn on the car to leave. He couldn't stay there all night.

Then, it happened.

A flicker of light, like from a lighter, briefly lit up inside the home, and Casey made out a shape through the window. He narrowed his eyes and waited for further confirmation of what he thought he was seeing. The lighter flickered again, and Casey saw it for sure. Not just any shape.

Tucker.

CHAPTER TWENTY-NINE

C asey was sure that's who he saw through the window. Well, almost positive. The light had only illuminated the person for a second, then went out, but it looked like Tucker's weasely face. Casey sat in the dark and considered his options. He could bust through the door and go face-to-face with Tucker, however, that would put Casey at a disadvantage. He had no weapons, didn't know if Tucker did, and didn't know the layout of the house. He could be putting himself in more danger than he was ready for.

After a few minutes, Casey decided it was best to go home and make a plan. If Tucker had broken into that home, it was clear he was holed up there. Hiding from Ernesto. Begrudgingly, Casey started the car and eased it away from the curb, leaving his lights off. He didn't want Tucker spying him and making a run for it.

On the way home, Casey thought about ways he could take Tucker down. He'd need some kind of weapon; that was a must. Then, he needed to figure out what to do next. He wanted Tucker dead, but that was more Hollywood than reality. He was pretty sure he couldn't kill someone point-blank. Then again, as soon as he thought about Tucker threatening his family, Casey thought maybe he could.

Casey vacillated between being sure and doubtful. He didn't want anyone to know his plan, but he also needed a sounding board. Smith was too close to the situation and would try to stop him. Casey opened his phone and dialed a number he didn't think he'd ever call. They'd exchanged numbers when he left, but he thought it was more symbolic than anything.

"What's up, Casey? Fancy you calling," Miranda said, her voice more chipper than when he last saw her.

"Hey, I need someone to talk to. About something confidential. Can I trust you with secrecy?"

"Oooh, juicy. What you got?"

Casey pulled up outside his home and cut the car off. "Can you promise me this stays between us?"

"Uh, sure?" Miranda replied, sounding less than.

Casey needed to take the risk she'd keep it between them. "Okay, I know where Tucker is. He's been hiding out because Ernesto is looking for him."

"He didn't leave town? That was fucking stupid of him," Miranda said in disbelief. "Ernesto will end him."

"You know Ernesto?"

"Johnny? Yeah. Friend of my mother's."

That explained a lot. "Yeah, so, he's squatting in a house nearby. I don't know if he thinks this will blow over or what, but I saw him in there. He didn't see me."

"Damn, that's crazy," Miranda whispered. "His ego was always a lot bigger than his brain. Did you tell Smith or Ernesto about this?"

"No."

"Why not? I thought you wanted Tucker gone?"

"I do, but I want to do it," Casey said, realizing he sounded childish. "He threatened my family."

"Fuck, Casey, this isn't a movie. You could get yourself killed. Then what would happen to your family? They'd be devastated." Miranda was weirdly being the voice of reason. After all, she probably knew Tucker best.

Casey chewed his lip. All of a sudden, his plan seemed stupid and implausible. "Look, please don't say anything to anyone. Let me think this out. Thanks, Miranda. I wish we had gotten to know each other better when you were here. You're actually pretty cool."

Miranda laughed. "You always thought I was Smith's bitch friend."

"A little. Not so much anymore. I see the shit you were dealing with," Casey admitted.

"Ah, don't worry about it. I was a bitch. I did fantasize about getting you naked, though."

Casey blushed at this and stared at his house as he thought about her naked for a moment. "Uh, yeah. Are you ever coming back this way?"

Miranda was quiet, then sighed. "You know, I thought I'd drop Brittany off here and make my way back as soon as I could. Now that I'm away from there, I feel like I might have a future. Crestview is a trap. Believe it or not, I'm thinking about going to school for nursing."

"Damn, that's awesome. Maybe one day, I can get the fuck out of here, too."

"Well, you know where I am. Oh, and Brittany's doing a little better. Serious detox and she's going to the free clinic for some STDs she picked up from that shit, but she's starting to talk more again."

Casey wanted to say that was good, but he knew Brittany had a long road ahead of her and would never be the same. "At least she has you looking out for her."

"Don't be a stranger, Casey. And leave the Tucker thing for Ernesto, he'll know what to do."

They hung up, and Casey rubbed his forehead. He knew Miranda had the best of intentions, but this was his battle to fight. Even so, it was good talking to her. He felt less alone with that.

After a late dinner and movie with his family, Casey went to bed. He made a plan for the next day. He still had keys to the restaurant and knew Natalie kept a gun locked in her top drawer for the nights she worked alone. She'd kill him if she found out he took it, but he didn't know where else to get one. Besides, if he took it after they closed and returned it by morning, she'd never know.

After a fitful night of sleep, Casey got up and put a pot of coffee on. It was going to be a long day of waiting until the restaurant closed, and his mind was all over the place. Could he kill Tucker? If he did, how would he hide it? What if a neighbor heard the shot?

He was running over each scenario in his mind when he heard someone behind him in the kitchen. Getting spooked

by the sound, he jerked around, eyes wide.

"Hey, Casey, just me," Issac said, grabbing a coffee cup out of the cabinet. "Smelled coffee and thought you might be up. Mind if I join you?"

"Sorry, didn't mean to wake you. I made plenty of coffee," Casey said, following suit.

They sat down at the kitchen table, and Isaac eyed Casey. "Your mother told me about the conversation you had with her when you got home from seeing your father. About what happened that night."

"Mark. He's not my father," Casey interjected. "You are, Isaac."

Isaac nodded, his brows knitted, understanding how hard it was for Casey to say that. How much it meant. "Mark, then. She told me you know about what he did to you and her. About the baby, too. I'm so sorry."

Casey didn't respond but bobbed his head. Isaac set his coffee cup down and reached over to place his hand on Casey's. "I know all of this has come as a shock to you, and you didn't do anything to deserve it. Sometimes, bad people slip through. My father was an abusive man, as well, which is why I swore I would never lay a hand on my boys. You and Aidan are everything to me, I hope you know that."

Casey did. He supposed he always had. Isaac never treated him as less than his own flesh and blood. He met Isaac's eyes and nodded. "Thanks, Isaac. I know I've given you a lot of shit over the years. I apologize for that."

Isaac laughed. "Comes with parenting. Aidan will, too, when he's a little older."

Casey waited until the rest of the family was up, then headed back to bed for a few hours. By the time he woke up again, it was early afternoon, and he was anxious to do what needed to be done. He went downstairs and saw everyone had left for the day. He was glad because he felt like he had it written all over his face what he was about to do.

In the kitchen, his mother left him a note that she was taking Aidan for school clothes and a haircut. Beside the note were the prayer beads he'd given to her while he was gone. Casey slipped them over his head, liking the weight against his chest. He ran his fingers over a few beads, finding unexpected strength in them.

He left before anyone came home, so he didn't get caught in explaining where he was going. Not that they ever gave him a hard time. They trusted Casey. He wandered to the beach and sat drawing for a while. At one point, he swore he saw Smith coming down the beach toward him, but when he looked back up, he was gone.

Once the sun set, Casey put his sketchbook in his parked car and waited for Natalie to leave the restaurant. Like clockwork, she locked up and headed out with the cook at the same time. Casey crept up alongside the restaurant and peered in. It was dark and empty. He unlocked the door and slipped in, making a beeline for the office. The door was open, so he went in and sidled around the desk to get to the drawer. It was locked, but Casey knew where Natalie kept the spare keys. He put his hand on the top shelf of her bookcase and reached back, feeling the key ring with the tips of his fingers.

The gun was right where he expected it, and the bullets were on another shelf. Casey grabbed both and shoved them into the backpack he'd brought. He had a doubt for a moment but pushed it away. It was his only option.

Slipping back out into the night, Casey peered around. The beach and parking lot were empty. He planned to leave his car and walk, so no one knew where he was going. The heaviness of the backpack matched the heaviness of his steps. This wasn't him. Or, at least, he hoped not.

Would killing Tucker change him?

He rounded the bend to the street where he'd seen Tucker and hid in the bushes across from the house. Like before, he saw a light flash in the house and realized Tucker was in there smoking meth. Miranda told Casey it was Tucker's drug of choice. Casey crept across the street and ducked behind a tree near the front porch of the house. He unzipped the backpack and put his hand in, feeling the cool metal of the gun. He took it out and loaded bullets into it, convincing himself he could do this.

He stepped out from behind the tree and started for the porch, setting his resolve. This was for Brittany. This was Miranda. This was for Aidan. For anyone else whom Tucker had hurt. As he got to the bottom step, Casey eyed the door and grasped the gun in his palm.

It was time.

He never made it to the door, however. Casey was grabbed from behind and dragged to the side of the house, his captor muffling his yells. No matter how hard Casey fought, he couldn't get free.

Then everything went black.

CHAPTER THIRTY

His head was pounding when he came to, and Casey instinctively touched his skull. No obvious injuries, but still, his head throbbed. He was lying down, which confused him even more. He sat up and peered around. He was in a room he didn't recognize. He put his hands down beside him and attempted to get his bearings. The sound of someone clearing their throat startled Casey, and he scanned the room to find the source of the noise. Smith was sitting on a chair in the corner watching him, his face twisted in concern.

"Fuck, Casey, you had me worried."

"Someone attacked me. Where the hell am I?" Casey croaked out.

"Ernesto's. You don't recognize the room?" Smith

asked, his voice strangely flat.

Casey glanced around again, realizing it was the room where he and Smith found the drugs in the ceiling. "I don't understand. Why am I here? How did I get here?"

"Couldn't take you home in your condition. Ernesto offered to bring you here."

Ernesto? Casey was even more befuddled than before. Last he remembered, he was outside the house he saw Tucker in. "How? Did you find me somewhere after I was attacked?"

Smith lit a cigarette and leaned back in the chair, his long legs stretched out in front of him. He eyed Casey for a second, biting his lower lip. "Casey, man, don't freak out. I'm really sorry about this."

Casey frowned and put his hands in the air in confusion. "Sorry about what?"

"Fuck. So, we followed you tonight. Ernesto put you into a sleeper hold, and we brought you here."

Now, Casey was pissed. "What the hell are you talking about, Smith? You followed me? To that house?"

"Yeah. Ernesto wanted to deal with Tucker on his own terms and knew you would get in the way if he didn't stop you," Smith explained.

Casey was floored. He thought Tucker or someone with him had attacked him, but it had been his best friend and Ernesto? That didn't make any fucking sense. "Smith, seriously back the fuck up. How did you know to follow me? You knew Tucker was there?"

"No. Not at first, anyway. Then, Miranda called me and let me know what you told her about finding Tucker. She confessed what you were up to. I knew I wouldn't be able to convince you that taking Tucker down on your own was a bad idea. I didn't want you to get hurt or in trouble."

Fucking Miranda. Casey never should have told her anything. "Why didn't you come talk to me?"

"Would you have listened?"

No. "Maybe. Probably not. But you're my friend, goddamnit! How could you go behind my back like that?" Casey railed. He tried to get up, but his legs felt wobbly, and he sat back down. "You told Ernesto?"

"Look, Casey, you don't have to believe me and I get you're pissed, however, Ernesto is skilled at all of this. You're just a kid with a grudge. Do you want to go to prison for the rest of your life?"

Casey had been so blind with rage at Tucker, he hadn't thought out the long-term consequences of his actions. "I wouldn't have. I was going to..."

What? What was he going to do? That's where the plan fell apart.

Smith leaned forward, his hazel eyes tired but kind. "You're my little brother, dude. You have been since we were kids. I couldn't let you make a decision that would've affected you for the rest of your life. Imagine what it would have done to Aidan had you been killed or arrested. Hate me if you want, but I'd do it again."

Casey deflated. Smith was only looking out for him, and if he had come to try and talk Casey out of going after Tucker, Casey would only have fought him on it and done it, anyway. A soft knock came at the door, and it opened a crack. Ernesto peered in and gazed at Casey, worried. Once he saw Casey sitting up, he motioned to Smith with his head to go out of the room with him. Smith watched Casey for a moment, then followed Ernesto into the hall.

Casey could hear them talking in low tones back and forth and heard Tucker's name come up multiple times in the conversation. He couldn't make out any other parts of what they were saying, however. He was about to get up and go out when Smith came back into the room. Smith stood by the door and ran his hand through his light golden-brown, shoulder-length hair, his face unreadable.

"I need to leave with Ernesto for a bit. Do you want to stay here or go home?"

"What are you doing?" Casey asked.

"Running an errand. You want us to drop you off at your house?" Smith replied, clearly hiding something.

"Smith, how long was I out?"

"I don't know. Like, about fifteen minutes or so. I was worried you weren't going to wake up, but you were breathing alright."

Fifteen minutes. What happened in that time? Casey glared at Smith, needing answers. "Tucker?"

Smith shook his head. "Your guess is as good as mine. Ernesto had me bring you here. He stayed behind."

Casey had so many questions but knew he wasn't getting anywhere with Smith. He stood up, more steady this time. His bag with the gun was missing. "Where's my pack?"

"Safe. Where'd you get that gun?"

"It's Natalie's, so I have to get it back before she knows it's missing and reports it stolen to the police. I need it." Casey wasn't ready to give up yet.

"Casey, please just listen," Smith's voice was pleading for his friend to stop. "If you had used the gun, the police would have traced it back to Natalie, and she would have gotten in serious trouble. There's nothing left to do tonight. You need to go home and forget about this."

Casey hadn't considered the risk he was putting Natalie in by taking her gun, however, he didn't like Smith lecturing him. "Fuck you, Smith! Fuck Ernesto, too! Give me my shit and leave me the hell alone. I can't believe I ever trusted you! You were supposed to be my friend."

Smith flinched but didn't budge. "I'll put the gun back tonight, I have your keys to the restaurant. The alternative is Natalie finds it missing and questions anyone with keys to the place. Which narrows it down to you and like two other people who work there."

Casey knew he was out of moves. He hated Smith for it. He seethed and walked up to Smith, almost losing his balance. "Don't ever fucking speak to me again."

He pushed past Smith and found his way out of the house. Ernesto was standing on the front porch and touched Casey's arm as he stormed past. His hand on Casey's arm made Casey pause. Regardless of his anger, Casey was afraid to cross Ernesto.

He glared at his father's former friend. "What?"

Ernesto smiled, his eyes pained. "Your anger is understandable. Something you may not know is that when you were a baby and your mother had to call the police on your father, she reached out to me and asked me to protect you and her in case he showed back up. I swore on my life I'd do my best to make sure no harm came to you. I've watched out for you throughout the years until you were about thirteen, and I thought you were able to look out for yourself. I knew who you were when you were delivering my newspapers and later when you showed up with Smith. Your life and family seemed to have come together, though, so I didn't need to worry about you anymore. I never had cause for concern for your safety. Until tonight. I fulfilled my promise to your mother."

Casey pulled away and narrowed his eyes at Ernesto. "I'm sure my mother will be very happy about that."

He stomped down the path and flung open the gate to the sidewalk, causing the rickety frame to bend. He headed for home without looking back. He'd been robbed of his chance for revenge, and he couldn't let it go. He hated Smith, Miranda, and Ernesto, even though a tiny voice inside him told him they were only trying to protect him.

When he got home, everyone was asleep, so he crept up to his room and shut the door. Hot tears flooded out of him, and he punched his pillow until his arms were tired. Casey was so sick of everyone deciding what was best for him. He had no one left to turn to, so he took enough ketamine to pass out.

Casey was woken up by the sense of someone sitting on his bed. He opened his eyes and saw Aidan grinning at him. Aidan bounced on the bed, all legs and arms. Casey watched him, his heart hurting. He hadn't been the one to make sure his brother was safe. He hoped even so, Aidan was safe. He nudged Aidan with his foot.

"What's up, little dude?"

Aidan bounced some more, then leapt on Casey, giggling. Casey grabbed him and pinned him, tickling the squirming boy. Finally, Aidan begged for mercy between squeals of laughter, and Casey let him go.

Aidan stared at him, his face red from laughing so hard. "Can we do something today?"

Casey sat up and checked the time. It was after ten in the morning. "What did you have in mind?"

"Skateboarding?"

They didn't have a park, but they always found places to skate and do tricks, much to the dismay of the local older folks. "Sure thing. Can I get dressed first, or do you expect me to go naked?"

Aidan wrinkled his nose. "Ew, Casey. Are you naked under your covers?"

Casey wasn't, but he wanted to mess with Aidan. "Maybe, and if you don't leave right now, you might see more than you bargained for."

That did it. Aidan bolted out of the room. Casey dressed and fished around the nightstand for pills. He had a stash, which he was grateful for since he'd burned any bridges with Smith and Ernesto. He didn't know where he'd find shit, now. He considered taking a pill, then decided he'd need to conserve them until he could find a new source. He shut the drawer and slipped his shoes on.

Aidan was waiting by the door with their skateboards when Casey came down. Casey shook his head, chuckling. "Am I not allowed to eat first?"

Aidan shoved a toaster pastry in Casey's direction with a grin. "Here."

Everything seemed so normal, considering the night before, he was planning to blow someone's brains out. He took the pastry, slightly sticky from being in Aidan's hand, and took a bite. "Alright, let's go. You tell Mom?"

Aidan turned his head. "Mom! Casey is taking me skating. We'll be back later."

Casey laughed, shaking his head at his little brother. He could have done *that*. They got out to the street and got on their boards, pumping their feet to pick up speed. It felt good. They darted between cars and went on and off the sidewalk. Aidan was getting incredibly good, maneuvering the board with precision.

Casey felt a moment of sadness, thinking about how one day they'd go their own directions in life once Aidan grew up. He never wanted this time with his brother to end. If he could just hold onto it for the moment, maybe he could slow the speed of time.

They made it out to the main drag and crossed over to the park, whizzing past people strolling along the path that bordered the beach. A few people griped at them, but neither Casey nor Aidan cared. They made it to the end of the walking path and hopped off their boards, grinning and out of breath.

Aidan looked at Casey. "Can we get something to eat?"

They were near By the Sea and the lifeguard stand. Casey panicked, wondering if Smith had indeed gotten the gun back to Natalie's drawer. If not, he was sure Natalie would see it all over his face. He sighed. "Sure."

They went into the restaurant, and Natalie was behind the bar washing glasses. She eyed Casey with an odd expression on her face and pointed toward the office, letting him know she wanted to speak to him alone.

Fuck. His heart raced, and he felt himself flush with panic. There was no way he could hide it on his face from her. He followed her back as Aidan took a seat at the counter. Casey was ready for the worst. He might be going to jail.

She was dangling his keys in her finger when he got to the office. Casey didn't offer any explanation and stared at her, waiting for the fallout. She tossed him the keys. "Smith dropped these by this morning. Said you left them in the lifeguard stand."

"Oh. That all?"

Natalie frowned, reading his face. "Should there be anything else?"

"Uh, no, I just didn't know if you needed me for something more. I dropped by to buy Aidan lunch."

"Look, Casey, be careful with those keys. The last thing I need is for someone to come in here and rob the place. You understand? I trust you."

He nodded. "Sorry, Nat. I'll be more careful."

"Please do."

He went back out, counting his lucky stars. Aidan was spinning on the stool and waved the menu at Casey. "Come on, I'm hungry."

They ordered food and ate, Aidan talking almost nonstop. Casey could see the lifeguard stand when he turned his head and saw Smith standing on the deck, staring out over the ocean. Casey pushed down the ache in his heart and focused back on his baby brother's ramblings.

When they left, Smith glanced at them, his face grim. Casey dropped his head and walked in the other direction, not making eye contact. There was once a time he considered Smith his best friend, his other brother. Now, he wanted nothing to do with him.

At least, that's what he tried to tell himself.

CHAPTER THIRTY-ONE

C asey spiraled for the next few months. Nothing seemed to make sense, and he began to lose control over even the simple things in life. He let his family down time and again, forgetting to follow through on promises and completing tasks. He used up all his ketamine, then started using whatever he could get his hands on since he couldn't go back to Smith for more. He began showing up to work at the restaurant high, and Natalie took notice. One night, as they were closing up, she pulled him aside.

"Casey, we need to talk," she said as she cleared the last table. The doors were locked, and it was only the two of them left in the restaurant.

Casey wasn't surprised and wondered why it had taken her so long to call it out. He nodded and set the stack of plates he was carrying on the counter. "Okay?"

Natalie watched him, her face showing the wisdom of what was really going on. "Honey, I know tracking your father down didn't go as planned, and since you came back, you've been all over the place. I tried to let it slide to give you time to work things out, but I can't have you working here fucked up like you've been."

"I haven't-" Casey began, but Natalie put her hand in the air to cut him off.

"I'm not judging you, kiddo. You've been through a lot, and I know it's tough to deal with the world sometimes. I like you, Casey. You're a good person with a big heart. Maybe that's why you are trying to bury yourself, I don't know. I have no way to catch you, and you're going to end up hurting yourself or someone else if I continue to let you work here. Do you understand what I'm saying?"

Casey did, but he didn't want to admit it. "I work hard, I always show up, Nat."

"That you do. However, I have been catching some pretty major errors with your work, and I can't risk it."

"Like what?" Casey asked, indignant.

"For example, tonight a customer told you they were allergic to dairy, and you put cheese on their salad. Not a huge deal because they caught it before they ate and said it would cause hives and upset their stomach but wasn't life-threatening. Thankfully, but you didn't know that, and it could have been serious."

"It was just one mistake, it won't happen again. I promise," Casey insisted.

"Casey, it already has. This wasn't the first time I caught you doing something that could hurt someone.

You served food on a plate that had raw chicken on it last week. Luckily, I caught it before they ate."

"Why didn't you say something?" Casey asked, attempting to deflect the blame.

Natalie sighed and leaned against the counter, her eyes kind but firm. "We aren't doing this. I care too much about you to turn it into a fight. I think it's time to take a break. Get your shit together and you are welcome back once you do. For now, though, I need your keys. Please understand, I don't want to do this, but you aren't leaving me a hell of a lot of choice here."

Casey was ashamed and dug the keys out of his pocket. At least she hadn't done it in front of customers or other staff. He handed her the keys, his eyes burning with humiliation. As he reached out with the key ring, Natalie took his hand, getting his attention.

"I've known you since you were a baby. I consider you one of my own. Your mother and stepfather are good people, but you have Mark's blood running through you, as well. He was an addict and an abuser. You're no abuser, but I can see you are struggling with the other. Am I right?"

Casey met her eyes, then let his drop. He shrugged. "I'm just experimenting, you know?"

Natalie squeezed his hand. "No, I don't know. You're running from something but are treading water. Eventually, you'll drown if you don't get out of this. Don't let Mark own you for the rest of your life. Let him go. Set yourself free."

Casey fought back the sting of tears and cleared his throat. "He's dead."

"What do you mean? You found him, right?"

"I did. He told me I was a mistake and he never wanted me in the first place. That I messed everything up."

"Casey, don't-"

This time, Casey stopped her. He pulled his hand away and met her eyes. "Don't what? That's what he said to me. It's the truth. I was fucking in the way, a thorn in his side. Whatever you want to call it. I was *unwanted.*"

Natalie watched him, her face twisted in concern. "Maybe he didn't want you, but everyone else did. Everyone else *does.* Never forget that. He was a shell of a human; his hatred for himself seeped out to everyone he was around. It had nothing to do with you. You were simply an easy target for an angry man."

"It sure the hell feels like it had to do with me. He tried to kill me. He murdered my sibling."

Natalie frowned and tipped her head, her expression trying to understand what he was saying. "Your sibling?"

"My mother was apparently pregnant when he beat her up that night and tried to get to me. She lost the baby from the abuse when she got to the hospital. He told me when I found him, and my mother confirmed it."

"Oh. Damn, Casey, I'm so sorry. I didn't know."

"Neither did I, until I confronted him, and he threw it in my face. So, there's that," Casey replied, his voice tired and flat. Saying it out loud sounded strange, like it happened to someone else's family.

"I want you to come back to work once you get yourself straight. I need you to know that, hon. This was a hard decision for me to make. I want you to know that it has nothing to do with me not wanting you around."

Casey nodded and shrugged. "I'm getting used to it."

"What?"

"People pushing me away." Casey knew he sounded defeatist, but at the moment, that's how he felt.

"Aw, Casey, I know that's how this feels, but I promise you it isn't the case. Everyone except Mark has your best interest in mind; know that. We all care about you and want you to be alright. Also, know he isn't worth the energy you are giving him."

"Well, since he's dead, I guess I'll never know. He blew his brains out right after I left."

"Jesus. I'm sorry, I don't understand. How do you know that?" Natalie asked, confused.

"I heard the shot as I was leaving his trailer but didn't go back. Later, I looked it up online, and the police said he died by suicide. The day I was there."

"Oh, shit. That's a lot of baggage to unpack there. Look, why don't you take a week or two off, then let's sit down and see if we can work this out together," Natalie suggested, switching gears.

Casey shook his head. "No, you were right in terminating me. I'm not in the place to be in charge of anything. I'm a fucking wreck, right now. I need to go. Don't tell anyone what I told you about Mark, though."

"You're mother doesn't know?"

"No one does. I left that day after I heard the shot and came home. I didn't tell anyone."

"I see. I won't say anything, but, Casey, you shouldn't be carrying this alone. That's way too much for anyone to shoulder. If you ever need to talk..."

Casey gave a half smile and glanced at the door. "It is what it is. I'll see you around, Nat."

Not giving her the chance to respond, he headed out

the door into the night. He could smell cigarette smoke and knew Smith was at the lifeguard stand. For a moment, he considered stopping by, but he was still pissed about the betrayal and moved on. They hadn't spoken since that night, and Casey preferred to leave it as it was. Cut ties and run. He hurt less that way.

Tucker hadn't resurfaced, either, and Casey suspected Ernesto followed him to that house that night to do what he had been wanting to since he discovered what he thought was Tucker ripping him off. Casey was simply in the way of the plan. So, he'd been removed temporarily to clear the way for Ernesto's revenge.

Casey was unintended collateral.

Casey drove home, swinging past Ernesto's on the way. A single light burned in the home from the back bedroom. Casey pictured Ernesto in bed reading and pushed down his anger. Everyone else got what they wanted, while he was stuck on repeat. Surprising himself, he parked by the curb and got out of the car. His feet carried him up the sidewalk, and he banged on the door.

Not expecting Ernesto to answer, Casey was shocked when the door swung open and Ernesto stood there in a bathrobe and a tired expression. He pushed the storm door open and waved Casey in. "Come on, then. I suppose we have some things to talk about."

Casey followed him into the living room and sat down when Ernesto gestured to the couch. Ernesto sat across from him, lighting a pipe. It was all a little too quaint for a drug dealer's house.

A drug dealer who took people out of the picture when they got in his way.

Ernesto took a puff, then leaned forward. "What can

I do for you, Casey?"

What *could* he do for him? Now, Casey wasn't sure why he was there. He glanced around the room for a moment, considering. He met Ernesto's eyes. "Why?"

"Because it had to be done. That's all. Nothing personal, you see. I had to send a message."

"You used me to find him," Casey spat.

Ernesto laughed, a weirdly kind and comforting sound. "I get it. You feel like you did something, and I swooped in and stole it from you. Fair enough, but it doesn't change anything. I couldn't risk you failing, and Smith couldn't risk you not failing."

"What does that even mean?" Casey asked, frustrated with the course of the conversation.

"It means I needed to make sure Tucker went away for good, no questions asked and no trail to find. Smith didn't want you going away for killing him."

Smith *was* protecting him. He'd been telling Casey the truth about that, at least. Fine, but Casey was still angry that he was treated like a child who didn't know any better. They could have worked with him to take care of Tucker instead of removing him from the situation.

He fiddled with the fabric cord that ran along the edge of the cushion, thinking about how to ask the next question. "Can I ask if you took care of it?"

Ernesto's face became serious as he leaned back in his chair, eyeing Casey. "No, son, you may not. However, I will say that your family is safe. We will leave it at that. For good. Now, is there anything else I can do for you tonight?"

Knowing he had exhausted the conversation and wouldn't get anything about Tucker out of Ernesto, Casey

DONE.

decided to put his own interests first. He cleared his throat as he met Ernesto's eyes.

"Can you sell me some ketamine?"

CHAPTER THIRTY-TWO

The months rolled one into another. With each passing day, Casey felt himself slipping more and more away from who he used to be. He watched his younger brother change, going from a little kid to almost a teen as he turned twelve years old. Aidan started to distance himself from Casey and the destructive path he was on. Casey couldn't blame Aidan for it, he was only protecting himself from Casey's unending chaos.

Ketamine became a daily need, obliterating any dreams Casey had been holding onto. His mother was concerned but couldn't reach Casey. When he was high, he was funny and approachable. The more he used, though, the less high he got. It was a cycle he couldn't break, nor did he want to. It was the only way he could face each day.

A series of menial jobs kept him from completely sinking into oblivion, but he used his money only on one thing. Ketamine. His motivation. Casey stopped surfing and floated between working his crap jobs and sitting in his room getting fucked up. The day his parents finally realized they weren't helping him by enabling it, they told him they loved him but that he needed to make plans to move out. His mother cried. Casey felt nothing. He wanted to, however, detachment had become his new normal.

He found a room to rent above the auto shop he was working at. It was small, smelled like auto grease, and had one single window looking out over the street. He suspected it was an old manager's office, as the hot plate, microwave, and mini fridge were shoved awkwardly into a corner like they didn't belong. He couldn't deny the parallel to the shithole Mark had been living in before he blew his brains out.

Casey felt like he was on a train heading in one direction, and there was no way back to the place he'd been before. His dreams of leaving faded into the ketamine haze he lived in day in and day out. He had no friends, no family, no hope. His mother invited him to dinner a few times a week, but Casey never took her up on it. He was ashamed and didn't want to face them in the state he was in.

Ernesto had become his source, even though every time Casey showed up for more, Ernesto looked at him like Casey was sinking. Most other people didn't see through the facade Casey had up. He joked, he flirted, he acted like life was worth living. Not Ernesto, though. One day, he asked Casey to stay for coffee, and Casey was too afraid to lose his source to say no.

Ernesto poured them each a cup of coffee out of a French press as they sat in his small living room. Casey stared around the room, wondering if Mark had ever been in there. Maybe sitting on the very couch Casey was sitting on. He didn't know why, but his mind kept going back to trace over the brief interaction Casey had with Mark in West Virginia. As if he'd remember some tidbit he'd missed to think differently about what Mark said.

Ernesto handed Casey a cup of coffee and watched him for a moment before speaking. "Casey, I appreciate your business and discretion. However, I'm concerned about you. You seem to be spiraling out."

Casey eyed him, then laughed dryly. "Drug dealers care about their users?"

Ernesto flinched. "You may not know this about me, but I didn't see this becoming my future. Any more than I imagine Mark thought he'd end up the way he did."

"So?" Casey could hear the hardness in his voice as if it was another person talking. He backtracked, knowing burning this bridge would only hurt him. "I mean, I get it, but it's not like that. I'm not like Mark."

"How is it, then?"

"I'm fine. Just having a good time," Casey lied.

"You don't seem like you are having a good time. Look, I made a promise to your mother. I thought I'd kept that promise, but now I'm thinking I haven't. If you using ketamine is causing you harm, then I'm not living up to my end of the bargain, am I?"

The promise to keep Casey safe. "You did that. Now I'm an adult, and no one cares about that anymore. Like I said, I'm fine. I don't need protecting. You did what you were supposed to, so we're good."

Ernesto could see he was getting nowhere with Casey and sighed. He still held the ace. "I don't think I'm comfortable selling to you anymore, kid. I know you don't want to admit it, but it's getting out of hand."

Casey felt his anger flare and met Ernesto's eyes. "Because of some stupid fucking promise you made to my mother years ago?"

"No... because I do actually care about you. When you started coming around at first, you had a light in your eyes. You talked about leaving here and doing something with your life. Hell, you talked about spirituality and meditation. What do you believe in, now?"

Ketamine. Casey believed in ketamine. "Stuff. Look, Ernesto, I appreciate your concern, but this is my life and my choice. We aren't friends or family. You're my drug dealer, so you lecturing me on my life is weird and to be honest, fucking out of line."

Ernesto's eyes flashed, and he set his coffee down. "I see. No, you're right. I can't sell you drugs, then act like we're friends. It's a conflict of interest."

Casey nodded; he'd won. Then, he saw the shift in Ernesto and realized he, in fact, hadn't won. Ernesto picked up his coffee cup and stared at Casey until Casey became uncomfortable. They sat in this awkward state until Casey finished his coffee and stood up. "So, uh?"

Ernesto eyed Casey warily, then tossed him a pack of pills from a sewing box beside his chair. "On the house, this is the last time. I'm sorry, Casey. For everything. You can see yourself out."

Casey got what he came for and left before Ernesto changed his mind. Moving forward, he wondered how he and Ernesto would do the transactions since clearly, he'd pissed Ernesto off. He'd cool down, he wouldn't lose a paying customer, Casey believed. Casey would apologize, and they'd get back on track. He was sure of it.

He didn't have to wonder for long, as the next time he went by the house, Ernesto was gone. Not temporarily. His house had been packed up and sat empty with a for sale sign out front. Casey felt like he'd been punched in the gut.

Did Ernesto leave because of him?

No. He was a nobody in Ernesto's life. Just another customer. Casey wanted to ask Smith about it, but they hadn't spoken since that night he went after Tucker. It was like they'd never been friends. However, that was the least of Casey's concerns these days.

How would he get ketamine now?

He scoped out the party scene, careful to avoid Smith's circles, asking people if they knew where to find any. Most people shrugged and told him to talk to Smith, not knowing they weren't on speaking terms. The partiers went back to their vices of choice. None of which was ketamine. Casey floated around, trying different drugs, but nothing beat back the depression and anxiety like ketamine had. Even so, he couldn't go cold turkey and went back to using whatever he could find to keep reality at bay.

The tables turned in his relationship with Aidan, and Casey was the one trying to convince Aidan to spend time with him. Finally, one day, Aidan met him at the door, not ready to go skate.

Casey cocked his head. "Hey, little dude, did you forget I was taking you skateboarding today?"

Aidan scrunched his nose. "I don't want to go."

"Not feeling well?" Casey asked.

"I'm feeling fine. It's just..." Aidan's voice trailed off, and he looked away.

"What's up, Aidan?"

Aidan stared at Casey, his dark brows drawn down. "Casey, you aren't the same. It's like an alien replaced my brother. You aren't fun anymore. I'd rather hang out with my friends. I'll go skateboarding with TJ."

While Casey had most people fooled, he wasn't pulling the wool over Aidan's eyes. Which was fair; he had no less than three substances coursing through his veins at that very moment. Casey scuffed his sneaker against the stoop and sighed. "Alright, no worries."

He turned to leave when he heard Aidan sniff. He glanced back and could see Aidan was fighting back tears. He put on a strong front, but he was still just a kid with a fucked up brother. Casey went back and wrapped his arm around Aidan's thin shoulders. Aidan cried, then pushed back, rubbing his nose. He looked at Casey for assurance Casey couldn't give him. Casey felt like shit but didn't know how to turn things around. Instead, he gave Aidan a play punch on the chin and left. It was always easier to run away.

He completely stopped going by to spend time with Aidan. Casey could deal with everyone else's disappointment but not Aidan's. That one hit home, and he knew Aidan was better off without him.

Hell, everyone probably was.

Without friends or family, Casey sunk deeper inside his own mind, spending more time at the library and reading to find the meaning of anything. No matter how much he read, however, none of it hit home to help him understand the path he was on.

Casey was struggling with full-blown depression, and nothing seemed to help. He thought about sobriety, but that was a cliff he wasn't willing or able to leap off. It terrified him.

Miranda tried calling him many times, but he never answered. He could never forgive her for telling Smith about him going after Tucker. That was what started all of this. At least, that's what he convinced himself. It was easier to believe that than to see that he was causing his suffering. Not Mark, not Miranda, not Smith, not even Tucker. What Casey was dealing with came from his own mind. He was knocking on a door he'd locked from the inside.

After he ran out of all his fixes and wasn't finding the relief he needed, Casey finally accepted he'd need to talk to Smith. Word had it only Smith was dealing ketamine since Ernesto left, and Casey wondered if Smith and Ernesto were still in contact. He'd approach Smith as simply a customer, not as friends. He'd make that clear from the beginning.

Sucking up his pride, Casey went to a party under the pier, with the intent of approaching Smith to buy ketamine. He smoked a joint and chugged a few beers to get his nerves up. When he got to the party, however, Smith was nowhere to be seen. Casey had word Smith would be there, so he began asking around.

A very drunk girl shrugged when he asked her and waved her arm around like she was giving a tour. "He was here. I don't know, maybe he went to piss." She dragged out the 's' on piss like she was a snake, then stumbled forward. Casey caught her and made sure she was stable before letting go. She smiled and tried to bat her eyes at him, which ended up looking like a double wink.

"Thanks," he replied as he let her arm go. He departed the party and started wandering down the beach toward the lifeguard stand. Smith usually left parties and went there when he was done with people.

The stars seemed to be twinkling at Casey, and he stopped to stare up at them, remembering a time when those were enough for him to feel like he belonged there. Belonged anywhere. He drew in a deep breath and let it out, trying to recapture the innocence he once felt.

None came.

Still looking up, he began walking again. His feet caught up on something, and he pitched forward, landing face-first in the sand. He rolled over, shaking his head, to see what he'd tripped over when he saw what it was.

Smith was half in, half out of the water, vomit splattered on the beach by his head. He was cold and unresponsive. Casey reached out and shook Smith. Smith was known to pass out on the beach a lot, but this was different.

Smith was dead.

CHAPTER THIRTY-THREE

C asey froze, not knowing what to do. He tried CPR on Smith, but it wasn't working. He scanned the beach looking for someone who could help, however, he was alone. From the coldness of Smith's body, he'd been lying there awhile. Casey panicked, dragging Smith's body up the beach away from the waterline.

He lifted Smith under the arms and leaned with all his might as he dug his feet into the sand and moved backward. Smith was heavy and almost impossible to move. Casey strained and pulled, making progress in inches. Finally, exhausted, he dropped Smith's body and flopped down on the sand next to his friend.

His friend. His brother.

He began to bawl, realizing they had let some bullshit

tear them apart. The one person who understood him. Rage filled him, and he began to pound on Smith's chest, trying to get a response.

"Wake the fuck up!" he screamed into Smith's lifeless face. He grabbed Smith by the shoulders and shook him as hard as he could.

This couldn't be happening.

Casey rolled Smith onto his side and beat on his back, remembering the vomit around Smith's head. He stuck his fingers down Smith's throat and scooped out chunks of remaining vomit, then continued to perform CPR as much as he could remember. He'd taken a class to work for the town, but the details were hazy.

He couldn't tell if there was a pulse or breathing as he leaned in close. As far as he could see, Smith had no life in him. Casey covered Smith with his body, trying to create warmth. Nothing was working. He didn't have the phone Smith had given him, having long since thrown it in the trash.

He was just about to leave to get help when he felt something. A vibration of some sort. His body heat had transferred some to Smith's, making Casey shiver. He waited but felt nothing. Maybe his own shivers had given the sense of vibration. Casey rubbed Smith's arms, trying to stimulate warmth.

He felt it again. The vibration. He leaned in close to Smith's face to see if he felt breath, but the wind prevented him from feeling anything. He began compressions on Smith's chest as he called out for help. No one came to the rescue. It was only him out there to try and save Smith's life. Casey's arms were shaking as tears rolled down his face. Fuck.

How did it come to this?

Casey could see the lifeguard stand in the distance and wondered if there was anything in there that might help. However, it was locked up at night. He felt helpless. He'd let a grudge drive a wedge between him and Smith. Now, he was out of time to fix it.

"Is anyone out here? Please help me!" he screamed. Only the breeze answered. "Please, please, please. I'll do anything. I'm sorry, Smith. Please."

Nothing else mattered. Not Mark, not ketamine, not Ernesto, not Tucker. Nothing but his friend. At that moment, Casey knew he was losing the one person who never gave up on him. Who had his back, who kept his secrets. He bent down, placing his forehead on Smith's, willing him to breathe.

Casey collapsed next to Smith, his arms giving out. He laid his arm across Smith, out of ideas and out of hope. No one was coming to save them. Sitting up, anger washed over him for all the times he'd been let down, been abandoned. He realized he wasn't Mark and didn't need to hold himself prisoner over someone else's perception of him. He raised his arms together in one large fist and slammed them down on Smith's chest with everything he had in him.

Vomited spewed out of Smith's mouth, splattering Casey's arms. Smith's eyes flew open, glazed and terrified. Casey grabbed him by the shoulders and shook him. "Smith! Smith! Can you hear me?"

Smith's eyes darted around, filled with panic, and Casey realized he was still choking. He got Smith up as best he could and began doing the Heimlich on him, his knees digging into the sand. After a few sharp thrusts, chunks of vomit came out, and Smith drew in a loud gasp, followed by a series of smaller gasps as he tried to catch his breath. Casey let go and hit Smith on the back over and over, helping to clear his air passages. Finally, Smith was able to catch his breath but began shaking violently.

He was in shock.

Casey knew he had to get Smith warm and peered around. He needed to get into the lifeguard stand. He got up and ran as fast as his legs would move, scaling the ladder in record time. As he suspected, the door was locked, so he grabbed a flotation device off the outside wall and used it to break the window closest to the door. He reached in and flipped the lock, shoving the door open. Once inside, he gathered a handful of blankets and jumped down the ladder, landing painfully on his ankle.

He made it back to Smith, who was lying in the sand, not moving. Casey yanked him up and shook him, trying to get Smith to respond. Smith's head lolled, but he made a sound, a moan. Casey wrapped a blanket around his friend and leaned him against him.

"Dude, I need you to fight to come back. Smith, can you hear me?"

Smith didn't respond, but he was breathing. Casey considered moving him, however, he didn't have the strength left in him. He kept talking to Smith, shaking him, making him stay close to the surface. This went on for hours until Smith began holding himself up and responding.

His first words hit Casey to the core. "Casey, I fucking missed you so much, dude."

"I missed you too, man. You gotta stay with me."

This was the worst it had ever been. Smith was often

found passed out on the beach after a party. People in the town were aware of it and held him at arm's length because of it.

Smith had been dead when he found him; Casey was sure of it. He would bet his own life on that fact.

He stayed up the rest of the night, keeping an eye on Smith. Smith fell asleep on and off, but Casey would wake him repeatedly to make sure he came to. By morning, Casey could barely keep his eyes open anymore and wrapped one of the blankets around himself to rest his eyes for a moment. He fell asleep almost immediately.

Waking up a bit later, Casey realized where he was and what happened. He jerked and whipped around, sure he'd let his friend die. Instead, Smith was sitting up, watching the waves with a blanket wrapped around him. Dark circles lined his eyes, and he shivered continually. Casey put his hand on Smith's shoulder to make sure he was really there.

Smith turned, his face sad and exhausted. "Fuck, Casey, I don't know what I'd do without you. You're the only family I have left these days."

Casey shook his head. "I don't know. I thought you were dead for sure."

"I was."

"How do you know?"

"I just know. Had you not come along, they'd be dragging my body off the beach about now. Or, I would've washed out to sea, and no one would even know I was gone," Smith replied.

Casey didn't disagree. They'd both successfully pushed away everyone around them who gave a shit about them. No one would even have noticed Smith was missing until they wanted more drugs. Smith would've washed out to sea without anyone caring for a while.

Casey wasn't sure that didn't happen and he was only dreaming. He pulled his knees up to his chest, tugging another blanket over him. "So, what do we do now?"

Smith glanced over at him, his lion eyes looking lost. "I don't have a fucking clue. I can't keep doing this. It's out of control. I don't want to be like this. I don't know how to stop."

"Yeah."

They sat in silence for a long time, neither knowing what to say, aware they'd hit a crossroads. The sunrise was beautiful, surrounding them with gorgeous brushes of color. A painting for only them, or so it seemed.

After a bit, Smith turned to Casey. "I'm sorry, man. I never meant to make you feel like I didn't respect you. I do. I didn't want you to go to jail or end up dead. You mean the world to me, and I would've done anything to keep you safe. I still would. I should've talked to you that night. Before you went after Tucker."

"It wouldn't have stopped me. I hate it, but you were right to do what you did. I wasn't thinking it through. I just fucking hated Tucker so much, I was seeing red, you know? I was pissed at you, but now I understand. I would've done the same thing if the situation was flipped," Casey admitted. The weight of carrying a grudge toward Smith had taken its toll, and Casey was ready to put it down.

Smith sighed. "How the fuck did we end up here? It started out so fun and became such a nightmare."

"I don't know, but, Smith, I really want us to be friends again. I know things can never go back to how it was, and maybe they shouldn't. I'm tired of hating you and want us to stop being away from each other."

Smith looked at Casey and frowned. "I never hated you, if that matters."

Casey nodded. "I know. This was all my shit. I should never have looked for Mark or gone after Tucker. I was so angry about both of them, I wanted to have some vengeance. I guess you were in my line of sight."

Smith laughed. "I have a way of doing that. I truly am sorry, Casey. Please believe me."

Casey got up. "Think you can move? Let's go someplace warm."

Smith made it to his feet, the blanket still over him like a cape. He stumbled, so Casey braced him as they made their way off the beach like an elderly couple. By the Sea was open for breakfast, so they went in and sat down. Natalie wasn't there, which Casey was glad for. He didn't want her seeing them like this. He ordered coffee at the counter and chatted with the waitress while she poured two cups. He noticed shelves being put up behind the counter.

"What are those for?" he asked. The girl glanced back and waved her hand. "Oh, Natalie is getting her full liquor license. More than beer and wine. She says it's the only way to keep this place going. The locals, you know?"

Casey did. The restaurant did alright serving food and beer, but Natalie was constantly behind on the bills. Booze would definitely change that because the locals liked to drink.

A lot.

He took the coffee back to where Smith was sitting and slid one over to him. Casey sat down across from

Smith and met his eyes. "It's not just us."

"What do you mean?" Smith asked, sipping the steaming coffee with a grimace. The coffee wasn't good, but it was hot.

Casey leaned forward, wanting to keep their conversation private. "It's this town, you know? It's like sitting down to a feast, however, everything is made out of paper. It looks good but tastes like shit and leaves everyone feeling empty."

Smith laughed, shaking his head. "Only you could explain it that way, Casey. I get what you mean, though, and you're right. It's all a mirage we can never reach. Always just over the horizon."

Casey nodded and added creamer to his coffee. "We all are trying to fill that hunger with whatever we can get our hands on. Some people, like Tucker, Mark, maybe even Ernesto, want to control that hunger, so they keep feeding us the bullshit."

Smith set his coffee cup down and stared out the window. "You could put me in that group, too, I guess. Since I sell drugs."

"Nah. You do it because you're hungry, as well," Casey offered, knowing it was true. Neither of them profited off of the other's struggles. That's what made them different. They were doing it to fill a void in themselves they couldn't heal.

The others were doing it to open the wound.

CHAPTER THIRTY-FOUR

After a few cups of coffee, Smith started looking a little more alive, spots of color returning to his cheeks. Not wanting to run into Natalie, Casey suggested they move on. Smith ran to the bathroom as Casey paid the bill. He waited by the door, anxious to get going. Smith came out, his long frame looking thinner than usual. They walked across the boardwalk toward the parking lot. People were beginning to mill about, creating a weird sense of two realities.

"You have your car here?" Casey asked, looking around for the beater.

Smith shook his head. "Nah. Don't have it anymore. On foot now."

"Oh. What happened to it?"

"Sold it."

Casey stopped. "What's going on, man? Why?"

Smith shrugged, seeming nonplussed. "Needed to eat."

Clearly, that wasn't all.

Casey started walking again as Smith shuffled on beside him. They hadn't talked in so long, Casey felt he'd missed key pieces of Smith's life. "Talk to me, Smith. What's going on?"

Smith turned to him. "Parents cut me off. They won't even speak to me until I 'get my life together'. With Ernesto gone, I had to front more money for K than I did with him. He got me in contact with his person in Jacksonville, but they are charging me way more out the door. Anyway, I used my paycheck to get a supply and didn't have money to eat. So, I sold the car. I'll figure it out. I mean, for the most part, I don't need it. Except to pick up supplies now and then."

"Damn. Let's head back to my place. I have some burgers we can fry up."

They walked to the auto shop and climbed the stairs. Casey unlocked the door and pushed it open, letting Smith into the one-room space. Smith sat at the card table Casey used as a dining table and put his head down, clearly exhausted. "Thanks, Casey."

Casey threw a couple of burgers in a frying pan on the hot plate and grabbed sodas out of the fridge. It wasn't much, but it was his. "So, uh, what happened with Ernesto? I saw his house is for sale, now?"

"You know he left, I guess. He took care of the problem, then decided he didn't want to be Ernesto anymore. So, Johnny left to start a new life elsewhere. He didn't tell me where, and I didn't ask."

The problem being Tucker.

Sort of. The town had more problems than one person. Casey recognized this more and more as time went on. "Have you heard from Miranda? She's tried calling me a few times, but I didn't answer. I feel like shit about it, however, I guess it's better in the long run. Is she doing okay?"

"Yeah. She's doing well. Enrolled in nursing school. Brittany is doing okay, too. Miranda says she is struggling with nightmares and shit, but is back in school and putting all that hell behind her."

"Damn. Poor girl," Casey muttered. He took a gulp of his soda, letting the sugar coat his tongue. "I'm glad she got away from here."

Smith watched him, his eyes wiser than they should be. "Here, there. No matter where it is, there is a world of shit to deal with. You know?"

Now Casey did. He thought about the kid at the trailer park where Mark lived. There was toxic garbage everywhere, and kids were paying the price. He pulled the burgers off and handed Smith a plate. "Here, man. I'm not hungry. Make yourself a plate of food. I need to go do something. If you want to sleep, feel free to use my bed. I'll be back in a bit."

Smith frowned, tipping his head. "Aidan?"

Casey nodded, appreciating how tuned in Smith could be. "Yeah. I've let him down so much. I need to see if he'll let me in and give me another chance to be his brother."

He went to leave when Smith reached out, placing his hand on Casey's arm. "Casey, thank you. For being there for me. I... fuck. I don't think I'd be alive if it wasn't for you. I'm sorry it took that for you to forgive me."

Casey sighed. "Smith, you didn't need my forgiveness. I was being selfish, and you were only trying to help protect me from myself. We need to stop trying to destroy ourselves, though."

"That is true and trust me, I plan to chill the fuck out. It's good to have you back, dude."

"Same. I'll see you in a bit. Get some rest."

"One more thing, Casey," Smith said seriously.

"What's that?"

"You have never let Aidan down. I wish you could see that. He might be pulling away, but that's his age. It's what he's supposed to do to find himself in the world. Remember being that age? It's what happens. He'll come around. Give it time, and stick around, no matter what."

Casey chewed his lip. "I hope so. I've given him plenty of reasons to give up on me. He deserves better."

"Keep letting him know you're there for him. That's all you can do, you know? I'm going to crash for a few hours. You want to go surfing later?"

It had been so long since they'd surfed together, and Casey could think of nothing he wanted to do more. He smiled at Smith. "Damn, dude, I have missed you. Yeah, I'll be back this afternoon. We can go then if you are up for it."

He left and closed the door behind him. He took his car, hoping he could convince Aidan to take a ride with him. When he got back to his mother's house, fear overtook him. What if Aidan didn't want to see him? Taking a deep breath and setting his resolve, Casey walked up the path. He knocked a few times, then pushed open the door.

"Hey, Aidan, are you around?"

Aidan came down the stairs, his dark eyes framed by the thick black eyebrows they both had. "What's up, Casey?"

"You want to take a ride?"

"For what?"

Casey could feel the coolness coming off Aidan but pushed through, anyway. This was on him to make it work. "I really want to talk to you, let you know what's been going on with me. Please, Aidan?"

Aidan nodded, even though his face was still unreadable. "Sure."

They drove out to the pier and wandered down the long, wooden structure. Casey knew he had to come clean with his little brother to bridge the distance between them. He bought a couple of hotdogs from a cart vendor and motioned to the bench at the end. "Sit there?"

Aidan followed him and plopped down. Casey handed him a hotdog and stared out over the water. This was one of his favorite spots. "I need to tell you some things, Aidan. I think you're old enough to understand. First, I want to tell you how sorry I am."

Aidan took a bite of his hotdog and stared at Casey for a second. "About what?"

Casey paused as he formed his words in his head. "For not being the big brother you deserve. For letting you down over and over again. I've been dealing with so much shit and lost sight of what was important, you know?"

Aidan didn't respond. Casey looked at him, noting how quickly his brother was changing. The baby face was disappearing, being replaced by angles and a more serious face. Before long, Aidan would be an adult and off on his own. This made Casey sad.

He wanted to keep Aidan little forever.

Casey set his hotdog down and wiped his hands on his shorts before he went on. "When I went to see Mark, my biological father, I found out things I didn't want to know about. I should've stayed away from him, like Mom asked me to. I have such a good family with you, Mom, and Isaac. I didn't appreciate that enough, but I do now. That's not why I wanted to talk to you, though."

Aidan cocked his head. "Why, then?"

Casey pushed down the anxiety coming up. "Aidan, I sometimes struggle with things. Depression, anxiety, things like that. I know it makes me distant, but I want you to know it has nothing to do with you, and I'm working on it. I'm facing my own demons the best I can. Okay?"

Aidan cocked his head, looking like a little kid again. "Is that why you leave me behind all the time?"

That one stung. Casey felt like shit but nodded. "I'm sorry. I really am. I can be a real dick, sometimes. You don't deserve that, and I promise to do better. You're honestly my favorite person in the world."

"More than Smith?" Aidan asked, needing Casey to prove what he was saying again. It was a sensitive spot for Aidan, and Casey didn't want him feeling like he was second best to Smith.

"Yes. Smith is my friend, and I care about him very much, but you are my baby brother. We're blood, Aidan. You are part of me, do you understand that? Like we are the same person in a way. I see you as my heart."

Aidan smiled almost to himself, accepting the

answer. "Okay. What's it like?"

Casey frowned. "What?"

"Depression."

"Oh. Like the world looks black and white all the time. Like your feet and heart are covered in concrete, I guess," Casey explained, trying to keep it simple. It wasn't easy to explain in a way that made sense.

"Is that why you take stuff?"

Casey was genuinely surprised by the question and sat back. How much did Aidan know about his drug use? He chewed his lip, knowing he was on slippery ground. He wanted to be honest, but he didn't want Aidan to think he was a drug addict, either. "What do you mean?"

"I know you used to have pills in your drawer, and you'd act different at times. Like you weren't really here," Aidan answered.

"You didn't ever take any of those pills, right?" Casey asked in a panic.

Aidan shook his head. "I'm not stupid."

Casey was.

He put his hand on Aidan's shoulder. "Don't tell Mom or Isaac, okay? I'm working on that. Trying to do better... but, yeah. It's a dumb thing to do, and I'll stop. I've already cut back."

"You swear?'

Casey focused on the horizon. At that moment, he meant it. "I swear."

Aidan ate the rest of his hotdog, satisfied with Casey's answers. He got up and went to the end of the pier, staring down at the water. Casey joined him, and they stood side by side. The seawater sprayed them as the water hit the pilings, making Aidan laugh. Casey wanted to believe what he told Aidan. He wanted to put ketamine and all the other garbage behind him.

It almost cost Smith his life.

He put his arm around Aidan and drew his brother to his side. This had to be enough. If he could bottle the moment and drink it down, he'd never need anything else in life. He thought back to being Aidan's age and how he found joy in simply being alive.

He also remembered being that age and the grayness finding him sometimes when he was alone. He didn't know it was the start of his depression then, but he did now. He never wanted Aidan to feel that way. Aidan grinned up at him, and Casey believed he could do anything.

Casey dropped Aidan off at home a little bit later and headed back to his apartment to meet up with Smith. He was committed to changing his ways and being the person Aidan thought he was. Smith was asleep, so Casey crept around, getting his stuff ready for surfing.

Smith woke and sat up in bed. "Hey, Casey. Thanks for letting me rest. You still want to go surfing?"

"Yeah. Where's your board?"

Smith blushed and shook his head. "Sold it."

"Oh, shit. I think there is a spare board in the auto shop. We can grab it on the way out. So, do you have anything left, or did you sell it all?"

"Not much. I sold anything of value. Pretty much down to my clothes and a few necessary items."

"How much K do you have left, then?" Casey asked, not out of interest to use, but rather understanding what situation Smith was in.

"Some. I used a bunch last night. Enough left to sell

and turn around to buy more. Make a little profit."

"I see. Let's get going, we can walk with the boards to the beach. What's your plan moving forward?" Casey asked, eyeing Smith.

Smith shook his head. "I fucking don't know. After last night, I think I need to rethink what I'm doing with my life before I end up dead."

Casey thought about that. How easy it was to make promises when rock bottom was level ground. He wanted it to be true. For both of them to turn things around and make their lives worth living. He grabbed his board and gestured to the door. Smith slipped on his shoes and joined Casey.

They snagged the extra board from the shop and headed to the beach. The weather was warm, and the air carried change on it. They took off their shoes and made it into the surf with their boards. Casey let everything go, allowing the waves to ease his worry. To keep him in the present. Within a few minutes, he was immersed in the ride and forgot about everything else except catching the next wave. Smith was weak but seemed to have found the same peace.

After a couple of hours, they sat on the beach, their muscles spent and their minds clear. Casey watched the sunset and turned to Smith.

"Do you think you'll ever leave here?"

Smith shrugged. "Sometimes. Other times, I don't care. Just trying to survive day to day."

Casey nodded. "I used to think I'd save money and leave as soon as I could. Now, I don't know. After going to West Virginia, I see things differently about my life. I don't know where I'd even go. I'd miss Aidan, too, though

I think he'll leave this town one day and never look back. I hate to think about that. Me here without him. Then again, sometimes I think I won't live to be twenty-five."

Smith laughed. "Man, Casey, everyone thinks that. Every person at every party I've ever met says they won't live to be twenty-five years old like it's some far-off destination. It's coming faster than we realize."

Casey chuckled at that. Smith was right, he'd heard it time and again from everyone around their age at parties. Thinking that was all there was to life. Getting fucked up with no plans for the future.

He lay back on his elbows in the sand and stared up at the colorful sky. He had a lot to live for, whether or not he left their small town. His family, Smith, surfing. He slipped his strand of beads over his head that he'd taken off to surf. He stared at each carved bead and smiled to himself. At that moment, he felt home. Like he belonged where he was. He was on a soul journey, no matter where it took him. He was where he was supposed to be.

At least for the time being.

Everyone's got to face down the demons
Maybe today you can put the past away
Third Eye Blind, "Jumper"

Police Report 12/4/2003

Crestview State Park

On the morning of December 4, 2003, a group of hikers called in a report of finding possible human remains in the marshland at the state park. Police were dispatched to the area to investigate.

An autopsy confirmed the bones were human remains. Male, approximately mid-twenties. A single gunshot to the head is determined to be the cause of death.

No missing people have been reported in the region.

Dental records were matched to a Tucker Peters of Durham, North Carolina. The Peters family was notified, and the remains were transported to the Basset Funeral Home in Durham for interment.

Due to the decomposition of the body, police suspect the body had been there for at least a year. Police have ruled the death to be accidental or suicide, as the weapon was registered to Mr. Peters.

No foul play is suspected.

Resources:

If you or anyone you know is struggling:
American Foundation for Suicide Prevention:
Anxiety and Depression Association of America:
National Suicide Prevention Lifeline: 1-800-273-TALK
(8255)
En español: 1-888-628-9454
Crisis Text Line: Text "HELLO" to 741741
National Alliance on Mental Illness: nami.org
To Write Love on Her Arms (suicide/addiction help):
twloha.com
7 Cups of Tea Foundation (emotional online support):
7cups.com
Never Alone Initiative (tools and resources): neveralone.love

You are not alone.

Acknowledgements

A big thank you to my son, Jack, for his honesty about his experiences and struggles. He contributed the chapter art of Zorbak, the skateboarding skeleton. It's never easy to open up about addiction or depression, and I appreciate your ability to talk about it with me.

Thank you also to my husband, Justin, for sharing his journey with addiction and family trauma.

For my big brother, Scott, who protected me as a kid but forgot to protect himself. You will always be my big brother and friend. You can do this.

To those adults who stopped to pay attention and listen when I was a child, to see through the facade I presented to the world to hide what was happening.

Thank you to my readers for having an open heart and an open mind to the reality that not everyone is given a fair shot. I write to show a different side of reality. Thank you for reading and supporting.

Books by Juliet Rose
Do Over
We Don't Matter
Prick of the Needle
Through the Surface
Trigger Point
Carrying the Dead
Catch the Earth
In Dreams, We Fly
Stitched Together
By the Dimming Light
Expectation of Pain
Done.
Please visit my website for upcoming books and news:

authorjulietrose.com